# ONLY THE HUNTED RUN

**ALSO BY NEELY TUCKER**

*Murder, D.C.*

*The Ways of the Dead*

*Love in the Driest Season*

# ONLY THE HUNTED RUN

A NOVEL

NEELY TUCKER

VIKING

VIKING
An imprint of Penguin Random House LLC
375 Hudson Street
New York, New York 10014
penguin.com

ISBN: 9780525429425 (hardcover)
ISBN: 9780698198081 (ebook)

Printed in the United States of America
10  9  8  7  6  5  4  3  2  1

Set in Adobe Garamond Pro
Designed by Alissa Rose Theodor

*for my parents*
*who did not throw me off the fire tower on hwy 12*
*though*
*god knows*
*i gave them reason*

*And indeed there will be time*

*For the yellow smoke that slides along the street,*

*Rubbing its back upon the window-panes;*

*There will be time, there will be time*

*To prepare a face to meet the faces that you meet;*

*There will be time to murder and create . . .*

—T. S. Eliot, "The Love Song of J. Alfred Prufrock"

# ONLY THE HUNTED RUN

HE COULDN'T COUNT the shots for the screaming. It was coming from every-where. Jesus, the noise. Bouncing down the marble steps, over the stone floors, around the columns, echoing down the long corridors. Women. It was mostly women screaming, but there were men yelling, too, all bass and fury, bellowing that they'd been hit.

The woman across from him in the Crypt of the Capitol building was bleeding out. Shot through the chest. She had been screaming but now she was just whimpering. The blood oozing over the stone floor beneath her was darker now, a maroon tidal pool, moving steadily outward.

The shots had been *pop pop popping*, an automatic at work. But now they were sporadic and far away and seemed more to be echoes than original sound and he had no idea how many gunmen were in the build-ing or where they were.

Sully Carter, tucked between two of the double columns that formed the outer ring of the Crypt's sandstone beams, looked toward the center of the circular room, then to the outer walls. Ten, maybe a dozen others, cowering between columns or under display cases. Some wounded, some taking cover. Nobody said anything. They were all breathing heavily. Looking, the lot of them, like passengers on a plane with no pilot.

Well, fuck *this*.

He blew out his breath and scrambled on all fours until he got to the shot woman. She was flat on her back. He took her hand and knelt beside her, breathing hard with the effort, the adrenaline. She had two hits, the upper chest and the abdomen. The blood pumping out of her was a river. She opened her eyes when he squeezed her hand, but the light in them was faint.

"Can you hear me?" he whispered. "Hey? Squeeze if yes. We'll get out the door." He jerked his head to the right, toward the exit. Which, when he looked at it now, with the prospect of carrying her, looked a mile and a half away.

She had curly brown hair, green eyes, little blue stud earrings, and too much makeup. Her mascara was running. Early thirties. A lanyard around her neck with a badge. She was wearing a navy skirt and a white blouse, untucked and gone mostly red, with a smart navy jacket over it. One of her shoes, black pumps, had come off. Heavyset. If he got one arm under her knees and another behind her back . . . no. Never. She'd be limp as a dishrag, and forty pounds too heavy. He'd have to heave her over a shoulder.

"You squeeze me? Like this?" He gave her a series of rapid-fire squeezes. She blinked and her mouth parted. A gossamer-thin bubble of saliva, tinged red, came up from her lips, ballooned, and—as Sully watched, transfixed—burst.

She did not squeeze.

"Goddammit," he said.

The blood pumping through her blouse settled into a desultory flow. She stared at him, and there was the stillness, the letting go, the hand coming off the trapeze bar, and she was floating, floating, the ground a forgotten thing, just floating into the void. He felt dizzy for a second. He did not want to let go.

There was scrambling behind him. The rest of the survivors were coming out of hiding, abandoning their safe spots, running like hell for the exit or back down the hallway to the Senate side, away from the gunfire.

Somewhere, someone pulled the fire alarm.

Sully looked at his watch. A little after five. He had been in the building maybe an hour, filling in for Clarice. It was August in Washington, the worst time of year, the absolute worst. Everybody who was anybody was on vacation. Sully, who was not quite anybody, was working, like the stragglers in the Capitol building: stuck in the city, the heat a hammer that hit you in the face.

He'd been assigned a bullshit story about environmental regulations governing oil drilling in the Gulf. The desk handed it to him because the Gulf was back home and they thought he'd know something about it. And because he was a warm body dumb enough not to be in the Outer Banks or the Caribbean this time of year. Then, in the sagging hours of this afternoon errand, there had come the burst of automatic weapons fire, the bleeding and screaming, everything going out of focus and off kilter, the modern American nightmare. The national anxiety during the Cold War had been a Russian nuclear strike, millions of god-fearing Americans vaporized in an instant. By the turn of the century, the national anxiety had devolved into a crazy man with a gun, god-fearing Americans picked off half a dozen at a time. Slow motion suicide instead of instant annihilation.

The woman on the floor beside him had, no kidding, stopped breathing.

The hand in his was still warm but it wouldn't be for long. He gave it a final squeeze and then pushed himself up, shaking a little now. Looked down the hallway to the exit. Sunshine and safety. Part of him, at this point in his life, longed for it. But he was at work, and you did your job because nobody ever made anything better by running from it.

Sitting up, he slid his hard-soled shoes from his feet and left them beside the dead woman. The last thing he needed, going to find the man with the gun, was his shoes telling the bastard where to shoot.

Quickstepping in his socks, he gimp-legged it into the heart of the building, finding a circular marble staircase. He brought his eyes up, brought his eyes up *hard*, and his feet followed, hewing close to the rail, back hunched over to lower his profile, hitching his bad leg along as best he could, up the steps, now six, now eight, the screaming getting closer—Sully Carter alone in the core of the building that symbolized America's allegedly invincible power, and his isolation telling him with every step that something had gone terribly wrong.

## TWO

CRISSCROSSING HIS STEPS, watching the shooting angles, he made his way up the marble staircase, lowering his hips, bending his knees. Two more *pop pop*s stopped him. The acoustics of the building, the stone and marble, the arched ceilings, turned it into an echo chamber. You couldn't tell what was coming from where.

He felt some nameless thing creeping up his spine and spreading out through his nervous system, little Day-Glo electrical dots flying down the bundles of the nerve fibers buried under his flesh, conducting not a knuckle-whitening sense of fight or flight, but of . . . calm.

That was it. The sensation flowing through his body, right down to the tips of his fingers and the far reaches of his toes, was that of antifreeze in a running engine, a coolant, like what bourbon so often had done for his kicked-around and possibly damaged brain. His heart rate slowed and his breathing deepened. Day-to-day stress drove him up the wall.

Chaos suited him.

He came out of the crouch at the top of the steps and, gaining the edge of the Rotunda, his eyes scanned the upper reaches of the atrium. Sounds, colors, stillness. Also: a bloodied mess. Five, six, seven bodies lay in the open, tiled expanse. Two were in uniform. The grand statues looked on, mute. Light streamed in from above.

One body, that of a man in a brown suit, lay in almost the center of the floor. Another, in seersucker, was across the way, the blast to the face taking out the back half of the man's skull, the body facedown. Wet speckles and clumps of gore, gray and red and brown, were everywhere, like grotesque confetti that had showered and settled. The two officers lay on their backs a few feet apart. They were both just inside the House entrance to the room, not forty feet in front of him, slightly to his left. They had come running from the Senate corridor, Sully thought, shot from the front. It indicated the shooter or shooters were in the House wing, to his right.

The screaming burst out again. It had sounded like a woman when he was coming up the steps but now that he was here, he could see that it was a young man. Slumped against the far wall, half hidden behind a tall marble statue, the kid kept his left hand on his right shoulder, trying to slow the spewing. Blood came up through his fingers and over his suit. He had to be a page, an intern. His wing-tip-clad feet were clawing at the floor, trying to push himself farther into the wall.

The shriek lasted until he ran out of breath. Then, chest heaving, still looking at the bloody pulp of his shoulder, he started up again. A long, high-pitched wail, seeming to start at the base of his lungs and, shuddering once in the open air, to bounce off the walls, until he coughed, and coughed again. Vomit bubbled out of his mouth, onto his suit. He spat. Then he started another wail, half an octave higher than the one before.

Sully got his eyes up again, scouting for an arm, a rifle, a gun held over one of the balconies above. Nothing. Then he came out of his crouch at a full clip, running, sidestepping one body, ignoring the others, his eyes fixed on the bleeding kid by the Grant statue until he was right up on him, dropping into a half slide, like he was coming into second base, slamming into the wall with a grunt.

The kid's lips were slightly apart, dried out. The tongue was pulled back in the mouth. Sweat drenched his forehead, dampened his hair, dropped from his chin. He had pissed himself, given the aroma, but Sully accorded him the dignity of not looking.

"Hey, hey now," Sully whispered, forcing his voice to be heard over the alarm. "You good? You hear me okay?"

This was greeted with a blink and the bobbing of the kid's Adam's apple.

"Where," he said, a little louder, "where did they go?"

The kid looked at him, his blink-blink brown eyes looking like a puppy's on the front porch. Sully put his age at twenty or twenty-one. The kid licked his sweating upper lip and looked at Sully like he was an escaped zoo exhibit. At least he had stopped screaming.

"You hear? The words coming out of my mouth, you hear that?"

The kid blinked and licked his lips again and nodded.

"Okay. Kinda crazy weird, hey, you know?" Sully smiled and ran a hand through his hair, letting the kid know it was a long day, okay to be tired, okay to be a little freaked. The kid was so deeply in shock that if Sully bounced a basketball off his head, all he would do is nod.

"Can you tell me your name? Try it out."

The kid shook his head, no. Now he was staring at the scars on Sully's face.

"That's cool. That's cool. For real. But hey, you're going home now, you know that? You'll be home before dark. Okay? Okay? Home before dark. We're going to get you on your feet and outside."

The kid was nodding, exhaling a little, his body still clenched tight. *Enough* flashed through Sully's mind. Soldiers were younger than this. Guys with guns who would shoot you at a hundred and fifty meters and then come over and pop another in your brain, they were younger than this.

"But, seriously, how many, man? I got to know, you see that? How many men with guns we talking about today?"

The kid held up one finger.

"One. What he look like, this guy?"

"He had a gun." The voice, tremulous, halting, but it was there.

"Right. Tall, short, white, black, wearing what?"

"The gun."

"Okay. Okay. That's good. We can deal with one gun, right? Now. What I want you to do, you're going to head down this hall right behind us, okay? You'll see some stairs? You go down them, you see a long hallway, you get outside. Tell the police that the first floor is, like, clear, and what we're probably talking about is the second floor, House wing."

The kid nodded and did not move.

"Guy, gun, House, wing," Sully said.

The boy had on a purple tie. It was still knotted. He was hit high on the right shoulder. It probably burned like hell but the rest of everything around it should be going numb. It wasn't serious. Still, without a foot up his ass, the kid might sit there until the next term was over, still saying "gun."

Sully leaned over and took off the kid's shoes, one by one, slip-ons with little tassels—the fuck was that even about. The kid looked at him and Sully said, "So you don't make any noise running, okay?"

Then Sully stood in front of him and bent into a crouch and lifted him from under the armpits until he, too, was standing.

"Time to go home," he said. "Go for the stairways. Back there. Quick like a bunny rabbit. Now." Sully pushed him, gently, and then harder. The kid stood there, immobile.

"Run, goddammit," he said, finally, shoving, and the kid staggered away, stiff-legged and straight upright, knees barely bending, one palm clapped on the bullet wound. But he was moving, out of the Rotunda and down the steps, silent as a cat on the kitchen counter, leaving Sully behind.

## THREE

IT WOULD HAVE been better if he knew a goddamn thing about the building layout. He cursed himself for his ignorance but he had always avoided Congress like it was an infectious disease, a parliament of prostitutes, the building ostentatious beyond belief. He'd been in red velvet French Quarter whorehouses that had more restraint. Jesus, you'd get a wart on your dick, hanging out in places like this.

That last *pop pop*, two, three, minutes ago, that had come from somewhere near Statuary Hall. But the alcove just before you got to it led to a hallway that led to the Capitol office of the Speaker of the House, third in line to the presidency. He knew that much, but Christ, you couldn't miss it. A wooden sign above the hallway designated it as such. The problem was that it was a corridor, a shooting gallery. You went down that, the guy was waiting? You were fully ventilated and done.

Now the hitch in his throat, the tingle of urine at the tip of his cock. Fear.

He blinked and all the paintings on the walls shifted from heroic scenes of the Revolution and Freedom to grotesqueries by Greco or Bosch or the murderous masterpieces by Caravaggio—the blood running, the perspectives shifted, the world tilting off its axis, nightmares painted on the walls in colors that ran and bled and spread over the luminous tile floors in front of him, the sunlight streaming from the arched windows above going from sunshine yellow to a sclerotic orange.

"God*dammit*," he said, rubbing his forehead with the palms of his hands, pain building behind the temples. Cupping his hands in front of his mouth, a deep breath. Another.

On the exhalation, he pushed off and came out from behind the Grant statue, sticking to the wall, humping it around the statues, keeping an eye on the upper reaches of the Rotunda. By the time he reached the corridor to the Speaker's office, he'd made up his mind. Full tilt and no excuses, all the cards on the table. Halfway down, suddenly, there was a door on his right. He lowered a shoulder and reached for the handle, timing it just right, barreling into a meeting room with a long wooden conference table and chairs in front of him, a chandelier, the walls painted Republican red.

Empty, thank the Jesus. He got under the conference table and let the door close behind him. Where was the phone, his phone. . . . Here. The inside pocket of the sport coat. One bar. Fuck. But he punched the buttons and it went through, the Metro desk answering on the second ring. He asked for R.J., his editor, and the man himself was on the line in milliseconds.

"Sullivan! You're where?"

"The Capitol. There's been some—"

"AP bulletin says shots fired. What, what?"

"We got bodies, brother, we got six, seven, this is minimum, this is in the Crypt and then the second floor, I'm talking the floor the Rotunda's on, more hit. Ah, what, I got two police officers dead in the, the Rotunda, one gunman reported—"

"—slow down, down, give it to me again, I got a file, I got a file, where, now now now. Seven bodies? Dead, wounded? You're *inside* the building?"

"—with a semi, I, I got, I wasn't taking pulses. One guy, his head blown open, he's gone, that's in the Rotunda, this lady in the Crypt, she's gone, the cops and this other guy in the Rotunda, all head shots."

"Where are you?" Sully could hear R.J.'s hands flying over the keyboard, banging out the dictation.

"A meeting room in the hallway to the Speaker's office, just off the Rotunda. You know where—"

"You're inside the building?"

"Did you hear me? Write this down: In the fucking middle of it."

"What can you see right now? What are you looking at?"

"The underside of a desk."

"Goddammit—"

"Calm down. I know, I know. I can—"

"The shots, man, the shots. Did you see anybody with a gun?"

"You got to slow down. I ain't seen nobody with a gun. It started down low, though, I can tell you that, the shooting, I mean. The Crypt, from that entrance. The east side. The shooter came in from the east side. Moved up to the Rotunda, seems to be behind me in the Speaker's office, but I can't confirm the last. May be just the one shooter."

"Basis for the observation?"

"This kid, this intern? He got tagged on the shoulder, there in the Rotunda? He said one. The shots I've heard, from a distance? They've all seemed to be in one place. I think it's here. You know, the Speaker's office. But I can't hear shit from in here, this room. Calling in to dictate."

"Go, go, go."

"Okay, let's go with, ah, Jesus, okay." He took a deep breath and closed his eyes. "At least one gunman fired dozens of rounds in the U.S. Capitol building this afternoon, killing at least four—ah, it's gonna be more, but let's stick with four for the minute—and seriously wounding several others in an attack unlike any other in the nation's history. . . . With me?"

"Keep going."

"At least four bodies lay in the Crypt and the Rotunda in pools of blood. Shots rang out. The screaming of women and bellowing of men was, what, what, it was *pronounced*, the raised voices echoing down hallways of marble and tile. A fire alarm was activated, adding to the confusion, though no flames or smoke were immediately present. Two security officers were hit by gunfire at the east entrance to the Crypt and they fell, perhaps fatally wounded. Two more officers were hit, fatally, in the Rotunda, one floor above. Also in the Rotunda, at least two other victims had been shot to death. A witness in the Rotunda, a young man hit in the shoulder with at least one bullet, said he saw only one gunman, and that the man had gone toward the Speaker's office. Time that at, what is it, 5:37 p.m."

Running his palm over his forehead, through his shock of black hair, "Okay, okay, how we doing? What else, what else you guys getting—"

"Complete and total fuckery. First AP bulletin was, was eleven minutes ago. 'Shots fired at the eastern entrance to U.S. Capitol building.' A follow six minutes later, reporting Capitol police officers down at that entrance. Something about a confrontation at the metal detector, guy pulls out a gun and goes all Columbine."

"Ah, shit."

"Television has some cameras outside, but they're not close. Everybody was down at the federal courthouse. I'm looking at long-range lens stuff on the screen. People running. Did I say fuckery yet?"

"Is there a wide shot of the building?"

"What? Yes, yes. CNN."

"Is there smoke?"

"Not that I can see."

"Good. Then somebody just yanked the alarm; it didn't go off because of some sort of fire I can't—"

"When can you get—"

"—get to, look, keep an eye on that body count, right, particularly the officers? My numbers are all over the place. I saw two dead, two dead cops, in the Rotunda. Didn't see any other reporters, or anybody else at all, so I wouldn't think those two are included in the AP's count of three. So we may have five cops down."

"Networks and the cables are on air now with people calling in from the building, hiding in offices, like that."

"The kid I saw, the one that got tagged? He should be outside by now, but he's catatonic. He's not going to make it to the cameras. Too bad. He saw the shit firsthand."

"You're sure about the female fatality in the Crypt, though?"

Sully closed his eyes. The blood, the bubble on the lips, the way she'd looked not at him but in him. He could not let that in, not now, maybe not ever. You could not do this job and let the eyes of dead and dying see into you.

"Yeah," he said, "I'm pretty goddamn sure."

"Okay. Okay."

Sully's eyes popped open, the thought just coming to him.

"Wait, wait, wait. Isn't Timothy in the building? I saw him upstairs about an hour ago."

"Timothy is in the press room. He's on the line with the National Desk. Says they've barricaded themselves in there. He's calling, looking for the leadership."

"Barricaded?"

"Says they locked the door, moved chairs and couches."

"The fuck is he doing in the press room?"

"Timothy has been in the press room for approximately forty-three years."

"You're saying the press corps locked themselves in the press room when the shooting started."

"Yes."

"To keep themselves from getting to the news?"

"I don't think they want the news getting to them."

"Jesus the fucking H."

"Are you going to get over this?"

"Tell Timothy to find his dick—it's usually right below the belt buckle—and get *out* of the press room and do some gotdamn reporting."

"Not happening. Turtles in the Galápagos move faster than Timothy. He's—wait, National sends an all-newsroom message here." There was a pause. "He saying he's got the House Speaker on the line."

"Who is where?" Sully said, startled, sitting up straight.

"At home in Georgia."

"That's going to help."

"Nobody is in town. Nobody."

"Where's POTUS and Vice POTUS?"

"West Texas and a secure location, respectively."

"Is Al Haig in charge?"

"Can you get out?"

"Of what?"

"The building!"

"Why, why would I do that?"

"An outburst of common sense?"

"You pay me to—"

"Then stay put. Now gimme the rest of what you've got. Gimme, gimme the narrative, walk it through."

"—to, what, okay. Look, I was stalking Evans, the senator lady from back home who approved these drilling rights, like I'm supposed to be doing—*fuck* Clarice, why am I the pinch hitter? I'm walking to this hearing Evans is supposed to be holding, but like three people are in there and, and nobody is up at the stage thing or wherever they sit, right? The dais, is that the word? So I'm going back the other way, going through the Rotunda, thinking I'm in the wrong place, and then there's this noise, this rumpus from way off, it's like you're at the beach and somebody a quarter mile down starts yelling 'Shark!' but you can't hear them for the wind? But something's obviously going south? This was downstairs at the time. Absolutely downstairs. People start running like a cattle stampede, screaming 'He's got a gun! He's got a gun!' Like that. Bursts of shots, one, two, half a dozen, you can't really tell because it's all marble and tile and everything echoes. So I ran downstairs, heard some fire, hit the floor, but then the next volley was from upstairs be-cause—"

"Clarifying. You were going *toward* the gunfire?"

"—it, what, yes, what? For all I knew it was firecrackers. Didn't see a body till I got downstairs. Shooter ran upstairs after I went down."

"So, wait, did you come in through that east entrance to the build-ing, same as the shooter?"

"Yes. Peaches and cream at the time. But that was a couple hours ago. Look, I can't hear shit in here. I got to move."

"Sullivan. Sit tight. The SWAT team, the Navy Seals, the fucking cavalry, is coming. We'll get eyewitnesses, survivors, from outside. What you—"

"Did you see the video from Columbine?"

"—gave me just, wait, what?"

"The video. Columbine. You mentioned it. Did you see it?"

"Yes."

"Then you should know I'm not going to sit under a desk and hope the douche bag with a gun doesn't come find me. I'm going to do my job, with a reasonable share of prudence and concern, and report in. What did you think I was doing abroad all that time? We need the scenery from when they take this guy down, the—"

"I am telling—"

"—visuals of that. Do me a solid though, hey? My nephew, Josh? He's staying with me for the summer? Call the house, tell him not to freak about the news. There's stuff in the freezer he can microwave for dinner or—"

"Sullivan!"

"—just get whatever. Gotta run, brother. Turning this thing off. Keep 1-A open. I'm coming back to you, and it's gonna be a freight train."

## FOUR

HE OPENED THE door to the conference room a few inches. Nothing but the endless, bell-clanging alarm. His head was really thumping now. It was jabbing at his vision, shards of light. You'd think somebody would shut that fucking thing off. Down he went to his good knee, to bend and—"Ay!"—he staggered, his good leg bent beneath him and the other, gimpy, suddenly splayed out. His head clipped the edge of the door. Beads of sweat burst out on his forehead. He wiped them away with a shirtsleeve. His scars itched.

His fingers found the edge of the door. He pulled it open an inch, then another. He peered out, looking far to the right and to the left. Empty. A deep breath. In through the nose and out through the mouth. Calm. He was calm as fucking little white clouds above a flat blue ocean.

Exhaling, he shoved off and was sprinting to the Speaker's chamber, completely exposed, nowhere to hide—and then the door to the chamber burst open. A herd of humanity shot out of it, ten or fifteen or twenty of them, struggling to get through the doorway all at once, arms here and legs there, women in skirts, men in suits, nobody in charge, faces tight and drawn, everybody coming at him so hard he couldn't register what anyone looked like. They swept past him helter-skelter, churning hard, no one speaking, just grunts and gasps, the last guy through in his sixties but a hard-ass, had to be former military, you could tell, that gait. Sully reached out from the wall to take his arm.

"Where is he? How many?"

The man snatched his arm back. Never slowed, but half turned in his retreat. Hissed, pointing: "Down that hall! White. White male." And he was gone, the herd stampeding ahead of him, out of sight down the corridor.

Sully waited a beat, then two, to see if there were footsteps coming in pursuit of the herd. None. He shuffled forward, now almost flat against the wall.

The corridor made a ninety-degree turn to the right up ahead, a hard L. Across the hall was the entrance to the Speaker's office. The left side was a dead end. To go down the hallway to the right, he'd have to make a full turn, blind, and gamble the gunman was not waiting in the hallway.

This seemed reasonable—the man hadn't opened fire on the group that just ran past, nor had he pursued them. The problem for Sully, if he made the turn, would be finding a safe spot in the next hallway. No idea what it looked like, no idea of where to look for a safe haven.

R.J. was right. The troops were coming. The last group down, they would tell them where to find the gunman. It was no longer a blind search through the massive building with its Brumidi corridors of gold and stone, the marble stairs, the open chambers, the Old Supreme Court and Statuary Hall, the tucked-aside meeting rooms and back stairwells.

There was a target, there was a destination. He could just sit tight and wait.

Gunfire and an echoing scream jolted the air just then, coming from around the corner and down the hall. Scream after scream now, long and gurgling. Goddammit goddammit goddammit. The gunman was not in the hallway. He was in a room, an office, down the hall, and some poor bastard was paying for it.

There wasn't any more time to think. Sully rounded the corner, bending at the knees, coming on the run, staying next to the wall. Down the hall in front of him—maybe forty, fifty feet ahead—there was a thump and another scream. Far behind him, Sully heard the hoofbeats of boots on stone. A door, a door, he needed a door. . . . There was a small one, on the right.

Hit it with his shoulder, his full weight behind it. It gave and he was falling, stumbling inside. He regained his balance and pulled a pen from his jacket pocket. He came back and wedged it between the door and the frame, keeping it open just that much. Turning back, disoriented, what the—he was in the women's bathroom—how do you figure. . . . He took two steps toward the nearest stall, making himself count by Mississippis now, because it wouldn't be long and it was hard to keep track of time.

Then the lights went off and the world went black.

*One Mississippi, two Mississippi, three* . . . it was absolute, crystalline, total darkness. Little purple motes popped into view, dancing away from his eyes in the void, the retinas trying to adjust. He blinked, like that was going to help, and then turned to look back at the door, to see if light was streaming in from the crack. None.

The lights in the corridor, if not the building, had been cut. The SWAT team was coming hard and soon now. Lights out had to mean they were coming with night goggles. He was in the process of kneeling down on the floor, getting low, when he heard a door open, somewhere down the hallway. He froze. Over the fire alarm he could hear grunting, cursing, dragging. A disembodied voice, from out there in the darkness, said, "Well ain't this some shit."

The voice gave him a locator beam. The noise was coming from down the hall, to his right. He waited until he heard more dragging before he moved again. Easing down onto his hands and knees, then bringing a knee forward, setting it down gently, an arm and hand extended in front of him, waving gently, like a blind man in a crystal shop. Then a touch of cold tile, the front wall of the bathroom. He swept the hand toward the left and hit an outcropping. There was a small gap between the two. The door, wedged open by his pen.

He waited, listening for any sound over the fire alarm. Nothing. Slowly turning, sitting, he pulled himself up to the edge of the door.

There was something—shuffling, rattling, things being moved—but nothing he could make out. There was no flicker of a flashlight. The shooter, or whoever was at the end of the hall, was as blind as he was.

A heavy settling and then, "C'mon, c'mon, answer." Sully sat very still, closed his eyes, concentrating.

"Hey, um, 911?" a man's voice warbled. Sully missed the next string of words, the man mumbling. He held his breath to hear better. "No, no, not a prank. Um. It's, uh, me. Terry Waters. From Oklahoma. The guy with the gun in the Capitol."

*Terry Waters Terry Waters Terry Waters Oklahoma Oklahoma Oklahoma*—the words shot through Sully's mind like quicksilver, turning this way and that, seeping down into the well of memory, repeating silently over and over. No way he could write anything down. Not now, maybe not for hours.

A pause, this fucking fire alarm making him strain to hear.

"No, hey, seriously. What's with the attitude? I'm up in the Speaker's office, or area, or, um, whatever they call it. Down that hall. You listening now? I shot two guards downstairs, and look, I mean, sorry about that. They wanted to check my backpack, like I was straight out of St. E's or something, you know? And they just couldn't do that. Also, I shot some people as I went through the building. Maybe I shouldn't have. That was probably wrong. But Barry Edmonds, you know him? The representative from Oklahoma? I had to kill him. It got messy. He's right here."

Dust, the tension, something, tested the end of Sully's nose. He squinched his eyes shut to keep from sneezing. How far away was the shooter? Fifty feet? Sixty?

"I don't know why you're being this way. I really thought you guys would be here by now. Okay, so I'm sorry, I got to hang up then."

Silence followed, some muttering, and then the sound of a match striking. A flare in the darkness and a sizzle. *Whoomph whoomph*, something flew by him, sparkling, and hit the tiled floor. It slid past him, sparks of red and white light illuminating the hallway. A flare. A roadway flare. Then movement. Scuffling sounds, a grunt, a zipper closing, a clatter, something hard and metal hitting the tile floor. Then, soft as a rose petal, footsteps.

Christ. He did not breathe. The steps came slow and steady. As he peered out the slit in the door—his one chance to eyeball the shooter—it dawned on him. His pen. His pen was stuck in the door, providing his narrow window. It would be sticking out in the hallway, knee level. Obvious now in the flickering light.

The footsteps came alongside him and then passed, the man's body between Sully and the flare, illuminating him by backlight. The ponytail, that was the first thing Sully noticed. The man bent by the flare, the hair frayed and pulling loose. Sully breathed as slow as a swimmer.

The man reached out and took the bottom of the flare, holding it in his left hand, the light dancing around the hallway. He rose and turned back. Sully could pick out jeans and a black T-shirt, no facial hair.

Just for a second—a fraction of it—Sully thought the man looked over toward the bathroom door, at the pen jutting out. But then he underhanded the flare back down the hallway from which he'd just come, a sparkler spinning backward, throwing shadows that somersaulted and pinwheeled. It flew past the door until it *clack-clacked* on the floor and slid, coming to a rest far down the hallway.

When Sully looked back, the man was gone.

There was nothing. No shadow, no footsteps, no clatter. The hissing of the flare, the pale light fluttering down the hall, the sound of his own breathing. That was all. He kept an eye on the slit in the door. It was possible the shooter had flattened himself against the wall and was waiting for Sully to open it and step out, but he doubted it. If the guy had wanted to bang in the door, he would have already.

Still, standing up required planning. He leaned forward, off his ass and onto the balls of his feet, bringing his weight over his heels. Pressing down on them, raising up—a knee joint popped loudly on the gimp leg, making him hobble forward and cringe—he was on his feet.

Now. The door.

Two careful, contorted steps, like he was playing Twister, then he was behind it. Slowly, he reached down with his right hand to hold the pen stuck in the door opening. His left hand found the door handle. He eased up and stood back, pulling the door with him, sliding in his socks, until it was wide open and his back was against the wall, the door pressing against his nose.

Nothing. He counted to twenty. Nothing. *Where is the fucking cavalry?*

He came from behind the door. The ghastly reddish-white flare hissed. Briefly, he waved a hand into the hallway to see if it would draw fire. None. He slid out into the hallway, moving backward toward the flare, his eyes fixed down the hall where the shooter had disappeared. There was nobody and nothing. Just the flickering light, his breathing, the floor cool beneath his feet.

Sliding, taking his right foot forward, then bringing his left to catch up with it. Again. Moving in this way, he came past the flare. He swung his eyes to see the body that the killer had left behind.

"Oh, shit," he whispered.

A man in a suit. On his back. The mortal remains of Barry Edmonds. Smears of blood on the floor. Duct tape wrapped around his ankles, upper thighs. Arms bound at his sides. A strap of tape across his mouth. The crotch of his suit dark, wet.

He had been shot in the upper right leg, but that was hardly the problem. Sully blinked and looked again.

A stainless steel ice pick was driven through each eye. The shiny handles, catching the gleam, were flecked with blood and gore. They stood up out of his head like two antennae. Viscous fluid from each eye slid down his temples, puddling on the floor.

"Sweet baby Jesus," Sully whispered.

He turned and looked back down the hall, to see if the killer had reappeared. There was just air and empty space and, at the end of it, a dark sense of foreboding that something was just beginning rather than coming to a bloody end.

He had no idea how long he crouched there, but another clattering sound brought him out of his reverie. He whipped around. There was only darkness punctuated by—

*Fucking cavalry, now they . . .*

—bouncing bits of light coming at him. Too late, he knew. He turned and flung himself backward, tripping over Edmonds's corpse, clamping his teeth, trying to get his hands over his ears before the concussion grenades detonated. The floor came up too fast and he took the fall full on the chest, eyes squinched—

*Whoomp whoomp whoomp*

—flashes of light and Sully felt his eardrums dimple in against his brain and his temples explode and blood spurt out of his nose—

Floor vibrations running blistering ears forehead arms legs dragging feet feet feet floor sliding

—and it dawned somewhere in the dark recesses of his mind, somewhere below articulate thought, that before he even opened his eyes, before they'd even finished dragging him down the hall, before he'd even asked anything, he knew that these SWAT motherfuckers or Navy Seals or Army Rangers or who the fuck ever had stormed past the shooter, that they had missed him, and that he was still free and loose and gone, baby, gone.

## FIVE

"I, I DON'T know."

"Hair color?"

"Don't know. I told 'em an hour ago I don't know."

"Dark? Light?"

"Are you thick?"

"The ponytail. Long and wispy? Short and heavy?"

"Sort of wispy. Sort of long. Christ, my head."

The sketch artist dropped his hand away from the paper. "They told me you were a reporter."

Sully looked up. He'd been holding his forehead in the palms of both hands. The headache, the nosebleed from the concussion grenades making him dizzy and nauseous in a wobbling sort of way, like you were drunk and fell over but still thought you were standing upright. A crust of blood still held on to his upper lip; he could feel it, flaky and dry. He scratched at it, elbows still on his knees, and eyed the man up again.

Black hair perfectly combed, a neat little mustache, thin. Wearing a black Windbreaker with "FBI" emblazoned on it big enough to be seen from space. Through the arced light coming through the tent on the grounds east of the Capitol, set apart at a little table and easel a few feet from the milling crowd of uniformed cops, federal agents, witnesses, and

Hill staffers, the man was looking at him dull-eyed. Didn't give enough of a damn about him one way or another to give him shit. Sully was just a cog in the machine that had information that needed to be gleaned and he wasn't—what—gleaning.

"Then we're both fucked," Sully rasped, keeping eye contact, " 'cause they told me you were a sketch artist."

"I can't sketch without a description."

"I can't describe what I didn't see."

"You said you were within ten, fifteen feet."

"Yeah, Pocahontas, I was. And then your friends cut the lights. All I saw was him lit by a flare. Maybe five foot ten, could be six feet, thin but obviously strong, jeans or dark pants, a dark pullover. Ponytail. Clean shaven."

"We're trying to get a sketch to broadcast."

"Know that."

"This guy is still out there. The sketch might help someone recognize him."

"Know that too."

"He was wearing a baseball cap when he came through the security screening, so the cameras didn't pick up much of his face."

"Okay."

The man frowned. "The other people who saw him, mostly around the Speaker's office, were very frightened. What they said, it's more impressionistic, and somewhat contradictory. I was hoping you, given your background, might provide better detail."

Arms folded across his chest, his breathing steady but his left eye developing a tic, Sully nodded. He sat up in his chair. His ass hurt. Everything hurt.

"I would have thought the commando team, whoever, would have gotten a good look at him on their way in. The man just walked out. He wasn't in a hurry. He told the 911 operator his name and where to find him."

"Apparently there was some confusion."

"Not on my end."

The man didn't respond.

"Look at me like that all night," Sully said, lowering his head back into the cradle of his palms, closing his eyes. "It ain't changin' nothin'."

After a moment, the man with the black hair said: "He's not in the building, we know that. He's beyond the perimeter. He's loose. And armed. Which is why the description is critical. Anything jog your memory? Anything at all?"

The man waited. Sully heard the chair creak. The man was leaning forward, expectant. Sully recognized the drill without opening his eyes. He'd done it a million times to a million people himself. The patient interviewer looking for that last detail. Coaxing it forward with body language.

The noises of the night, the other conversations, the crowd of people in a small space, the light patter of rain tapping on the tent above, all these began to register on his conscious thought. But the image that danced on the back of his eyelids, the thing that he saw, like a still frame from a snuff film, was Edmonds's face, his eyes, the gore-spattered ice picks sticking straight up out of them.

"Well?"

"I done told all I'n tell."

The easel snapped back and there was the clatter of pencils on the table and the man walked away. The table and chair sat empty. Nobody else came.

The sound of the rain grew louder.

After a while, still bent over, still holding his forehead, he fished the phone out of his coat pocket. He pressed the green button and waited for it to come on. Once it did, he ignored the notice that he had six million missed calls and instead called the desk. Elliot, the news aide answering the call at this hour, immediately put R.J. on the line. Sully spoke for some time as the old man's fingers flew over the keyboard, a loud clatter, keeping up with the narration.

Then R.J. stopped and said, "You are shitting me."

"No."

"Got to be."

"It was pretty gotdamn original," Sully said, talking with his eyes closed. Every now and then he leaned over to spit, trying to get the taste of the explosives out of his mouth. The jitters, now that the shit was all over, were starting. He could feel the tremors at his elbows radiating down to his palms. He shook his free hand to try to rid himself of the sensation and finally stood up, walking in a tight circle, over and over again. Sometimes, as they talked, he wandered outside the tent to feel the spattering rain. All the survivors or witnesses or what have you were quarantined out here in the shadows and humidity, standing around in clumps, waiting to be interviewed or reinterviewed or debriefed or whatever the feds were calling it.

Hours, this had been going on. Fucking *hours*. They'd let him use his phone once earlier, for five minutes, in which time he'd called the desk and given them the shooter's name and a heads-up that a narrative was coming.

"Cooperators necklaced in South Africa," Sully was saying. "Seen that. Serbians cut the cocks off the mujahideen. Seen that. Liberia. Fuck's sake, man. *All* of Liberia. But this today, nah, I ain't seen this. Ice picks through the eyes."

"You're positive?"

"Seriously, you ask me this?"

The hour was going on ten. Deadline, that merciless bitch, was moving in for the kill. It always got later faster than you thought. Sully would swear, actually give a sworn affidavit, that on some days the hours between seven and ten p.m. lasted twenty-three minutes.

"What about the name?" R.J. said. "Waters? The feds will neither confirm nor deny."

"It's what he told 911. It's what I'm reporting."

"We have to be one hundred percent," R.J. said. "What you gave us,

Terry Waters, from Oklahoma? We ran it. Got a hit out of central Oklahoma. An hour and change south-southwest of Tulsa. Indian Country. One 'Terry Running Waters' has been certifiable since high school at the local Native American reservation, which appears to be the Sac and Fox. He dropped out. In 1982. As a junior. In and out of wards and the local jailhouse for a year or two, then apparently kept at home. Something like two decades. He was a suspect in some animal mutilations. There are a couple of clips."

"What you mean, 'kept at home'?"

"I mean, like, kept at home," R.J. said. "He's the Boo fucking Radley of the res. Like nobody's *seen* him in years. Except for, you know, the 'shadow at the window,' that sort of thing."

"Come on."

"We wouldn't print it if it wasn't true."

"Who's reporting that?"

"Ellen, from the Chicago bureau. Quoting tribal officials by phone. Nobody else has the name, at least for now. Feds have a presser skedded at eleven; I'm guessing they'll give it then. But nobody else has this for now. So you're right, right?"

"As rain."

Tulsa, Sully thought. Take out the "s" and you had his hometown in Louisiana. "Ellen's solid," he said. "And this guy, he told the 911 operator that was his name. Wanted credit. Couch it like that and we're golden."

"The feds aren't releasing the 911."

"I guess not. It sounded like the operator thought it was a prank."

"Were you taking notes?"

"In the dark?"

"But, I mean, the name, the details of the call, sometimes it's hard to remember—"

"Terry Waters and Oklahoma and ice picks. I can remember that much. What's the town Terry's from?"

"They're calling it Stroud, which I personally have never heard of, but apparently he lived way out on or near the Sac and Fox Reservation, which is apparently in your greater metropolitan Stroud."

"In other words, East Jesus."

"Jim Thorpe grew up there. I learned that today."

Sully, staying outside the tent now, took a seat on the curb, a blanket draped over his shoulders—what was with paramedics and blankets?—in a grove of trees in back of the Capitol, emergency lights throwing crazy shadows, ambulances and police cars, lights revolving. There was still a light rain falling, but it wasn't bad under the trees that lined the drive. The Capitol was fully illuminated now—but depopulated of everyone save for the techs inside poring over blood spots and counting ejected shells.

Outside, a huge phalanx of police had herded the last staffers and tourists into this more-or-less pen, marked off with yellow crime-scene tape. It was a rough square among the trees, with officers a few feet apart, setting the perimeter. Everyone had been screened and screened again. Law enforcement had slowly come to the obvious conclusion that Terry Waters was, in fact, long gone.

On the streets framing the Capitol complex—Independence and Constitution running east and west, and First Street SE and NE running north to south—Sully could see dozens of squad cars, lights revolving. Armored trucks parked at intervals. Two choppers beating the air in the near distance.

The paramilitaries who'd pulled him from the building were more pissed off than inquisitive; the detectives and the feds who questioned him were demanding and impatient; and the medic, who couldn't have been more than twenty-five, kept telling him, 'Mister, you're in shock,' until Sully ran his fingers across the scars on his face, then raised his sweat-soaked shirt to show the railroad track of shrapnel scars from Bosnia and said, "It's not my first dance at the prom."

He had told the feds enough but not everything. Certainly he didn't mention that he'd heard the man give his name—they would have that from the 911 call, anyway. He didn't imagine they'd be thrilled to read it in the paper tomorrow, but that wasn't his problem. Neither was it his problem that they'd missed Waters in the Capitol. It probably hadn't been hard to do, people running out of offices all over the place, so many warrens and back stairways, the subway running to the House and Senate office buildings—had anybody sealed that off?

Now the manhunt story was galloping ahead, dominating television, radio, and the Web, with newspapers holding their final editions to the last minute. Sully could play no part in the manhunt—he was locked in the safest part of the city for the foreseeable future—but he had the first-person firecracker narrative of the shooter's path.

"What's our body count?" he asked R.J.

"Nine confirmed, four critical, five serious, thirteen admitted. One of the fatals is a heart attack. Two of the admitted were people tripping, twisting an ankle, like that, running out."

"Who we got working it?"

"Everybody but Sports, and I'm including Jesus Christ in that. Keith is anchoring the lede-all with, I'm serious, something like forty, forty-five people sending feeds. It's the whole damn paper. Your narrative is the 1-A centerpiece. The art is great, a shot of the eastern entrance to the Capitol, all these people sprinting out, looking like they just saw Charlie Manson."

"Read me back the lede."

" 'The killer came prepared,' " R.J. said, reading from the story they'd been editing.

"Go on," Sully said.

" 'The gunman who killed U.S. Rep. Barry Edmonds and at least eight others in the U.S. Capitol yesterday afternoon first stormed into the building by shooting guards at the eastern entrance,' " R.J. continued. " 'He sprinted down a hallway, apparently shooting at random in the Crypt. Ascending the steps, he killed guards and civilians in the circular Rotunda, one of the most famous public spaces in the United

States. Then, with a hard right, he zeroed in on one of the most powerful offices in the U.S. Capitol: that of the Speaker of the House of Representatives.' "

"It's obvious but not awful."

"We give his ID to the 911 operator, and a bit on his background, but most of that is in the lede-all, not your narrative. And down below, later, the killing of Edmonds reads like this: 'He had come not only with semi-automatic guns, but with duct tape, flares, a cell phone, and ice picks. He shot Edmonds in the leg, bound him with the tape, hand and foot, then drove a steel ice pick through each of Edmonds's eyes, killing him.' "

He paused. "Okay, wait. How do we know he shot him before the ice pick business?"

"Because the picks were mortal. The leg had bled a lot, the pants were soaked, all that. You shoot somebody post-mortem, they don't bleed so much."

"Hunh. But, I mean, he could have tied him up and then shot him, right? That could be the sequence?"

Sully closed his eyes. He was going to throw up soon, he could tell. The throbbing.

"I guess so, R.J. Edit as you wish. I'm not hung up on that."

"Okay, okay, just a second . . ." and R.J. drifted away, the keyboard clattering, the old man breathing softly into the receiver. Sully wondered if he had a concussion. Blown up in Bosnia, beaten up at a motorcycle race track in the spring, now this. The paycheck wasn't matching the effort. He was pretty sure of that.

"Now then," the voice, bright and hard, back with him. "Let's pick it up at: 'Waters was in no hurry. He lit a common roadside flare—he had apparently brought it with him—to illuminate the pitch-black darkness. By the light of the flare, he appeared as a man of average height, perhaps five foot eleven, with a ponytail of dark hair, dressed in jeans and a dark shirt. When he was leaving, he tossed the flare back toward Edmonds, but did not speak. His path after that is unknown.' "

"True, fair, and accurate," Sully said. He leaned forward and spit.

"Did he say anything?" R.J. asked. "Did you hear him say anything to or about Edmonds, about why he had to kill him, and in that manner?"

"No. But they're saying out here that Edmonds was on the House Committee for Indian fuckovery or whatever."

"He's the ranking member on the House Committee on the Indian, Insular and Native Alaskan Affairs," R.J. said.

"Which is, what, the new name for the Bureau of Indian Affairs?"

"Bringing you Wounded Knee and other atrocities since 1824."

"Well. Any evidence of a more direct connection?"

"You mean like Edmonds was fucking his girlfriend?"

"That would put a bow on it. Tells you something, the way a man kills another. This thing, they had personal history, that's my guess."

"None apparent," R.J. said. "We got Susan and Audra up in research, and the entire congressional desk, going over Edmonds's voting history, like that, see if there's some legislation that our shooter might not have liked."

"Nothing on the manhunt?"

"Sweet fuck all. The city is locked down. Metro is shut down. So is Amtrak, the MARC Train, National, Dulles, and BWI. Traffic checkpoints everywhere. You should see the aerials. The Beltway, 66, 495, 295, the BW Parkway, the George Washington. Every on- and off-ramp. World's biggest parking lot."

"Jesus," Sully said, the last of the adrenaline oozing out of him, a physical sensation, like blood had been drained from his arm. He closed his eyes against the dizziness. The ice picks buried in Edmonds's face materialized in the blackness. He popped his eyes back open.

"How much time we got?" he said.

"We're five minutes over."

"Punch the button. We're sewed up tight."

R.J. paused, silence on the line. "Sullivan," he said quietly.

"Da, sahib."

"You're sure about this? All of it?"

Sully looked down at his socks, worn through at the heels now, his shoes lost and long gone, at his right hand, which had dried blood on it. He guessed it was from the kid in the Rotunda or the woman in the Crypt. The night had a bright electric feel to it, something metallic on the tip of the tongue, a penny in a socket.

"One more time, R.J. I swear to Christ and sonny Jesus, you ask me one more time—"

"Okay, alright already. We can*not* be wrong. We have *tons* of exposure. *Nobody* else was up there. This thing is gonna be huge and you're out there all alone. Eddie, Eddie Winters—you remember the executive editor of this establishment? He's behind you on this but nervous. The feds are going to want to pick you apart, you were up there before them. It's not going to be—"

"I don't see it that way," Sully said.

"—pretty, wait, what? Enlighten me."

"I'm not the one with the exposure. I didn't let the fucker get in the Capitol. I didn't let him get out. I got within ten feet of him without a gun, pistol, or badge, and had the drop on him, besides. The police and the feds, they can't say that. They don't correct us on this. We correct *them*."

## SIX

THE POLICE WERE taking witnesses and survivors over to Union Station, or to hotels at the foot of the Hill. By the time Sully was finished talking to R.J., the crowd was almost all gone, nothing left but stragglers. So when he was herded with the rest to the east entrance, right across from the Supreme Court, he figured he'd walk home. It was just six blocks up East Cap and two north on Sixth Street.

But when he walked past the waiting bus and got a dozen steps up the street, every cop on the block started screaming at him, shouting, uniforms running, boots on the wet asphalt. Two of the tacticals on the corner, beneath floodlights, had M-16s trained on him.

This set off a five-minute pissing match about who could go where and orders and states of emergency and what defined a public street. The bus pulled away and left. The cop said that he'd throw his ass in D.C. Jail. Sully, the cavity behind his eyes feeling like it was about to explode, pulled out his phone and called the cell of John Parker, head of D.C. Homicide, who didn't pick up. Sully, still holding up a wait-a-minute finger at the cop in front of him, called right back. Parker picked up this time and said, "If this caller ID is right, it better not be."

Sully gave Parker the ten-second summary and said he'd count it as a personal favor and handed the phone to the cop. The cop listened and didn't say anything and handed it back to Sully. The cop waved his hand and said, "Let the fucker get shot then." He waved his arms back and forth to get the attention of the cops a block up, at the end of the Supreme Court building. Then he told Sully to walk his bony ass down the middle of East Cap all the way home and that if he got shot, all they'd do is stand there and watch him bleed out.

Sully limped to the first checkpoint, the cops there eye-fucking him, then moved from the brightly lit part of the city immediately into the neighborhood of narrow row houses and brick sidewalks and overhanging trees, the hush descending.

The cell in his hand buzzed.

It never failed to astonish him how vast the seat of power on the Hill was, a center of clout, senators and representatives who could change the lives of the entire nation, if not the world . . . and, one lousy block east, you crossed a two-lane and you were in a Washington neighborhood of row houses and corner markets and alleyways, where streetlights didn't work, air-conditioning units hung out of most of the windows, you could buy dope in the parks, and nobody gave a rat's ass about who you knew.

The tremors—he felt them start at his fingertips.

The cell buzzed again.

Still in the middle of the street, he was approaching the checkpoint at Third Street, the police cruiser blinding him with its spotlight. He clicked to accept the call without looking at it, expecting Parker or R.J.

"This is Carter."

Lucinda's high-pitched voice burst out of the phone.

"How could you not even *call*," she said. "I trust you with my son and this is what—"

He came up even with the cruiser and shielded his eyes to click off the call, his sister still at full volume. The cops cut the searchlight and stared at him.

"Family," he smiled, twiddling the phone back and forth. "We good, gentlemen?"

*    *    *

Ten steps past the checkpoint, the cell buzzed. Arizona area code. He clicked it back on. "Lucinda, I got to tell you," he said, before she could speak, "you scream in my ear like that one more gotdamn time, we won't talk again."

She was quiet now but seething. He could feel it coming through the line.

"Sullivan. Sullivan. Sullivan. Let me breathe. I send my only child to you. Only child. And you go gallivanting after some crazy man with a gun. Leaving him alone. He called at least five times tonight, scared to death. And now this lunatic is loose? Blocks from my son? What, I ask you, *what* are you doing to keep him safe?"

There were times he wished he smoked, to give him something to do when he felt the world pinwheeling beyond his grasp, that out-of-control feeling that had taken over so much of his life since Bosnia.

*Bourbon* floated across his mind, just like that, and he unconsciously turned to look at the pub on the corner, but the red and blue neon OPEN sign was off, of course, the entire block shuttered. Even the houses were dark, people huddled inside, thinking that somehow Terry Waters was lurking by the Japanese maple in the front yard.

"*Sullivan*," her voice rising. "Did you *hear* me?"

He pictured Lucinda in the kitchen of her house in Phoenix, sitting at the breakfast nook—that's what she called it, honest to Christ— looking outside at the dry hills in the distance, still light there this time of year, the house quiet, Jerry off at the grocery store, overseeing all of them in the city or region or whatever.

He also made a mental note to pop Josh upside the head, soon as he got home.

"I would call it doing my job," he said, finally. "Josh was at home in the basement watching television," he said. "Boy was fine. Eating pizza. Is fine."

"You hung up on me just now," she said, sounding like she was reading from an indictment.

"You called me three hundred times already," he said, now nearly shouting himself. "Any one of those coulda gotten me killed, you know that? You coulda given this psycho a homing beacon to blow my head off. You knew Josh was gotdamn good-and-well safe but you could not wait, could not *wait*, to fuck with me about it. Calling me at work to start some shit about *your* kid at *my* house."

She took a breath down the line and he roared into it.

"You with me here? I call and ask *you* to babysit all summer? Nope. You called me and I got *your* boy in the flipping Corcoran, a summer session with Bill Christenberry, for God's sake."

"You keep saying that like I'm supposed to know who it is."

"You should."

"Don't lecture."

"How long'd it been since we talked, then you call me up asking if Josh could come?"

"Don't start."

"That's not a date on a calendar."

"A long time, Sully."

"A long time, you're fuckin' A. You didn't come to see me when I was in Walter Reed, after Bosnia, right? What, I was out cold and missed you?"

Silence, then: "No, Sully, you did not."

Long, slow, resigned, the same sibling waltz they'd been dancing since the family had collapsed and they'd been farmed out to different relatives. Lucinda to Phoenix, Sully to New Orleans.

Lucinda had found religion. Sully had found bourbon. Their bonds, stretched paper-thin, drifted apart like a spiderweb in the wind. The answer to the question he'd posed was five years, maybe six, and then seven or eight before that. Twice in fifteen years, call it that. Both at Christmas. They were, by any measure, strangers, but maybe even worse than that—

people who had once shared a bond and lost it. Now any meeting, any conversation, was filled with the shadows and silences of the intervening years and the weight of what had happened to their parents.

"You, you, you call, tell me the kid's a prodigy," he said, "asking me if there's a summer art program in D.C., something to boost his college application."

Silence.

"And I did you a solid. William fucking Christenberry, a summer class, ten kids, you got to be kidding me. And then, on a day when I damn near get killed, on a day I watch a lady spit a blood bubble out of her mouth before she dies, on a day I see a man with ice picks through his fucking face, on *this* day you call me, and your concern is not for your only brother, who was less than thirty feet from a mass shooter, but for your kid, who was half a mile away, in what amounts to a basement bunker. It's touching, sis. Touch*ing*."

"Sully, hey?" she said. "You chose to spend your life in a sewer of war and violence. Josh didn't. The rest of the world isn't like you. I turn on my television out here, the cable channels are screaming about mass murder on Capitol Hill. How do I know, from this side of the country, what the situation is unless I talk to you? And when I called? You wouldn't answer. So, really, what did you expect?"

The late-summer drizzle, coming down through the massive oaks, into the open spaces, pattering onto the asphalt, the brick cobblestone sidewalk, dripping off leaves and onto the patrol cars parked on the streets, it all seemed blurry, like it had been painted by Van Gogh. Head. His head.

Heading north on Sixth now. One of the warped bricks in the sidewalk caught his stockinged foot, causing him to stumble, cursing. Crossing A Street. No sound but a chopper in the distance. His house was one hundred and ten years old, at the edge of what his neighbors called "the box"—a rectangle on the east side of the Capitol building that roughly approximated the National Mall on the west.

The way the real estate market was exploding—a neighbor had her house on the market for three hours and sold it for $320,000, after buying it for less than half that eight years earlier—Sully sometimes thought, when he was in a good mood, that he was turning the corner in life.

This night, he was a long goddamn way from a good mood.

He shoved open the low wrought-iron gate, ascending the few brick steps to the front door. He dropped the keys once and then couldn't get the key in the lock until he stopped and took a long, deep breath. Once inside, he made straight for the kitchen, a glass, the bottle, and he was pouring. He made himself wait to add the ice to the Basil's but then he drained it in a long gulp, rattling the ice against his lips. Closed his eyes. Yes, Lord, yes. The burn in his chest, the blossoming percussion in his brain. He opened his eyes and poured another deep one, coughed, then went downstairs.

Josh was sitting on the sofa, television blaring, pizza carton on the beat-up coffee table, popcorn, a bottle of beer, half raising a hand in greeting but not turning.

Sully came off the last step, bourbon sloshing, "Hey, slick, you want to tell me that was about, your mother busting my eardrum just now?"

Josh turned, hand still half raised. "What, what?"

Sully grabbed the remote with a free hand, hit mute, threw it back on the couch. "Your momma. My sister. Screeching you were wetting your diapers."

"Oh, um, that. Mom. I switched off a movie? And it was all over every station, some shooting up there at the Capitol? So I thought I should call and let her know, you know, that I was okay and everything."

"She says you called like five times, blabbering."

"Blabbering? Two."

"Blabbering two what?"

"Twice. I called twice. And I wasn't crying, I can't believe she said that. That's just random."

"So, what I'm wondering is, why call her anyhow? You know how she gets—Christ, you live with her—and you set her off—"

"No, no. See, no. I, I wanted to let her know I was paying attention, calm her down, let her know I was okay. I thought it was interesting conversationally, the shooting. She asked if I was okay, and, you know, she likes to think I'm still seven years old, so I said, well, I'd feel safer if Sully were here, you know, or I was back home with her and Dad, 'cause I thought she'd like to hear that. Me being responsible."

"Responsible."

"Right."

"Move over. God. What is responsible about torquing your hysterical mother up another notch."

It wasn't a question and Josh knew it if Sully didn't. The couch was soft but, holy shit, his joints. His *bones*. He got a whiff of himself: musty, sweaty, stale. The kid was looking at him like he was out of a zoo.

"She's already *at* eleven," Sully said.

There was something on the television, a guy in an insane asylum, crosses all over his face and the room, the guy drawing like mad. Josh found the remote and turned the sound up enough that there were mumbles emanating from the screen. Sully closed his eyes and let out a long breath.

"Where are your shoes?" Josh's voice.

"What?"

"Your shoes? Your feet are soaked. The socks, they got all these holes."

"I don't even want to talk about it. Fetch me a bourbon, will you? Three cubes." He held out his glass with three fingers splayed. He did not open his eyes.

"You told me not to go get you bourbon when you asked for it."

"Never mind that now."

"You said it would help you slow down."

" 'Never mind that now' seems to be a phrase that most fifteen-year-olds who don't want their uber-evangelical parents to know they're drinking beer and binging on horror movies and certain pay-per-view titles I'm not going to mention would understand."

The weight lightened on the couch. Sully felt the glass taken from his hand. He let it fall back down in his lap. Breathing. He focused on breathing until it started to come even and slow. He'd forgotten to ask the kid for Advil.

When he felt the cool, heavy round circle of the glass back on his knee, he opened his eyes again. Three cubes. Another long pull and he felt his head ease, like somebody had loosened a too-tight belt. Still, the vileness in his gut from the explosives, that seasick feeling.

"Is the shooting thing all through?"

Sully looked at him, the slight frame, the my-mom-cuts-my-hair vibe, the shorts and the bare feet. "Yeah," Sully said. "Ain't you been watching the television? After you called Lucinda?"

"For a few minutes. But then it got boring. I put in a movie, one of those we got from the Blockbuster on Eighth. *The Evil Dead.* Your office called and this guy, he said you would be home late and to get dinner myself. He said I could order pizza or Chinese."

" 'This guy.' "

"He said that somebody shot somebody in the Capitol and you were there."

"That about covers it."

"Is your story finished?"

"I made it on the bevel."

"Are you okay?"

Sully, eyes still closed, wondered if the lady's bubble of saliva had made a sound when it popped. Just a tiny one. "Why?"

"Your left eye, it's doing this weird thing. And your right hand is shaking. Are you cold?"

Sully flopped his hand around. "Didn't you sort of get curious, the sirens, the helicopters?"

"There's always sirens going by."

"True enough." Exhaustion was hammering at his neck, his shoulders, his fucking knee. "1-D, the precinct, is a straight shot about ten blocks south. So any time they got to go rocketing north, up to H, I, those drug markets up there, they sail right on by."

"You're starting to slur a little."

"Forsooth."

"Also, somebody named Alexis called. She asked if you were home yet. She sounded like she knew you."

Christ, Christ, Alex, he hadn't called her yet. He would in a minute. In just one minute.

"She does. She's a shooter at the paper. May become an editor. She's in town for that."

"Okay."

"I been knowing her a while."

"That's good."

"Are you actually listening or just spouting one-word answers to anything I say?"

"Yes."

His ears were still ringing from the fire alarm. But it was all less now. Everything was less now. Bourbon was a wonderful thing. Coming down now, a plane for landing, altitude descending. All things shining.

"So tell me, what's this on now?" he said, forcing his eyes open. He didn't like yelling at the boy, clueless as he sometimes was. Must get all he could stand of that at home. Crazy-assed Lucinda. He ought to adopt the boy on general principle. "What are we, what are we watching here?"

"*In the Mouth of Madness.*"

"It has a plot of some sort, I just know it."

"It's awesome. This guy, this one right here—"

"Isn't that Sam Neill?"

"—he's supposed to go, no, yeah, that's him, see, he's supposed to go get the copy of this book that this other guy wrote, this horror-writer guy. . . ."

Later, a hand on his shoulder, shaking.

"Sully? It's over. The movie. You going to sleep here? 'Cause I'm turning out the light."

## SEVEN

DEEP BREATHING, SLOW drag on the respirator. Deep and slow.

Buzz.

Darkness reigned. He was somewhere, he was somewhere. He was three thousand feet underwater, that's where he was. No light at these depths. The cold, bitter, empty darkness of salt and water. Currents moved you with them; you could not see or sense them coming, they just waved you from side to side, like a little human palm frond, as they passed. There was no sound at all.

Buzz buzz.

That couldn't be, no no. No buzzing. No sound. That had to be some sort of weird jellyfish squid whale . . . one eye opened, and he was horrifically lifted from the depths of subaquatic oblivion to a roiling, light-shattered room and the jolt sent him upright, lurching, the heave coming from his gut but catching in his throat. He was awake and rolling sideways, upright, the basement a blur, then the sharp, hard edges of reality and right angles.

Light burst in through the half window. Josh hadn't pulled the shades. It was whiter than the sun, reflecting off car windows or something out front. He swallowed the bile, the burning.

There was the buzzing again. A bee sting, a dog's bite, a tiny tin hammer banging.

The phone. The motherfucking phone.

It was there on the glass top of the coffee table, humping up in the air on each buzz. He leaned forward on the couch, finding a paper towel by the pizza box, a lame attempt to wipe the worst taste in America out of his mouth. Wet cigarette butts in old ashtrays, rainwater in a motel gutter spout.

"Lucinda," he said into the phone, "I gotdamn well—"

"Mr. Carter? Mr. Carter?"

The voice cutting him off.

He closed his eyes again. Never answer the phone on a day you have a story on the front page. Never answer the phone on—

"Yes, this is." And after a moment, "Mr. Carter."

Coughing, throat clearing. "Okay. Okay. This is, this is Terry Waters."

It didn't make him jump, he would remember later. It didn't make him do much of anything. He just tried to lather his dried-out lips with his equally dried-out tongue and leaned back into the soft recesses of the couch, croaking with the voice of a hundred years, "Who thinks this is funny?"

"I, I thought I said," the voice came back, after a moment. It was like the guy was talking on a weird radio frequency that was only now beginning to come in clear through the static and sunspots. "This is Terry Waters. You, uh, wrote a story about me. It's right here on the front page. You, you were the one hiding in the bathroom."

The sensation came over him like a tuning fork struck on the spine, his nerve endings lighting up like a dormant Christmas tree. He stood up without realizing it.

"Mr. Carter? Are you there? I, I'm guessing this is a surprise. I'm sorry. Sorry sorry sorry. But I had to call. When I read about your mother. I think, I think we should talk. Is that okay?"

## EIGHT

"YOUR MOTHER?"

"Yeah."

"And his?"

"Yeah."

"That's very interesting."

"That's what I told him."

"And what specifically about them?"

"That they were both murdered."

This brought FBI Special Agent Gill's gaze up from her notes to his face. They were looking at each other across a conference table at the paper, a little after noon, maybe ninety minutes since Waters had hung up on him.

An agent sat on either side of her. R.J. and Lewis Beale, the paper's attorney, flanked him. Sully had called the paper after Waters's call and was transferred to Eddie Winters's office. Eddie had listened and told him to come in immediately. He'd also alerted the FBI, who got there almost as fast as Sully. Eddie had walked them all into the conference room, made the introductions, and then left to run the daily.

Now everybody had little water bottles and nobody touched them. They were on the eighth floor, the executive suite, far away from the newsroom below. The windows overlooked a parking garage. Haze and glare and shimmering heat.

She held the gaze—on his eyes, not flitting to his scars; it took discipline not to do that, he knew from past experience—and waited on him to elaborate.

He didn't.

"That is an unusual connection," she said, finally.

"Also," Sully said, "that neither of their killers were caught."

"I see." Another pause. "And how would you say it made you feel, when he said that?"

Sully tilted his head to one side, ever so slightly, and crossed his bad leg over his good one. All three of them, she and the men flanking her, looked like they ate nails for breakfast and shit steel before lunch. Suits, folders, and briefcases. Acting like they owned the place ever since they walked in.

After a while, he said, "What did you say your name was, ma'am?"

"Agent Gill."

"Do you have a first name, Agent Gill?"

"We seem to be losing the thread," she said.

"Your thread," Sully said, "and mine are not the same."

He got a glare this time, from the guy on her right. The guy's pen had been twitching the whole time, taking notes, and now he raised his chin and leaned into the table, like you do when you have to pull up your socks. "Look, Carter," he said. "This—"

"Special Agent Alma T. Gill," she said.

"Well then, Special Agent Alma T. Gill," Sully said, "the fuck business is it of yours?"

"Hey hey HEY," Chin Man said, bolting upright, his partner doing the same on her left, R.J. and Lewis matching them, everybody pointing and raising voices, tempers flaring for the second or third time now.

"I'd heard about you, Carter," the man on her right started in again, "and I'm not going to—"

"I wasn't talking to you, champ," Sully interrupted, not even glancing his way. "I's talking to your boss."

"—put up with, what did you say to me?"

"You heard. I'm not being deposed here. My boss calls to tell you we have likely contact with the nation's Most Wanted and you guys show up twenty minutes later all 'hunh who what,' like we work for you. Which we don't. So mind your fucking manners. Agent Gill here, she asked an odd question. You don't like my answers, yonder's your door."

Now he stood, pushing his chair back and taking three steps, no fooling around with this bullshit.

"I was asking," she said, her voice smooth as buttermilk, "because I wanted to know if you thought he was baiting you. Taunting you that your mother's killer was never caught."

Sully stopped, the room heavy, the hum of the air-conditioning the only sound. He eyed her for a moment, then sat back down.

"No," he said.

There was nothing else, her just looking at him, waiting.

"He was commiserating. In my opinion."

"How do you think he could have learned of your mother's death?"

"He would have seen my byline then looked me up on the Internet. It's not hard."

She nodded. No recognition in the eyes, though, that she knew what he was talking about.

"Like you could have, before you showed up."

"Sully," R.J. whispered, thumping a knee against his.

"We've had a rather busy morning," she said. "We came as soon as your editor alerted us to the contact. There wasn't, isn't, time for research. Apologies if you're offended I don't know who you are."

Sully gave her a half smile.

"Don't get it twisted, Special Agent Alma T. Gill. I know a misquote when I hear one. I said you could have found out who my *mother* was. I didn't say shit about me. But I got blown up in Bosnia. This being Washington and my employer being a fancy newspaper, it got reported. A couple of stories, some segments on the nightly news. My mother's murder was mentioned as biography. Nothing huge but it's on the Web. All I's trying to tell you is that he didn't have to be a genius, or take a lot of time, to get that intel."

"May I ask how your mother was killed?"

"Shot to death. Tula, Louisiana. In her hair salon, such as it was. Cash left in the register. No apparent motive, no suspects. Three shots, two to the head."

"Did he say how his mother was killed?"

"Thanks for asking her name."

"What was your mother's name?"

"Cyndy. Cynthia."

"I am sorry for your loss."

"You're so kind to say so."

"Did he say how his mother was killed?"

"No. I asked. He said he might could tell me later."

"Did he blame Representative Edmonds for her death?"

"No. You're getting ahead, though."

She gave him the full-on I've-about-had-it-with-your-skinny-white-ass look.

"Look, it's your interview," he said.

She sat back in her chair, listening.

"What he said, what he asked, was about my mother," Sully said, and as he spoke, his words came more slowly, more absently, as if he were forgetting the people in the room, that he was talking to anybody at all, save himself.

"He wanted to know, he asked, not so much about the method of how she was killed and what the scene was like, and where I was when I heard. That's usually what people ask about, you know. Details. Gunshots. People running. Like the last five minutes of their lives was all that mattered. People, they're interested in murder. They are. Grief? No. You want to talk about a killing, you'n do that on television. Grief, the long arc of it, you have to pay somebody to listen. Shrinks. Doctors. Counselors. He, what he asked, was about me, and what it was like living with that all these years. Growing up with it. He wanted to know how that ate at me. He wanted to know, if I had the chance, if I would kill her killer. If that would make me a bad person if I did."

The room had gone silent, everyone staring. He looked up.

"It's my two cents that you have to have that experience to be interested in that, those, questions. Our boy's mom died hard."

"You say that," Chin Man said, "like you feel sorry for him."

Sully looked at the agents. "I don't know I'd say 'feel sorry.' I'd say, talking to him, seeing him yesterday, he's a sick man. I'd say he's been corroding for a long time, bones wasted down to rust. You want to say that's feeling sorry, go ahead."

"He hurt a lot of innocent people yesterday," Chin Man said. "Killed several. That's the only reason we're here, the only reason anybody gives a damn about this guy."

"That's the problem with victims and perps," Sully said. "Line's so thin. Stop the clock yesterday morning, he's a sad story. By nightfall, he's a monster. I don't buy he made the transition in the afternoon. Grief is a patient bastard. It'll take its time, twist you into something you never were."

Gill put both elbows on the table, leaning in now. "So. The point. Did he blame Representative Edmonds for his mother's death?"

"Not exactly. Waters, he said he had to get *the* attention and get *his* attention. My emphasis, not his."

"Did he elaborate?"

"No. I didn't get it either. By 'his' I thought he meant Edmonds's, but there wasn't a lot of time for follow-up. He was scattered, he stuttered, he kept thinking somebody was going to trace the call. The whole thing was, what, three, five minutes."

"Did he seem in possession of his senses?"

"I would say so. Scared. But I mean, look, he had the presence of mind to pick up Edmonds's cell phone, either from his body or from his office, and use that to call 911, right? He saw my story, in the paper or online, looked up my name, then, I guess, called the paper's switchboard, got transferred to my line, got my cell from the message on the machine, and called me, again from Edmonds's phone."

Gill nodded, looking down the row of seats at their recorder.

"And then, then he quoted a poem?"

"Used a line. I wouldn't say quoted. He was talking about the killing—Edmonds—and he said that after he stabbed him, Edmonds 'lay there like a patient etherized upon a table.' He stopped, and then said, sort of to himself, 'as the evening was spread out against the sky.' It seemed like it just occurred to him. It wasn't a grand statement. Then he went back to the killing, and how he thought he saw somebody in the bathroom, which turned out to be me, and he said something about how we could have spoken when we were all but face-to-face, and then I said, because I had remembered the poem, 'but you went through certain half-deserted streets.' "

She looked at him.

"T. S. Eliot," Sully said. " 'The Love Song of J. Alfred Prufrock.' Then Waters sort of laughed. Sort of. Some noise. He said that he was glad he called and that he would call me back when he could. He said he was tired and hungry and then hung up. The end. It's the second time we been over this."

Gill nodded to the man on her left. Writing on his notebook, he got up and left.

"Agent Ginsberg will get research at Quantico pulling that poem apart immediately," she said. "Maybe he's trying to—"

"They'll like the line about there being 'time to murder and create,' " Sully said. "I looked up the thing, too."

"—tell us, okay, see, that's one of the problems here," she said. "We have an apparently mentally disturbed Native American, lightly educated and living in rural squalor, and yet he's broken into the Capitol, killed his target, escaped, and now he's got his feet up, calling reporters and chatting about dead moms and obscure poetry. How would you explain that, Mr. Carter?"

Irritated, like she had been since she'd walked in. The air in the room, it felt recycled, musty, run through rusting vents.

"I would say I don't have to," he said. "Terry Waters doesn't need me or you or a psychiatrist to explain him. Neither did Oswald or Booth or Manson. They just are."

"He's got help," she said. "He didn't do this himself."

"Possible. But, look, let's don't go calling this guy a criminal mastermind. I'm a mongrelized Anglo from eastern Louisiana, very lightly educated, to use your charming phrase, and grew up in rural squalor. You, you're an African American, the most trod upon of all Americans. Most of your accent is gone, but it's still got a trace of soft South to it, I'm going for Georgia, South Carolina, a big city rather than a small town, which means—given that people of your parents' generation were not moving from north to south but the other way around—your people have been down there a long time. And yet here *you* sit, a big-shot profiler for the FBI, at the center of the number-one criminal manhunt in the nation."

He took a drink from his bottle of water, swirled it around his mouth, aware that he was displaying a monstrous chip on his shoulder, and swallowed. "So how would you explain either of us? We shouldn't exist. Except here we sit. Ma'am."

"It's unusual because of his ability to plan, the escape, the poetry."

"I already done said. He told me he wasn't planning to escape. Walked down the hall, expecting to meet the cops, give himself up. Nobody ever stopped him, so he kept walking. Went down what he called a little staircase. Wound up with a bunch of people running out of their offices. Said they all went out what he called a side exit."

She and Agent Chin exchanged glances and Chin reached down and turned off the recorder. They started putting papers in folders and briefcases, not bothering to tell him they were finished. R.J. and Lewis finally exhaled.

"So, Special Agent Gill," Sully said, "you been asking all the questions. I got two."

She did not look at Chin Man before she said, "If I can," which confirmed his earlier impression of who was in charge, and thus allowed him to ask a better first one.

"You know of any place Waters has been since he left the res?"

"No. But it's early."

"You think he's going to call me again?"

"Absolutely. That's why we're putting a trace on your home, cell, office. It's why you're going to sit by one of them until he calls."

"Why would he?"

"That's three."

"Indulge me."

She flicked him a half smile, the first she'd allowed herself the entire interview, and stood up, looping her bag over a shoulder.

"Because a Spelman grad can see you're his loose end, Louisiana," she said, "not to mention a loose cannon."

# NINE

THE WHOLE WAY down in the elevator, walking back to the newsroom, R.J. was either pissing about the big-footing feds coming in the place with that attitude or riding him about popping off at them.

"You figure out she's smarter than you yet," R.J. said, looking over at him, "or you need me to tell you?"

"They on our turf," Sully said, ignoring the question. "You got to pee on your trees."

Yeah, R.J. was saying, but you can't just go peeing on every tree in the yard, and then he was bitching about southerners and their obsession with dogs. Sully, as they made their way through the cavernous newsroom, slowly tuned him out, the place was going a million miles an hour. Everybody had been called in from home or called back from vacation, nobody fucking around. Phones rang and reporters caught it before the echo of the first ring and talked low and fast, popping open a file, phone crooked between ear and shoulder.

At home, their spouses or girlfriends or boyfriends or children gave up hope of seeing them again for days. Across the city, the manhunt and the waves of heat and humidity rolled down deserted streets. People sat in front of their televisions and stared at the nonstop coverage and listened to what the killer had done to the congressman and decided that no, no, there'd be no taking the kids out for ice cream or to the movies or anything at all until this nutjob was dead or in jail.

In the newsroom, the televisions suspended from the ceiling broadcast images of retired cops and federal investigators, the sound muted, but all of them talking about facts they didn't have. The pundits yakked about what it all meant for the 2002 midterms. Some guy on the market floor was talking about how stocks were sliding. There was a real and actual police scanner blipping somewhere; Sully could swear he heard it.

"The daily budget, what, for today?" R.J. said, coming out of his rant, steering them to the main conference room. "It looks like a cross between D-day and a high-speed train wreck."

And then he was off on a new rant, about how this would involve, what, how many, between seventy-five and one hundred reporters, editors, photographers, graphic designers, copy editors, layout artists, and lawyers. Reporters were moving by foot, car, taxi, and airplane. They would, he went on, correspond by email, burn up phone lines, send faxes, file FOIAs, burrow into court clerks' offices, consult online databases, attend press conferences, consult experts, and—in a massive, strange, and somehow primitive act of coordination—all turn in stories, files, reports, and dispatches within minutes of one another, from all over the nation if not the globe, like they were a murmuration of starlings, like they were shoaling fish. They had to separate, align, and maintain cohesion while running at flat-out full speed, and then come together for a final presentation at almost the same time.

"The fuck-me part of it is," R.J. said, coming into the conference room, plopping down in a swivel chair, "is that it'll work. Does every time. *Challenger* blew up, Reagan shot, pick."

Sully, who had neither grown up in newspapers nor ever really cared to work in one before getting hired by the *Times-Pic* in New Orleans, said it was some sort of professional voodoo.

"When voodoo works," R.J. shrugged, "you leave the juju be." He flapped his printout of "Love Song" on the table. It was annotated in red, lines and arrows here and there. "The library has the rest of Eliot. Susan, Audra, everyone else, are going over it."

"Has Eddie decided when he wants me to write up something for the Web about the call?"

R.J. looked up, over his glasses. "I would score that one an 'if,' sport. Your new best friend at the FBI wants a sit-down with Eddie as to if we're going to use that. National security, encouraging a killer, etc."

"So why didn't we all do that just now?"

"The director wants in on it."

"Director?"

"Of the Feeb."

Sully stopped looking out the window to throw a look at R.J.

"You're serious."

"As cancer. Sullivan, the man just infiltrated the Capitol of the United States and executed a member of Congress."

" 'Infiltrating the Capitol of the United States' consisted of blowing past one magnetometer with two guards. Then he ran down a hall and shot his local representative."

"The ice picks."

"I'm trying to block the visual, thanks."

His stomach rolled over. Initially, he thought it was nausea. Then he remembered he had not eaten since yesterday, lunch. This morning, after the call from Waters, he had run upstairs, grabbed the small, heavy felt package holding the Tokarev from its hiding place in the closet, stuffed it in his cycle jacket, grabbed his helmet, told Josh to stay inside all day, and flew into the office on the Ducati. Now he was walking around the conference room, realizing he was in need of a shower and a burger in equal urgency. He wasn't going to get either for a while, he thought, looking at the big-ass whiteboard where all this was being mapped out.

It was a lunatic's scribbling of names and story assignments and headings and numbers, a lot of it in different colored markers.

There were stories assigned on Edmonds, his House career, his voting records, his youth back in Oklahoma, funeral plans, memories from colleagues, searches for ties to Waters. Did they meet at a shopping center campaign rally? Had Edmonds angered the tribe? Did Native Americans like or loathe Edmonds? Did a member of Waters's family work for one of his businesses? Rent an apartment from a property he owned? Did Edmonds fuck his sister? Did Waters even have a sister?

There was a link, there was a tie, and somebody somewhere was going to find it. They had to be first. Had to. This story. In this town. Getting beat on this would be professional humiliation.

The board also mapped out short memorial stories on each of the victims, longer ones on the Capitol police officers killed in the line of duty. Another quadrant was devoted to Capitol security, with "own police force" and "WTF" written in huge letters, with four exclamation marks.

Then, Jesus, there was another Old Testament assigned to Waters: his mysterious youth in Oklahoma, his alleged mental state, his juvenile arrests or misdemeanors or complaints or whatever about the animal mutilations. Did he or his family have any ties to protests or Native American causes? Had nobody really seen him for a decade? What was the state of mental health care out there? Could a doctor or nurse or aid worker be persuaded to comment? His old high school? Teachers, friends, classmates? There was at least one story on Sac and Fox, if not Native American, mysticism and the importance of eyes in folklore. What did the act of stabbing a man in the eyes mean? Did he stab the animals he mutilated in the eyes, too?

Washington being a company town, you also had the entire D.C. slice of the pie—stories about representatives and senators and staffers talking about their fears and safety, the outrage for once not partisan. There was a sidebar on a history of political assassinations and attacks in Washington (Lincoln, Garfield, Reagan), and assaults at the Capitol building (Jackson). There was a roundup of international reaction from other capitals, with feeds about attacks on other national parliaments and how security was handled in London, Paris, Moscow, Jerusalem, Tokyo, Mexico, Canada, South Africa, basically wherever the paper had a correspondent.

Investigative and Metro and the political desk were combining on a ticktock of the attack—tracking Waters's access to the building, Edmonds's movements that day until the two collided, the resulting chaos, and how Waters could have escaped.

Theories held that he'd used the subway that ran underneath the building, then popped out of one of the House or Senate office buildings. Others held that he'd taken a staffer's ID badge and just walked right past police. Bolder ones suggested he'd changed into an MPD uniform.

There were at least three stories on the manhunt, on how airport security was so beefed up that the lines were forever and flights out of National, Dulles, and BWI were all delayed, screwing up air travel across the eastern half of the country, and how yesterday's near-total shutdown of the Beltway had buggered traffic from Charlotte to Philadelphia.

This would amount to, more or less, Sully squinted an eye to figure, about fifteen thousand words, fifty pages in a book. It would all be reported and written—along with sports, features, local politics and zoning issues, the home section, movie reviews, real estate listings, classified ads, and wedding announcements, all adding up to a decent-sized novel—and then printed, more than eight hundred thousand times, for delivery to newsstands, gas stations, mini-marts, front porches, driveways, mailboxes, and apartment buildings in about, say, thirteen hours.

On the Waters story alone, any error, no matter how small, would have to be corrected in print and possibly to the detriment of the entire effort. Fifteen thousand words . . . and if, say, four of them were wrong—four errors—the paper's staff would look like douche-bag half-wits, mocked in the trades for blowing the big one.

It gave him the beginnings of a renewed headache, made worse by a single line of writing on the whiteboard that began glowing. It was circled, set slightly apart from the rest.

"Sully," it read. "Office/rewrite/phone."

"Hey," he said, walking to the board, tapping his name. "I'm the receptionist? I thought Special Agent Alma T. Gill was bluffing."

R.J. looked up, peering. "Calm down. You're writing the lede-all. If Waters has a hard-on for you, probably best for you to sit tight in the building. And answer your phone. Every time the thing buzzes. I don't care if it's a little old lady in Crystal City telling you that she's looking at black U.N. helicopters hovering over the White House. Answer. Waters calls again, you got to pick it up. That's from Eddie, that's from the FBI, that's probably from the fucking White House."

Out in the hallway, a crowd came out of the elevator and there was Alexis, tense, walking head down, studying a sheaf of papers in her hands.

"Be back," he said to R.J., then hustled out of the room, catching up to her in the narrow hallway. She stopped, stepping to the side to let the people behind them pass, raising her eyebrows half a notch. Sully stepped beside her. Her eyes were sharp, glittering, looking into him, reading what she could find.

"You look like shit," she said.

"Thank you for noticing."

"And—wait, is that you I *smell*?"

"Don't sniff me in the hall," he said, leaning back. "People might—"

"This fucker nearly kills you yesterday, then calls you this morning, and I find out both through a Nat-Desk message-all?"

"Josh, he told—"

"What's with your eye? What is *this* about?" Looking at him like he was falling apart.

"What, woman, what's wrong with it?"

"It's got a tic. The right one. Your other right."

He pulled his hand back and looked at it, like it might have blood on it. "Been doing that since yesterday."

"You're lucky that's the only thing wrong with you."

"One pursues the news of the day."

"From what I *read*, you certainly pursued."

"What does that mean?"

"You didn't run in the opposite direction."

"No."

"He had a gun, Sully."

"Most people in America do."

She rolled the papers in her hand into a tube and leaned back against the wall. "You weren't playing cowboy in the Capitol?"

"Look," he said, standing in front of her, a little off balance at the direct line of inquiry, "you said you wanted me to go back to being a foreign correspondent. So I act like one yesterday. Now you giving me flack about it."

"I didn't say be reckless."

"Gosh, I had forgotten."

"Don't try me with that attitude you give everyone else around here."

"Look," he said, trying to reign this back in, "you, missy, have come back from being a foreign hack to riding a desk job. I don't know that you—"

"We're not talking about me." A hair flip. Ah sweet Jesus, the hair flip. Now he was buggered. Now she was pissed. "And I wouldn't say I'm riding the desk. It's a promotion I'm thinking about accepting. You understand there's an upward trajectory to this business, that you don't always have to be out in the field eating dust?"

"Certainly not what I heard from you this spring, when we were eating at Jimmy T's. You were preaching at me to get off my arse and get back in the field with badasses such as your adorable self."

"They hadn't offered me the gig this spring."

"So how much more money is it?"

"Enough to think about," she said. "My mom's not getting any younger. It'd be nice to be on the same continent with her for a while. And, I've discovered, editors get stock options. Plus, you know, the business isn't overrun with women in management."

"So now you wanting to be on the masthead? Commencement speeches at the alma mater, all that?"

"Possible," she said, ignoring the jibe. "But it's not locked in, my side or theirs. I do it till December 31 and then Eddie and I sit down. If it's good, I'll take it. If not, I'll take the posting in London or Beirut, wherever they want me." Here she looked up at him. "And I'll be looking for you in the field. With shit like you did yesterday. That was great. Really sensational. I'm not riding you about it. And I didn't exactly expect you to return my call last night—"

"I had turned the phone off," he said.

"—but, wait, listen." Her voice softened, dropped a half key, making him almost have to lean forward. "I thought you would have called me. After deadline."

She looked at him evenly. Nothing about their physical relationship in those eyes, just a depth that spoke to their friendship. That stemmed back to Johannesburg, after Mandela's release from Robben Island. She, who had been posted in Central and South America, got sent to South Africa as part of the media mob on the only story in the world anybody wanted to read. He had met her at Jameson's on Commissioner Street. He saw a group of South African photographers he knew at a table toward the back and headed that way. She was sitting with them, this olive-skinned chick with thick black hair, all of them bellowing to be heard over the band.

She was drinking a gin and tonic and they were all laughing and she had giggled and it had come up through her nose and when he walked up she was facedown on the table, snorting and laughing, everybody howling, and she lifted her head and looked up and saw him and then sneezed and that sent them all into spasms, her leaning on the shoulder of Greg Marinovic, gasping and saying "Stopstopstop. My stomach hurts."

He had gone to the bar to get his drink and a fresh one for her. When he got back, he slid it across the table, and she looked up to see who was buying the round and it had pretty much been lust at first sight, the festive mood of the nation spilling into the air, a glossy-eyed giddiness infecting a tribe that reported war and death for a living. That they worked for the same paper but had not met gave him an excuse for chatting her up, and before Mandela was out he had taken a suite at the Kinton, a boutique hotel over in Rosebank, where prying eyes would not see them returning to the same room late at night or lingering for hours at the restaurant, sitting way too close, talking, whispering.

It had been a fling, but an adult one, as an actual relationship was not possible, given they had jobs on different continents. They had drifted apart. She had been polite but distant when she saw him again in Sarajevo, during the Bosnian War. By then he was living, and very much in love, with Nadia. The shell took Nadia not long after that, then he was blown up by a grenade, and Alexis had been one of the correspondents who helped load him, unconscious and mangled, onto a chopper.

Now they were based on the same continent, in the same building, feeling each other out, seeing if there were long-term commitments to be found underneath their shared attraction, that mysterious chemistry pulling them one to the other.

She was saying, here—at least he thought she was saying—that as a friend who'd been through the bang-bang shit before, she damn well knew he would have needed somebody to talk with, drink with, calm down with last night after deadline, and that person could, or should, have been her. That's what she was saying. He was pretty sure of it now. Since they were in the office, she was saying it from a polite, professional distance. Maybe she wasn't as pissed as he'd thought.

"Walk with me," he said, turning down the hallway, "get a Coke out of the machine."

She did, the corridor empty, just the two of them and the paintings on the wall, and he felt his shoulders relax. He didn't have to whisper, but he found himself doing it nonetheless. "If Josh wasn't with me this summer, I would have knocked on your door, had a few drinks, talked it out with you in a hot shower. As it was, I got home, looked in on him, passed out on the couch."

"Passed out?"

"Not drunk," he said, cutting her with a glance, "tired. On the couch. Shattered, the Brits would say. Facedown when Waters, this fucker, calls me this morning. Ran in here after that. Same clothes as yesterday."

The office kitchen was fluorescent lighting, old linoleum, the smell of burnt coffee, crystals of spilled sugar on the countertop, yellow plastic chairs at a couple of brown tables. She pulled money out of her front pocket, waving him off. "I'll buy hero boy a drink," she said, fucking with him a little bit now, a smile reaching to the corner of her lips. "I wasn't worried about your work on the story. I was worried, am worried, a little bit about you."

A Coke clanged down the chute. He fished it out, then pointed to the little pack of orange crackers with peanut butter stuck in between them.

"Spot me?"

She did, then bought herself a Coke, popped it open, slurping at the top to keep it from fizzing over. "Mmm. You can handle yourself, that's not what I'm saying. But when we, when we're working abroad, the big bads aren't looking for us. It's just that we get in the way. Like when you got blown up."

She reached forward, then, and touched his right temple, the welt of scar tissue there, the only person on the face of the Earth who could do that, and that sudden feminine grace had surfaced as if she'd called it up from the deep. She was close to him now, her perfume coming into his senses, the rustle of her blouse. It lasted less than three seconds. He closed his eyes at her touch, then opened them when she pulled her hand away, a little dizzy.

"This guy, he's calling *you*, he's looking for *you*," she said. "And you, you got a habit of leading with your chin."

"Thanks, Mom."

"I don't want you to get hurt again. And don't invoke your mother like that," she said, her eyes going dark, the only person on planet Earth who could say that to him, too.

"Okay, right, okay," he said, sipping his soda. "I was just—"

"You just watch your skinny white ass," she said. "You're in the deep end of the pool with this guy. This isn't some dimwit drug dealer in Frenchman's Bend. I can't come out there and save you every time you fuck up."

He sat back in his chair, telling her about Waters asking about his mother, the pissing match with the FBI that morning, how Waters had asked him if he'd kill the man who killed his mother, and how that had set off ten minutes of conversation that he'd neglected to share with Eddie Winters and the paper's brass, much less Special Agent Alma T. Gill.

"He talked about the years he'd been planning this, about how, you know, he thought the feds would get him and stick him in prison and that, since he was putting paid to his mother's death, he was okay with that. Totally okay."

"What did you say?"

"That it sounded reasonable to me."

"Sully!"

"Under a couple of conditions," he said, looking off from her now, not wanting to see her eyes while he finished talking. "I told him, look, that kind of thinking, it's acid. It'll eat right through you. And he said, well, it already has. And I said, see, that's the problem. You went off killing a bunch of people that didn't have nothing to do with your mother on your way to trying to set things straight for her, and you're not even saying who killed her, or why, and that's kind of bullshit, as to how I just told you about mine. He says, well, I will when I can. I said he should turn himself in, it's over, look, you made your point, and he said he was sorry about fifteen times, and kept saying he didn't expect even to be out right now. And I said, fine, just go turn yourself in. They'll be glad to have you. And he said, but yeah, answer me. What if you were sure, you were absolutely sure you could kill *just* the man who shot your mother. So, well, then, I said if I ever find *that* son of a bitch, or the soldier who launched the shell that killed Nadia? I'll do it between the breath and the sigh."

## TEN

THE VENDING-MACHINE crackers, he inhaled them all before he was back at his desk, rinsing them down with the soda. He settled in his chair, still hungry, spinning around a few times, bracing himself for the shit storm that was going to be his afternoon.

Fear hovered in the room, of getting beat, of being scooped. You could feel it, like humidity. R.J., he was hunkered down, phone in his ear, tapping away at the keyboard, looking up at the screen. He'd sent Sully a one-word note through the paper's messaging system, in all caps, a subtle reminder of what he was to be working on: "TICKTOCK."

The time line of events, the daily lede. Right right right. Like he already had something to fucking write—other than the call from Waters, which, for all he knew, he would be prohibited from using.

He clicked into the desk's copyediting system, found the TICK-TOCK slug that R.J. had created, and opened it. Nothing. He went back to the menu to see if other reporters assigned to the story, the ones who would file their reports, data, or sound bites with their initials tacked on after the slug, had filed anything yet. Of course not.

A drink, right about now, would be a lovely thing. Basil's? Or maybe Blanton's, with one big-ass cube in the middle of the glass?

He saw Keith over at his desk, moving in a hurry, picking up things from his desk drawer, putting them in a briefcase. Keith was a briefcase kind of guy. He covered Superior Court and was good at it, chatting up the lawyers and judges and pegging the cops who came through to testify, catching them all hanging on the second floor, leaning against the rail looking down into the maw of the first-floor lobby, the salmon stream of incoming people, perps, witnesses.

"What they got you doing?" Sully said, walking over, leaning on the cubicle wall.

Keith, never slowing: "U.S. attorney's office. Thoughts and reaction. Since they'll be handling the prosecution. Half the office is fighting the other half to get it, providing the feds don't blow Waters's head off first. You?"

"Rewrite. Lede-all." Sully looked down at the briefcase. "But you're headed back over to Super."

Keith looked back at him, his no-bullshit brown eyes flat but intense.

"Yeah. Terry Waters had been in D.C. before yesterday; you pick that up?"

"Dazzle me."

"Okay, that 911 call? He knew about St. E's, even called it that, instead of St. Elizabeths? You just blow into town, that place isn't on the tour."

Sully squinted. "Hunh. You ever been up there?"

"Couple of times. Hinckley's always looking for an appeal."

"I'd forgotten that asshole."

"It's a holdover from when St. E's had a national mandate, when it was the nation's premier mental hospital. All the presidential assassins were held there. Richard Lawrence, tried to kill Andrew Jackson. Charles Guiteau should have been up there but they hung him first. Celebrities, too. Mary Fuller, the silent film star. Ezra Pound."

"Guiteau. I remember Johnny Cash's song from when I was a—wait, what did you say?"

"What did I say what?"

"Pound? The poet?"

"Yeah, Christ, they had him for a dozen years or something. Mostly 'cause he was a communist with a hard-on for Mussolini during the war. So look, it's a straw, not a reed, that Waters has been living here, but I'll do the clutching thing since he mentioned the place. Check the records at Superior, the arrest records at MPD, then hit social services, see if he had any contact with the system, maybe he was living under a bridge. I got Susan in research started on real estate transactions, just to see if he bought something."

Sully nodded, deciding to keep it quiet, the details of the call that morning. He'd check if Pound and Eliot had been friends.

Keith put his sport coat on, the tie dangling, picked up his briefcase, and blew past Sully. "I get anything, I'll send you a feed about six."

# ELEVEN

**THE AFTERNOON WAS** a disaster of dead ends and might haves and sweet fuck all, a roller coaster of false alarms and bullshit leads. A dozen bogus hits, chief among them a raid on the Motel 6 out on New York Avenue and Bladensburg Road.

Half the afternoon, they'd all been watching it unfold on live television, transfixed, the anchors giving the play-by-play that Waters had been tracked to this dump in Northeast D.C. and was now holed up.

It was full-blown drama: helicopters two hundred yards up, hovering, intersection choked off, squad cars, SWAT vans, armored vehicles, an ambulance, canine units, guys in flak jackets, the parking lot blocked off.

Two tactical teams approached from opposite sides of the hotel. One from the front parking lot, the other from the back. The back unit went up the steps in the rear and came to the front via the second-story breezeway, about six doors down from the room in question. No doubt sniper units had it covered from across the street. Then the other SWAT unit came up the concrete steps in front in a flash, blew past their comrades giving them cover, and were down to the door in nothing flat, blowing it just that quick, the shock shattering the cheaply made plateglass window. It was just great damn television, Sully standing among the crowd in the newsroom, arms folded, chewing on the inside of his lip.

Twenty, maybe thirty seconds later, six guys came back out. They were like pallbearers, three on each side, a half-naked, ponytailed man between them, trussed up and carried like a casket. Down the steps they went, the man not appearing to move, and then they disappeared into the massed vehicles.

The paper had Chris, that sad sack motherfucker from Metro, out there breathlessly calling in updates. Keith had been rocketed out there from Superior Court and posted on the far side of New York Avenue, and Deena, who covered the Department of Justice, was there working sources, looking for that tip to get them an inside account.

And so it was Deena who called it in a few minutes later: Mr. Ponytail Man was a plumber from Gaithersburg who came to the big city to score some smack, shoot up, bang two hookers, and then pass out, dead to the world. The hookers had called it in, looking for a lifetime Get Out of Jail Free card.

"File it under 'horseshit,'" Deena was saying, her voice rising on her editor's speaker, so the assembled behind him could hear, and then she was saying she had to get fucking A across town to pick up the kid from the extended hours of summer camp she'd stuck them in this morning and she was twenty minutes late and being late meant a twenty dollar fine plus five dollars a minute and this had all turned into a steaming pile of crap—all this before the editor, Tom, could click the call from speaker to his headphones, the room getting a blast of maternal fury.

Deena's attitude sluiced across Sully's mind, wiping out any hopes of actual news. The raid, which had been shaping up to be the lede if the suspect was the Capitol murderer—they were going to nail the son of a bitch—slid south like owl shit on ice and now they didn't have anything at all.

The channel they were still watching cut to a live shot of Dalton Talmadge, the hard-right senior senator from Oklahoma, bellowing at a presser on the western steps of the Capitol. Talmadge was treating the murder of his fellow legislator, a "man I know, and know his wife and family," as a natural campaign platform for the reelection campaign of Dalton Talmadge.

". . . and this, this piece of human garbage will not deter us from the work at hand!" Talmadge was saying, actually shaking his fist. "I am not afraid to be here! I will introduce legislation on the first day of business to secure our great Capitol from this sort of terrorism! I will see to it that this sick killer is caught and that he gets every lash of justice he is due!"

He looked at R.J. and R.J. looked at him.

"'Lash of justice'?" R.J. said.

"Best quote I've heard all day. It's also the only quote I've heard all day."

"Story is slugged at seventy inches. That's about twenty-five hundred words."

"Are you trying to inspire me to greatness," Sully said, sitting on the edge of a desk, folding his arms, the newsroom crowd filtering away now, "or compel me to quit?"

"I am all about inspiration, fear, motivation, blackmail, gunplay," R.J. said, fiddling with his bow tie. Hand knotted. You could tell. Perfectly done. Probably had them tailor-made. "So how close are you?"

"To quitting?"

"Filing. You can quit tomorrow."

"Ten or twelve of the approximately twenty-five feeds I was supposed to have had in hand an hour ago are actually in. Half of them ain't worth shit and the other half *are* shit. I know feeds for somebody else's story aren't why anyone comes to work here, but Christ, man, a professional standard, I thought that sort—"

"So you don't have anything but your dick in your hand."

"Who said I'd gotten that far?"

Sully pushed himself off the desk, wandered into the hallway, threw his pen down the long, empty space in front of him, then picked it up and went down the steps and out of the building, the humidity assaulting him as soon as he pushed the glass doors open, coming out on the sidewalk.

To do, to do . . . what he wanted, what would fit the mental bill, was to be out on the boat, he thought, his crooked gait slowing, hands in his pockets, the din in his ears slowly being replaced by traffic, a jet overhead, the guy in the parking garage across the street, yelling for somebody pulling out to come back, come back.

The boat. Out on the Potomac in the gloaming, idling really, on that notch of the river just above the Key Bridge. The bluffs, densely green and overgrown this time of year, rose dramatically on both sides, but most prominently on the west, on the Virginia shore. The George Washington Parkway rose from river level beneath the Key Bridge to, what, a couple of hundred feet in less than a mile, the car lights winking in the oncoming darkness, flitting from behind the trees, emerging into an open stretch. Farther along, after the road turned inland, there were the mansions set on the bluffs, their patio lights barely visible this time of year, lost among the trees and the tangled overgrowth and shrubs.

That was the image that rose in his mind. Cut the engine on that notch of the river, just down from the rocks called the Three Sisters, letting it drift, bourbon on the rocks rattling in the glass, one hand on the wheel, not really thinking, night falling. . . .

As it was, he was stuck in the mosquito-breeding swamp called downtown, simmering at a low boil between the Potomac and the Anacostia. Looking up, taking in the snatches of sky between the buildings, it was all a hazy brown, not cloud-covered and not blue sky either, just heat and smog and asphalt and buildings of brick and concrete and glass, people walking around like clubbed fish, dazed but not quite dead. Washington in August. An Edward Hopper painting in three-quarter time.

*Deadline*, he thought, looking at his watch. It's what writers had instead of religion. He was three minutes late for a meeting in Eddie Winters's office.

*          *          *

"So what the FBI director wants," Eddie was saying, before he even sat down, "in addition to the wiretaps on Sully's line and our switchboard, is for Sully to *cooperate*"—he stressed the word, looking hard at Sully—"with their behavioral sciences unit. Go over any more calls the man makes. Assess tone, verbal tics, anything about his mother's killing, or alleged killing, that might help them out."

"Publication?" R.J. said, coughing, clearing his throat. "What's their position on our publishing the call Waters made to Sully this morning?"

"To squelch. To hold off and not use it. They're not thrilled, to master the understatement, about our using the 911 call that Sully overheard yesterday, his name, so on. The argument is that we're giving this guy a platform, his fifteen minutes."

Sully had plopped into the last available chair, which was right across from Eddie's desk and next to Melissa Baird, the Metro editor. Paul Laine, the National editor, bleary-eyed, sat next to her. Lewis leaned against the floor-to-ceiling window, as did R.J.

Melissa audibly rolled her eyes. Sully had not known that was possible. "Calls to 911 are public record, for God's sake," she said.

"Eventually," Eddie said. "Not necessarily during an active shooter situation."

"So that's what they're calling this, even today?"

Eddie patted the air with his right hand. "I'm just conveying their thoughts."

Lewis pushed up off the glass but Eddie cut him off before he could say anything.

"I don't think it's a legal issue, Lew. Or that's not the first issue. I think, before we get to that, we've got public safety, public service. We alone have information that may or may not be valuable to law enforcement in capturing a mass killer who is, if I may, making a mockery of national security. I don't see us just telling the FBI to stuff it. We cooperated with them this morning by alerting them to the call to Sully. Sully then relayed that information to them. We haven't published it on the Web yet. We've given them a head start, if nothing else. The question is if we continue to hold off until Waters is caught."

"I'm not saying we shouldn't take them into account," Sully said, "but they don't know any more about this guy than we do—or haven't told us if they do. Like you say, we've played ball, done our civic duty, given them a head start. But who's to say publishing the call wouldn't *help* catch him? I mean, the Zodiac Killer? The San Francisco paper got letters from him and ran them."

"Zodiac never got caught," Melissa said. "I don't know that's the example we want here."

" 'Hello from the gutters of NYC,' " R.J. said, eyes looking up and to the right, working to remember, " 'which are filled with dog manure, vomit, stale wine, urine, and blood. Hello from the cracks in the sidewalks of NYC and from the ants that dwell in these cracks and feed on the dried blood of the dead that has settled into the cracks.' "

"Son of Sam," Paul said. "a.k.a. David Berkowitz. The letter he sent to Jimmy Breslin. Hell of a column."

"And published while Berkowitz was on the lam," R.J. said. "It helped convict him."

"Ted Kaczynski, Eddie," Paul continued. "The Unibomber. The manifesto. Published by Brand X, the *Post*. With the urging of Freeh, who was then running the FBI, and Reno, over at Justice. Kaczynski's brother recognized the writing when he saw it in the paper, boom, arrest. Puts us on precedent, particularly with Freeh and Reno backing it."

Eddie leaned back in his chair. He had taken the time to put a suit on before coming in after R.J. had reached him at home with the news of Waters's call, but there was still no tie. His gray hair was unruly, and he had not shaved. His shirtsleeves were neatly rolled. He hadn't taken the time for cuff links.

"Do we know exactly how he tracked you down?" Looking at Sully.

"My cell," he said, "is on my office answering machine. 'And if it's urgent, you can call me on,' right there at the end. Available to any psychopath who has the nerve to call our switchboard and ask for me."

Eddie nodded. "But nothing, you think, nothing he said, what, followed you home, called you from across the street?"

"No."

"Okay," he said, "here's the deal. I'm going to tell the FBI we're going ahead, with reasonable prudence and concern. Lead the story with the call, but completely straight. Understated. Sully, quote him before the jump. Twice after. Nothing sensational. The rest of the piece, that's the manhunt, you've got everybody filing to you on that. We'll reconvene to look it over. For now. If this drags out over the next several days, and he calls you again, we'll decide case by case how to handle it."

Nods around the room, pursed lips, tension.

"Meanwhile, Sully," Eddie said, "there are now unmarked patrol cars at the top and bottom of your street, then on Constitution and A. They want permission for a shooter on your roof."

"On my *roof*?"

"Best to be safe. Isn't your nephew staying with you?"

"Until my sister has Jesus put a hit on me, yes."

"They'll also be giving you a ride home. Has Waters tried to reach you again?"

"No, but he couldn't get through if he tried. I got forty-seven messages on my machine and about that many on the cell. Every television producer and assistant booker on the East Coast started bombing them both after our story went up last night. Today, every half-wit on the East Coast is calling to tell me they were in the Capitol and saw the whole thing."

"No kidding," Paul said. "Our phones are blowing up."

"Is that what's been giving me a headache all day?" Eddie asked.

"Could be ours on Metro," Melissa said. "Every nutjob in town is calling to tell us they just saw Waters in their front yard, at the bus stop, in a blue Buick with a busted taillight, getting a Big Gulp at the 7-11."

By eight, a little after, Sully was neck deep in rewrite, the feeds coming in fast from all over, ten, fifteen, now twenty different reports. His shirt was untucked, his hair unruly, his scarred face set. As the writer of the lede-all, he was the black hole of newsroom energy, everything and everybody orbiting him, his desk, because it would all pass through his mind and fingers and onto the front page of the paper and it had to do that in the next ninety fucking minutes.

He felt like a tuning fork that had been struck on a gong the size of Nebraska, the tension from across the room pouring into him, like he had sensor panels in his palms, on his chest. Every half-heard conversation, every argument, every bit of fear from across town—on Pennsylvania Avenue, on the Suitland Parkway, on the evening commute on a nearly empty Duke Ellington Bridge—people wondering if the killer was in the car next to them, easing a pistol up to the window at the next stoplight.

The feeling he had this morning when Waters called, the fear on Capitol Hill yesterday, the gun and the blood and the smoke from the flare, the percussion blast sending a shock wave through his skull, the hands on him, the voices screaming obscenities, arms pinning him. . . .

Now, *now* it was all coming out of him, a sensation like ants crawling out of his pores. He was banging on the keyboard and sweeping his hands across his forearms to sweep the invisible little bastards away between keystrokes, his aching knee and the lack of a drink killing him.

```
The killer said he was scared, tired, and hungry.
```

Sorting through story files that were piling up now like corpses at the morgue, he pulled out quotes, cut and pasted lucid descriptions of street

scenes and police and political actions from the dispatches other reporters were filing as the evening wore on.

In a brief phone call to the paper, Waters said he
wasn't watching much of the televised hunt for him that
is riveting the nation and shutting down large parts
of the nation's capital. "I don't really like Washington," he said. "It's all disease and filth."

A tiny alert flashed in the top right corner of his screen every time a
new dispatch came in and he would have to stop what he was writing
and call it up, to see if there was a stark development that needed to be
plugged in high in the story. Or perhaps there was a lesser development
that, when taken together with other facts that were unknown to the
reporter filing the dispatch, changed or mutated the overall narrative.

"Barry Edmonds knows why I killed him. He and I
talked about that. Soon everybody else will."

Mood, like this right here. Robert Barnes, the mayor. God, if there
was a better synonym for a political hack than D.C.'s two-term chief
elected official, it was unknown to Sully Carter. But Barnes, when asked
about the level of fear in Washington, said, "My wife didn't walk the pug
today."

How brilliant was that? The political elite, the bastards who ran this
place, they were so unnerved by the specter of Terry Waters materializing
on the front doorstep with a pair of ice picks in hand that the mayoral
missus *wouldn't even walk the First Dog around the block*. Made him poop
in the backyard. You want a tangible, cut-the-meat-off-the-bones description of fear that would resonate from the white folks in Northwest
to the black folks in Southeast? That right there.

The manhunt was still centered on D.C., where bloodhounds tracked phantom trails in Rock Creek Park and along the Anacostia riverbank. But it also was radiating out into the Shenandoah, the low-slung but densely forested mountains and gullies an hour or so west. The Coast Guard was patrolling the Chesapeake, roadblocks were set up around the Beltway and on I-95, heading both north and south, and west on I-66, turning traffic into a monstrous, slow-moving worm. You could see the tie-ups from space. He heard that from behind him, somebody with a television, the evening anchor blathering. He flicked his eyes up, the clock. 8:30.

> One of the largest manhunts in the history of the nation's capital blanketed the region yesterday, as the gunman seemed to vanish into the humid August air. Checkpoints choked traffic, airports heightened security, Amtrak routes were delayed for hours, and commuter traffic grew into a monster so large that tie-ups, when viewed from satellites, took on the size and forbidding shape of something prehistoric emerging from the earth beneath.
>
> Terry Running Waters, as the gunman identified himself in a 911 call from the Capitol, apologized for killing everyone but Edmonds. He said what he wanted most, at the moment, was a "chicken sandwich and a cold beer."

Deadline. Now it took physical form. It was a beast that chewed into his right shoulder with a saw-toothed glee, gnawing deeper beneath the shoulder blade with each passing minute. The later it got in the newsroom, the more other reporters filed out, the more an invisible bubble seemed to grow around him. No one dared speak to him, so low in his chair was he slung, so furiously was he chewing on his pen, so intently was he staring at the screen, so violently was he whisper-cursing at each clunky bit of narrative that refused to be transmitted from mind to fingers to screen.

```
    Federal Washington all but ceased to exist. The Cap-
itol, site of yesterday's deadly rampage, was closed,
with armed officers and yellow police tape blocking off
the entire campus.
    All adjacent congressional office buildings were
closed, as was the Library of Congress. The Supreme
Court was flanked by armed guards at each corner. The
museums along the Mall were closed. So was the Wash-
ington Monument and the Lincoln Memorial. No tour
buses ran. Pennsylvania Avenue, long known as America's
Main Street on its route between Congress and the White
House, was largely deserted. Maître d's at its high-
priced restaurants leaned on the pulpits and awaited
anyone—anyone at all—to ask for a corner booth.
```

His solitude was broken only by R.J. coming over every now and again to whisper in his ear that Eddie loved the story, he did, but if Sully could maybe move the second sentence of the third graf into the lede, and move the second sentence of the lede graf into the fourth, that would be lovely, just lovely, and Paul had the smallest of concerns about the eighth graf because that was going to be the one right before the jump. This kept up until Sully loudly broadcast, at 8:58, spying R.J. getting up from his seat once again, "I'm taking a swing blade to the next dickless wonder who comes within five fucking feet."

R.J. sat back down without making eye contact, acting like he was straightening the crease in his khakis.

```
    Despite the massive police presence, despite the
assurances from the nation's highest levels of law en-
```

forcement, a gunman who was executing people in the Rotunda of the Capitol yesterday was still on the lam as night fell for a second day. Darkness came and a sense of safety, of national security, fell with it.

His cell buzzed at 9:26. The top of his head nearly fucking blew off. He let go of the keyboard—he'd been clinging to it for so long it felt like a life raft—and fished the cell out of his backpack. "This is Carter and this better be fucking good."

"Sully?" the man's voice said. "You know one of the things I discovered about paranoia today? That thing assholes say at bars, 'Just because you're paranoid doesn't mean people aren't following you'? You know, that, that, that's actually true."

"Hadn't occurred to me," Sully said. "So how you livin', Mr. Waters?"

## TWELVE

"I'M A LITTLE disappointed, tell you the truth," Waters said down the line, the voice clear and steady. Sounded like a landline, but Sully couldn't be sure. You got into trouble trying to overinterpret tiny impressions into major facts, and he didn't want to do that here. He just wanted to keep the guy talking long enough until he gave something away. Possibly gave something away.

"Welcome to America," Sully said, wedging the phone between his ear and shoulder, keeping both hands on the keyboard, typing furiously.

"I think my people should be saying that to yours."

"Touché," Sully said, "but you're going to have to be more specific. Everybody comes to America, hates it, but never goes home. It's like a bigger version of Washington."

Waters let out a long breath. Like he was a smoker and was blowing out the cloud. "I thought somebody would have caught me by now," he said. "I mean, how many dickheads do they have looking for me, about eight thousand?"

"I hear you," Sully said, standing, waving both arms above his head, making a huge X, then making it again, trying to get somebody's attention, anyone at all. "I thought that was you at the Motel 6 today."

A short bark of a laugh.

"Sully, look now. If we're going to talk, and I like talking to you, we've got to understand each other better. That hotel is for hookers and gangbangers."

No one was looking. It was like he was doing calisthenics and nobody could stand to watch.

"Apologies," Sully said, working to keep his breathing even. "I thought they left the light on for everybody. I figured maybe in reduced circumstances and all, you might, ah, be a lonely man in shirtsleeves, leaning out of a window."

In desperation, he picked us his stapler and fired it at R.J., missing the back of the man's head and his computer screen by inches, but hitting the framed picture of R.J. and Elwood dead center, shattering the glass and sending it clattering against the other tchotchkes in his cubicle. The man came three inches out of his seat, then turned, face going red until he saw Sully pointing his finger like a pistol, then pointed to the phone, then plunked back down, typing at knuckle-busting speed to try to keep up.

There was a sigh. Waters said, "'Lonely men in shirtsleeves.' You spent the afternoon brushing up on your Eliot."

"Well, sure," Sully said. "Thought you were trying to tell me something."

R.J. was loping across the newsroom to Eddie's office.

"I was, I mean, I am," Waters said. Not stuttering, more confident than this morning. Not apologizing about anything. "I was thinking, I mean today, and I decided it's a good thing we met. And that we meet again. We have things to discuss. *You* can tell my story *for* me. It's like it was meant, you know? I hadn't thought about this part of it."

Eddie was talking into the phone, standing up, looking out from his office all the way over to Sully, rolling his extended index finger around and around, telling him to keep the man talking.

"Don't know how you're going to do that, being on the run and all," Sully said. "Maybe you check in with the feds, then we can sit down and have a long chat. Your mom. Remember? You were going to tell me about her."

Breathing, down the line. Labored. Was he walking? Pissed off? "Sully, okay. You've got to understand this. It's key. Only the hunted run. I, me, I'm not the hunted. I'm not running. I hunt. I am the hunter."


"The hell does that even mean?" Alexis said, looking over her margarita at him, three or four or five tiny crystals of salt sticking to her upper lip. "The most hunted man in America thinks he's the predator?"

Her eyes were bright, despite the hour, despite the waning light of the outdoor café, and the shadows that fell and swooped across her face, the waving branches of the trees in the courtyard and light breeze that came down Massachusetts Avenue. She was leaning forward over the ceramic outdoor table, her hair undone, falling over her shoulders. Jesus Mary and Joseph, she was something. You could just feel her presence coming across the table. The tilt to her chin, the way she'd kicked off her shoes when they sat down, the direct nature of her gaze. Every now and again the breeze would catch and lift her bangs over her forehead and they would flutter down again, a little more askew each time.

"We're talking a delusional psycho," Sully said, settling his cycle jacket over the back of his chair, bringing it home out of habit, even if the bike was back in the garage at the paper. "So I wouldn't put too much into it. He's right about the hunting thing, though. Our boy has stalked some game."

"How so?"

It was closing in on midnight and they were sitting on the brick courtyard of La Loma. The Mexican place on the Hill. A converted two-story row house in a block of them. They were drinking margaritas on the rocks but the food hadn't come yet. The FBI had insisted that agents drive him home after the phone call from Waters, thinking he might be obsessing on Sully, trailing him. Since Alexis was still at the paper, and since she'd given him shit for not calling her the previous night, he'd invited her to come for a late dinner and then shack at his place.

On the short drive, Sully called Josh, who was happily glued to *Cheerleaders on Top*, or whatever he was watching that was sending Sully's pay-per-view bill into triple digits. Sully reminded him not to leave the house and if he heard clambering from the backyard, that was just the feds' sniper getting to the roof. He tried to pass this off as something that happened, like it was a regular thing, worrying the boy was going to freak. Josh just said that was awesome. Also, reading Sully's mind, he said that his mom had called but not to worry, he hadn't told her anything.

By that time, the car was moving up deserted Mass Ave., the yellow and red lights of La Loma gleaming off to the left. They pulled to the curb. Sully asked the agents if they wanted to eat. The crewcut on the right, chewing gum and staring straight ahead, said they'd wait in the car. Pissed, you could tell.

The tequila was going straight to his head. It was the best feeling he'd had all day.

He dipped a tortilla chip in the salsa and let it flit across his mind just how walk-into-a-wall gorgeous Alexis was, looking at him like this, just the two of them. He hoped she wouldn't go back abroad. He'd been thinking all summer, ever since she came back, of a way he could communicate this without saying it outright.

"Hunting, tracking game, if you're running? You can't hear nothing," he said, munching. "You can't hear what your deer or whatever is doing. You also can't see. You miss things. So. Whenever possible, you stop. You listen. You learn where your prey is and where it's going. Then you track until you can get a clear shot."

She flicked her tongue across her lips, taking care of the salt crystals, then sipped from part of the rim that was salt-free. "Sounds like your deer would just get away, great white hunter."

He snorted.

"I'll send you down to Mr. Gentry's hunt camp," Sully said, "like my daddy sent me. Out there off the bayou. You don't kill down there, you don't eat. You tell Mr. Gentry, you tell him he's got it wrong all this time."

He was loving the breeze, the shadows. Nothing was so wonderful as putting a monster piece on 1-A with I-can't-believe-that-shit detail. He wished La Loma stayed open all night. He'd sit here with Alexis till the sun came up.

"What did Eddie say?" she said. "The FBI?"

"About what?"

"The call, nimrod. Could they trace it?"

"I'd be sitting next to them if they could."

"Nothing?"

"It was a cell. Best they could do was narrow it down, that the call came from a tower in Northwest D.C."

"So, he hasn't blown town."

"Apparently not, but I don't know that's news. Look, he could have been tooling down Georgia Avenue on a bus, sitting on a park bench at Carter Barron, under a log in Rock Creek Park, holed up in a basement on the Gold Coast, or driving the proverbial late-model sedan, dark in color, on the inner loop of the Beltway, heading for a burger at Mickey D's. As I understand it, it's about a fifteen-mile range, radius, something. Since then? Assuming he's driving sixty miles an hour, forty-five on back roads? He could be anywhere from the Eastern Shore to West Virginia, from Pennsylvania to Richmond."

She sat back, holding the drink in her lap. It dripped with condensation, with melting ice, with the still-present humidity that was frizzing her hair, that was wilting her linen blouse. Tiny crow's-feet at the edge of her eyes, the years in the sun, the Third World.

The waiter came as she was finishing, the plates hot, both of them leaning back, breaking off the conversation, the man sliding the check by the side of Sully's plate at the same time. It was that late.

"Joey, hey hey hey," Sully said, reaching for the tab. The waiter, slim, tired, black slacks and a white shirt, already turning, coming back.

"Dos mas margaritas," Sully said, handing him back the tab, "before you close us out."

Joey, José, nodded, took the tab, and turned on a heel, gone before Sully could put a fork to his seafood burrito. Alexis sipped, long, slow, and lazy, on hers. She held the glass by its funky green stem—with a branch on it, like it was a cactus—in her right hand.

There were two other couples sitting outside. Maybe one or two more inside. Sully wasn't really paying attention. One looked like a Senate staffer and a man who wasn't her husband, the way they were sitting. The other was a gay couple he knew but couldn't name. They lived over on Seventh. He had nodded at them when sitting down and they had nodded back and that was being neighbors on the Hill.

Joey brought the revised tab back and Sully looked at it and pulled out his wallet and put down three twenties, covering the tip. The woman and her friend a few tables over got up and left. The wind blew and the shadows floated and danced across them all.

"We got great art of that situation at the Motel 6," Alexis said, "and then that went to shit and we had nothing."

"What'd you go with?"

"On A-1, the center art? A soldier with an M-16, in front of the Capitol. Dramatic. And nothing related to the news of the day at all."

"Hey, Sully?"

He looked up from his second margarita toward the door of the restaurant, expecting it to be Joey calling out something about closing up. But Joey wasn't there and Alexis was nodding behind him toward the street, the opposite direction. He turned and the first gunshot was loud and flat and the bullet exploded Alexis's margarita into a spray of flying glass and tequila

The second and third and fourth shots came in *blam blam blam*, the man with the gun standing fifty feet away in the street. The shots skipped off the tabletop, shattered the ceramic tile, clipped off the wrought-iron chairs. Alexis fell backward, screaming, hands at her face. The plateglass window at the front of the restaurant blew out. Sully overturned the table toward the shooter and fell behind it, crawling toward his jacket, scrambling to get the Tokarev from the pocket. The shots were coming wildly now.

His right hand closed over the grip of the Tokarev.

The shooting stopped. Sully pulled out the pistol and forced himself to take a deep breath. The woman across from them was curled on the ground, crying. A plate dropped and shattered inside the restaurant.

Then the gunman's voice arose in a guttural bellow, something primal and wounded and wretched that seemed to bounce off the pavement and echo off the buildings, filling Sully's head and burning into the well of his memory:

*"Sssssuuullllyyy!!"*

And then the feds were rising from behind their flung-open car doors, guns aimed into the street, yelling over one another, "Drop it drop drop drop it drop it motherfucker DROP IT." Sully, rising to his knees, saw the gunman lying in the middle of Mass Ave. bathed in an orange pool of light from an overhanging street lamp. He was putting his hands behind his back, his legs spread, assuming the position before the agents got there. The gun lay on the pavement, fifteen feet away. The man's mouth hinged open and the voice that emerged sounded like a hoarse carnival barker, "Don't shoot don't shoot don't shoot don't SHOOT me goddammit."

One of the feds pounced on him, planting a knee in his back, slamming his face into the pavement, pinning his arms to get the cuffs on. The other stayed five feet back, gun pointed, talking rapid fire into a squawking radio. Sirens in the distance.

Sully turned for Alexis. She was sitting up, dabbing at a slight cut across her forehead but otherwise unharmed. Sully rose to his feet and walked past the wrought-iron gate of the restaurant. He went over the brick sidewalk, finally remembering to tuck the pistol in the back of his waistband and let his shirt hang over it.

Then he was in the street, in the pool of light. The men on the ground were cursing and writhing. Sully kneeled on the pavement in front of them. The shooter looked up and saw him.

Blood dripped from his chin and poured from his nose. A knot rose on his forehead. Terry Waters spit a thin ribbon of blood from between his teeth.

"Still want to talk about my mom?"

## THIRTEEN

ALEXIS WAS STILL rattled, still pissed off, even in the shower. Getting over the shooting maybe, but channeling her anger and shock into a lecture.

"You actually carried that gun to work."

"I did."

"Fucking unreal. Where did you get it?"

"Bosnia."

"From?"

"The commander."

"Which?"

"The Bosnian. From the night on the mountain. On Igman."

She pulled the shower curtain back and looked at him, wiping the water from her eyes, shampoo thick and foamy in her hair. Her knuckles on the curtain trembled just slightly. "You didn't come down with it. I was there when they loaded you on the chopper."

"He sent it to me."

"For *what*? So you could shoot somebody in America?"

He was sitting on the closed toilet seat, drying himself off. Looking at his toenails, a bone-deep exhaustion settled over him, a blanket that weighed two hundred pounds.

"Souvenir. Or something. It's a long story."

She let go of the curtain and stuck her head back under the water. "I've got all night."

"I don't," he said. "I got to cover this fucker's hearing tomorrow. They'll present him in C-10. Superior Court."

She turned the water off and reached for a towel. She put it to her hair, not bothering with her body. Sully appreciated the view and said so.

"Don't you patronize me," she snapped. "You took a gun to work today. A. Loaded. Gun. I can't even."

"Prudent, I thought, the way it turned out." He felt thick-fingered, slow.

"Shots going everywhere, we go down on the ground, I look up, you're fucking around with your cycle jacket, I'm thinking you're trying to hide behind it, and then you pull out a pistol. For Christ's sake. You're lucky you got it back in there before the cops saw it."

"I got this rule? It's like, every time a psychopath kills people with ice picks and then calls me up to chat about our dead moms? I tote a pistol."

"That right?" Bending to flip her hair over her head, wrapping it in the towel, then wiping the steam from the mirror, looking at the scratch across her forehead, an inch above the eyebrow.

"I got it written down somewhere, like on the refrigerator: 'Get some milk,' 'Don't forget the dry cleaning,' like that."

"Sully. A gun."

"How's your head?"

"Fine. It was just a little bit of glass."

"Is Josh still awake?" Trying to change the subject. Opening the door a crack to let out the steam, pretending to listen for sounds from the basement.

"He barely woke up when we came in," she said. "Didn't seem fazed, a strange woman coming into the house late at night with his uncle, police cars out front. One wonders about the domestic environment."

"One does?" He moved his feet to accommodate her stepping out of the shower. The bathroom was tiny. Her stomach was just in front of his face. Breasts were peaceful things, it flitted across his mind, just like that.

"Look. You can talk to me," she said, lifting his chin up with her index finger. Just enough to make him raise his glance. It took him a second to get it.

"Later," he said. "I'ma tell you about it later. Or your boobs. I'm sorry about the gun. I'm sorry about that, that fucking insanity at the restaurant. But it's been a day, Alex. Two of them."

It was three, three thirty in the morning, maybe four. What his mother would have called the witching hour.

When they had come into the house—driven back from the 1-D precinct by no less than Homicide Chief John Parker, who had come to check on him—Sully had walked upstairs and got three of the pills the doctor had given him from the little orange prescription bottle in the medicine cabinet, walked back downstairs, poured a Basil's over ice, and slammed them home in three straight shots. He wasn't supposed to take more than one at a time but he gave himself medical clearance.

Alexis wouldn't let him drink after that but she was sitting up with him.

"I mean, you've talked to me, you've said, the nightmares, the PTSD things," she was saying, pulling one of his T-shirts over her head, opening the door all the way now. "I've woken up next to you, you're sleeping but sweating through your shirt, breathing so hard it wakes *me* up. You've had those ever since Igman."

On the street outside, there was a marked patrol car at the top and bottom of the block. Another unmarked FBI van in the middle. Another unmarked on Constitution, covering the alley that ran to his backyard, and another on A Street. Just in case there was an accomplice, they said.

He followed her out into the darkened hall, the house silent. She turned into his room and got into bed, him following. Sheets and air-conditioning and her next to him. *Don't be pissed, Alex*, he thought. This, this was nice. Fading fast now.

"That night in Bosnia," she said, "I remember them bringing you down the mountain, not even daylight, the U.N. choppers coming in to airlift you out. Nobody said anything about a gun."

"I was unconscious, so."

"It was a bad winter."

"Yes."

"You'd just lost Nadia, too."

"Can we talk about something else?"

"I was just saying I was worried about you. Am."

"I am fine."

"Said the idiot waltzing around with a gun."

"I *will* be fine."

"Where is this thing? As we speak?"

"Back in the closet. Alex, no kidding, can we sleep? I won't shoot anybody before tomorrow morning, I promise."

## FOURTEEN

THE HIGH CHURCH of the Misbegotten met six days a week in Room C-10, a small hearing room at the bottom rear of D.C. Superior Court, beset by a smell that no one could ever quite place.

It was where each and every person arrested the day and night before in the nation's capital was first presented to the judicial system. There was no bail in the District of Columbia. The brief services in C-10 were to determine if your lousy ass was a danger to the public.

If you weren't, the magistrate gave you terms (stay away from witnesses, don't get arrested again, don't be an asshole), and you got to walk out of the well of the court and past the bulletproof Plexiglas, up the aisle, past the pews, out of the courthouse and into the sweet sunshine of freedom.

But if the same magistrate said you were a danger to the American People? You did not go into the sweet sunshine of anything. The marshals stepped you back and took you right back through the Door to Hell and your lousy ass would go to D.C. Jail until such a time as your right to a speedy trial came due.

That C-10 was across from the cafeteria, the smell of one often wafting into the other, had not gone unnoticed among its faithful constituents. It made you think about the food in there before you ate, but particularly after.

Fittingly, considering the human waste that channeled through C-10 for long hours each day, it was also noted by the faithful that C-10 was set at the ass end of Superior Court. The massive, charmless concrete mass of the courthouse fronted onto 500 Indiana Avenue. The back of the building, facing C Street, was several dozen feet lower, down a small hill. Entering from the front, you had to go down two stories, usually by the escalator, to the bottom floor. C-10 was at the back of that floor, hence the tag. This lowly status added to the misery and squalor of the atmosphere, for it made the room seem like a funeral parlor, like the worst storefront church in Christendom, like the outhouse at the end of the rainbow.

On the morning after the shooting, on the day when Representative Edmonds's body began lying in state in the Capitol Rotunda, Sully slept late, staggering downstairs to make brunch for Josh and Alexis, who seemed to be getting along fine without him. He spent thirty-five minutes on the phone convincing Lucinda that the weird shit was over. Alex said she would drive Josh to his class at the Corcoran on her way in to the office. So he dressed and made the mile-long walk down Capitol Hill, his dress shirt soaked at the small of his back by the time he got to the courthouse. There were tiny rivulets of sweat at his temples, the base of his throat, swelling to a puddle at the small of his back.

Stepping off the escalator onto the bottom floor, turning the corner into a short hallway, he groaned. There was already a herd in the hallway, well-dressed reporters he'd never seen before, network and cable news staff, the cut of their suits—hell, that they were *wearing* suits in C-10— gave them away as one-timers, big-footers, here for the headline. They talked into their cell phones, walked around in circles, leaned back against the wall, killing time, the men outnumbering the women about four to one.

"How's church today, brother?" Sully said as he clamped a hand on the fleshy shoulder of Leonard Mahoney. Leo was a court-appointed attorney and a member of the flock in good standing. Right shoulder slumped against a wall, his plaid jacket, his sagging belly, his comb-over standing at a high wisp—Leo was instantly recognizable to any court-house denizen. Eons from now, when they were excavating the remains of this place, they'd find the petrified remains of Leo, halfway between C-10 and a courtroom, calcified finger in place, scratching behind where his right ear had been.

Leo looked at him, then went back to staring at his hand.

"Why'd they come up with these things?" he replied, wagging a knobby little Nokia in his left hand, never lifting his shoulder from the wall. "It's just another way for the ex to find me, is what it is. Wants to know, on a Friday morning in August, why our kids are going back to public school this year if I'm a lawyer. Says I have to be the only lawyer on the Hill whose kids are at Watkins. I say, nah, no, Jim Stevens, he's got his kids there, and she says to me, she says, 'I mean white people.' When did my ex turn into a racist lunatic, that's what I want to hear."

"Our boy's not up anytime soon is he?"

"How she gets a call *in* down here, I can't get a call *out*."

"I'm guessing we're not even close."

"What, Waters? You're here for Waters? Grab a seat if you can, hot-shot. Slummers were here at sunup."

The double doors swung open, some TV suit from New York coming out, walking fast, heading to do a stand-up out front. Sully tapped Leo's shoulder, adios, and slipped into the sanctuary before the door could close.

The room had the fluorescent look and feel of a tuberculosis ward, a dark, phlegmy, cough and passed-gas rectangle of a courtroom dungeon. It was accessed by the double doors behind him if you were a civilian and by the Door to Hell, the locked door at the back right side of the well of the court, if you were coming from the holding cells. There were a hand-ful of long wooden benches for observers, like pews, hence the room's designation as The Church. A central aisle led into the well of the court, with the magistrate on an elevated platform, lording over the proceedings.

The benches on most days were not more than scattershot full. They held the rear ends and crossed legs of dead-tired mothers and aunts and sisters and cousins, of exasperated fathers and pissed-off uncles, the bouncing bottoms of toddlers brought in to sit this out till Daddy or Mama's man came through his presentation to the court, him and a hundred other lunkheads, the tots there because there wasn't money for a sitter, or the time to find one, or that cousin who sometimes watched the kid was across town when Daddy got popped for a bullshit traffic stop, a handgun and a dime bag beneath the seat. So the babies bounced, chomping down on pacifiers and wiggling across the seats, the only people in the room oblivious to the slow-motion train wreck of humanity on the other side of the bulletproof glass.

This—thrown in with the court-appointed lawyers and the remora-like reporters, the bored-ass assistant U.S. attorney detailed here for the day, the magistrate, the marshals up front, everybody baking, the air assaulting one's nostrils if not one's sense of decency—was Sully Carter's world.

It was the bargain-basement realm of the criminal justice planet, the justice-by-mass-discount world of the black and brown and every now and then, at least in D.C., some random white dude, almost always picked up for solicitation or something to do with sex and, what do you know, today his perp, the one and only Native American. Terry Waters was the reason television trucks were lining the street outside, their antennae spiraling up into the stagnant heat, cameramen in shorts and T-shirts, sitting on the shaded side of the vehicles. It wasn't even noon, still *hours* before Waters would have his five-minute hearing, and the room already smelled of stale sweat, of the loss of hope, of desperation, of a three-year bid against a twelve-year charge.

He came around the back right of the room, behind the pews, catching the eye of Keith, sitting next to Dave, the WCJT reporter, both far off to the left. They raised eyebrows at him in recognition, but their bench was packed, nowhere for him to slide in. He parked himself on the front bench, marked LAWYERS ONLY. The U.S. marshal in the well of the court, who knew him and knew he wasn't a lawyer, gave him a bored glance, stifled a yawn behind a closed fist, and turned away.

By the time Waters finally emerged from the Door to Hell, six hours had passed.

The reporters packing the room had gone from a well-heeled group of professionals to a sweaty mob who had already filled out the *Times* crossword puzzle (with help from the entire bench they were on), studied the box scores until they had them memorized, stepped out to the bathroom, made a coffee run, made a sandwich run, made an I-can't-take-this-shit-anymore run. They did deep knee bends by the escalators, beating back the nodding-head monster of drowsiness. They called their editors and their spouses from the hallway, wandered over to the cafeteria, were asked to pipe down by the deputy clerk, were reminded that they could not bring food or drink into the spectators' gallery. One of their tribe, an Australian television reporter, was booted from the room after approaching the well of the court for the third time and asking Magistrate Raymond Estes, who was not having the best day of his life, exactly how much fucking longer could it possibly take to bring forward the one defendant anyone was there to see. Scattered applause followed him out the door.

Sully had been over to hobnob with Dave and his WCJT crew, stepped outside to call Josh and Alexis twice, and now, late in the day, everybody musky and irritable, looked up from his paper to see Janice Miller, the head of the Public Defender Service, emerge from the Door to Hell, make her way around the tables and chairs in the well of the court, and slide in next to him.

"You're not a lawyer, mister," she whispered in his ear, smelling of expensive perfume, coffee heavy on her breath.

"You ain't much a one," Sully whispered back.

Janice—she pronounced it *Jah-niece*—tucked her chin down and grinned, squeezed his hand and let go, easygoing, even today. Born and raised in the Five Points neighborhood in Denver. Full-ride scholarship to USC Law. She could ski double-black diamonds and then call in from the bottom of the slope to tell twenty-four-year-old fuckups—who were now having second thoughts about the plea deal she'd spent weeks negotiating—that they'd sign the papers in front of them or she'd cut them off from agency representation and they'd spend the next thirty in a federal pen wishing they goddamn well had listened to her. But, hey, she'd tell them, it's up to you. Totally up to you.

"What's been the deal," Sully whispered, "I mean, I know—"

"Floridly psychotic," Janice nodded, tilting her head toward the Door to Hell. "Our boy is *florid*. Can't get anything out of him for an hour, and then he'll spout about radio transmissions in his molars."

"Come on. I talked to him. He was, like, regular."

Janice held her right hand up, as if taking the oath.

"Can I use it?" Sully asked.

"Just state it as a fact, not sourced to me. This is going to be a problem."

"How you mean?"

"The state, they're going to want to force him to take medication."

"To make him sane enough to stand trial," Sully whispered back, shrugging.

She grimaced and shook her head, long brown hair, coming to rest on her shoulders. "Not happening."

"*Pero por qué, muchacha?*"

She looked over at him, bemused, slightly put off that he hadn't thought this through. Now her face was turning tutorial, the eyes expanding, the mouth elongating, talking to the slowest student in her Georgetown Law seminar. "The man is charged with killing ten people in the U.S. Capitol, four of them officers, one of them a woman," she whispered. "Does that sound like a capital offense?"

"I thought it was nine dead."

"One of the criticals died this morning, two hours ago."

"But the District doesn't have the death penalty," Sully said, eyeing her up, thinking. "The feds do. They'll claim jurisdiction, a case like this. So they'll kick it out of 500 Indiana over to 333 Constitution." He indicated this with a jerk of his head, the federal courthouse being catty-corner across Marshall Park.

"So the State," she said, nodding, "is going to want to medicate my client into sound mental health so that—"

"—that, that, they can execute him," Sully said, finishing the sentence, getting it. "They'll want to make him sane enough to execute."

She patted his knee, teasing, playfully patronizing, but her tone betraying an undertone of bitterness. "Exxxactly. Know what a legal conundrum is? When the best thing you can do for your client is to keep him mentally ill."

"Don't they call this a Hobbesian trap?"

"I thought it was a Catch-22. As his lawyer, it would be insane for me to make him sane. And no, you can't quote my quote."

He started to respond but she was already gone, the Door to Hell swinging open, her client emerging, the room coming alive, the air gaining a static charge.

Waters entered, flanked by two U.S. marshals, one on each side, holding an elbow, another walking close behind. They had him in an orange jail-issue jumpsuit, his black hair pulled back in a ratty ponytail. He had a scraggly beard. One eye partially swollen shut, deep bags beneath them both, like he'd been up all night. A red gash on the right side of his forehead. Sully put his height at about five foot eleven, not that tall, really, slender if not muscular, hard to tell with the jumpsuit.

His hands were cuffed in front of him and a chain ran down to a pair of leg restraints, making him rattle when he walked. But the most startling thing about him, the one thing that stood so wildly out of place, was his demeanor. He did not smile, he *beamed*, absorbing the energy of the courtroom. He moved forward by shuffling his feet in a kind of jig, looking out at the crowd, happy as a clam. For a second, Sully thought he was going to wave when they made eye contact.

The spectator gallery came to attention, the small talk dying, even the babies seeming to hush, people turning now to see. The courtroom artist, perched in the jury box, his charcoal pencil skittering across the pad with such speed that it could be heard across the room, the only image from today that the outside world would see.

The deputy clerk, seated just in front of the judge, scarcely looked up. Her monotone, born of a thousand days and a million defendants, had all the spontaneity and excitement of a washing machine clicking over to the rinse cycle. "Your Honor, now before the court, we have the United States versus Terry Running Waters, criminal case two zero two eight. Counsel, please introduce yourself for the record."

Sully had been so absorbed in the theater of Waters's entrance that he had not noticed that the regular bull-pen attorney for the U.S. attorney's office had stepped to the side, and Wes Johnston, a no-bullshit veteran, had materialized from a rear door and was now in the well of the court. He'd hoped Eva Harris would draw the assignment, his best source over there, but no such luck. Johnston was built like a linebacker, with a shaved head and a thin goatee; he looked like he'd just as well punch you out as prosecute you.

"Assistant U.S. Attorney Wesley Johnston, Your Honor, for the United States."

"Janice Miller, Your Honor, PDS, representing Mr. Waters."

"I'm Terry," Waters said brightly, leaning forward, nudging Janice with a friendly elbow. "Terry Waters."

Estes looked up, mildly, and said, "Thank you."

A nervous titter ran through the gallery.

"Your Honor," the clerk continued, "the defendant is charged with nine, no, make it ten counts of first-degree murder while armed, twelve counts of attempted murder while armed, multiple counts of assault with a deadly weapon, multiple counts of assault, illegal possession of a firearm, and," her voice trailed off, scanning down the sheet in front of her, "multiple other federal charges related to crimes of violence."

"Your Honor," Wesley started, "we have an affidavit from two detectives, which should be in front of you, stating there is probable cause in this case, on these and other charges—the charging document isn't complete—and we're going to ask you to find, ah, to find probable cause here. We're requesting Mr. Waters be held pending a hearing in federal court on Monday."

Estes looked down at the paperwork in front of him and said, "The pretrial services report? Do we have that?"

The deputy clerk turned and whispered to him, Estes leaning over the bench to hear.

"It's incomplete, I believe, Your Honor, if I may," Janice said. "It's been something of an exercise to get information from Mr. Waters."

" 'GALVESTON, OH GALVESSSTTTOOON,' " Waters burst out into song, the deputy clerk jumping in spite of herself, the judge's head snapping up as he sat back in his seat. "I STILL SEE YOUR SEA WAVES CRASHING . . . AH, SHE WAS TWENTY—"

And a marshal was up in his face, pointing a warning finger, Waters cutting off the singing but doing some little doo-dah, doo-dah dip with his knees, like he was about to segue into "Camptown Races," the spectator gallery erupting, reporters leaning forward, bursting into nervous laughter, elbowing the guy next to them, finally, *finally* something they could lead the broadcast with, top off the story, the long day not a waste after all, this guy was—

"Mmmiiisssstttteeerrr Waters," Estes said, patiently, leaning forward, the din in the spectator gallery dropping off. The judge looked over his glasses at Waters and cut his gaze to Janice, who was already nodding. "Are you with us today?"

"Yes, sir!" Waters said brightly. "Right here."

"Do you understand you're in a court of law?"

"Sir, I do, really. I do."

"Okay. Then you know we can't have any more outbursts like that, correct?"

"Sir, I just love the song. Also, I have seen many Negroes today. This is also what I have on my mind."

Another twitter from the gallery, this time drawing a glare from Estes.

"Ms. Miller, are we going to have a problem?"

"No, Your Honor." She turned and whispered to Waters, who nodded rapidly.

"Okay then," Estes said. "Okay. The pretrial report. Everyone just sit still a minute." He sifted papers, then settled on a sheaf of stapled paperwork, scanned the front of it, then flipped a page, it being so quiet you could hear the pages rattle.

Sully eyed Waters, shaking his head without being aware of it.

" 'I CLEAN MY GUN AND DREAM OF GALVESTON,' " Waters bellowed, this time more on key, as if it were coming back to him, the melody.

"Mr. Waters," Estes said, unperturbed.

The marshal got back in front of Waters, whispering fiercely, his face red with fury, the veins at the top of his balding forehead pulsing. The second marshal stepped in tight behind the defendant. The third marshal came from beside the Door to Hell, flanking Waters on his right.

Estes finally looked up. "Ms. Miller?"

"Your Honor, we're not going to contest probable cause. But this sounds like a random shooting, so we'll ask those first-degree charges be set as second-degree while armed, at most, as there's no evidence presented of premeditation, that Mr. Waters was carrying out some sort of planned act."

Wesley leaned forward to speak into the microphone: "He came to the Capitol building with two semiautomatic firearms, other weapons concealed in a backpack. Premeditation. First degree."

Estes nodded. "I'm going to find probable cause, which, by federal statute in the District of Columbia, requires me to order that the defendant be held until further notice."

"Could we get a twenty-four-hour screening at St. E's, Your Honor?" Janice said. "Mr. Waters has had lifelong mental-health issues, apparently, and has been without a fixed address for quite some time, at least since his father died. It's been difficult to communicate."

"You're saying he can't assist in his defense or he's psychotic."

"Either. Both. I would argue he meets both prongs of the standard. I think we're going to wind up with a thirty-day eval at St. E's, but for now, if we could just get the screening."

"Counselor?" Estes said, turning to Wesley.

"No problem with that."

"And, Your Honor," Janice said, "let me introduce this to the court now. Should the issue of forced medication arise, we're going to object as invasive and prejudicial to—"

"Okay, problem," Wesley cut in.

"—basic best interest, I know, I hear you, I'm just making sure we're on record as—"

"This seems preemptive, Ms. Miller," Estes said.

"—as, as, I, well, Your Honor. I suppose. It is. But this is very clearly going to come before the court, and I wanted our position clear."

"You can argue that over at 333 Constitution at the appropriate time."

"Of course."

"Other business?"

The attorneys shook their heads.

"It is so ordered that Mr. Waters will have a twenty-four-hour screen. This matter will be taken up on Monday by Judge Arrington, in district court, but we are likely looking at a full thirty-day psychiatric eval in St. E.'s, given this case's nature."

*Bang bang* went the gavel and it was done, Wesley and Janice putting away their papers, the deputy clerk asking the marshal, over an open mic, if there were any more cases. The man turned to ask his colleague and Sully saw it, even before it happened.

Terry Waters leaned back from the hips, as if he were a man leaning out of his window trying to see something on his roof. Then he rocked forward and snapped his forehead into the marshal in front of him. It caught the man off guard and in the temple. It made a sound like two croquet balls colliding. The marshal dropped, out cold even before his knees buckled.

Janice and Wesley turned. The marshals behind and to Waters's right came forward. The gallery audience bolted to their feet, the court artist dropped his sketch, the room off kilter and gone wrong, erupting, as Waters bunny-hopped in his leg chains toward the bench.

"DO YOU THINK YOU CAN CONTAIN ME, YOU BLACK-ROBED PIECE OF SHIT? DO YOU HAVE ANY IDEA OF MIRI-AM'S POWERS? DO YOU KNOW THE REIGN OF DEATH YOU—"

He was at the front of the dais by then, the deputy clerk ducking below her seat, Estes rising, banging his gavel and yelling, the marshals tackling Waters from the back and the side, Sully standing to see it, Waters's head hitting the wooden dais, going down to his left and side-ways, the two marshals piling on top of him. And still, you could hear him, cackling, bursting into a laugh that ricocheted off the ceiling and the cheap fluorescent lights, words that shot over those assembled in their spittle-flecked madness:

"THIS IS THE SHIT, WHOOO!!!"

## FIFTEEN

"THAT LITTLE SHIT STAIN is going to be at St. E's a lllonnnggg time," R.J. muttered, looking at the story on the computer screen.

Sully and Keith were standing behind him, looking over either shoulder, the newsroom all but empty at this hour. Eddie was in his office, reading the story on a printout, glasses down on the end of nose, copy editors at their desks, eternally slouched in front of their screens, the last barricade against reportorial failures of grammar, common sense, and third-grade mathematics.

The rest of the place, save for the guys in Sports, had gone dark. It gave the low-slung cubicles and filing cabinets a lonesome atmosphere, where sound traveled and the dimmed lights in the hallways absorbed the echoes.

"Shoots up the Capitol, goes ape shit in C-10?" R.J. rattled, twiddling the cursor back and forth. "He's going to be the next Hinckley up there at St. E's. An institution at the institution."

"Nobody is happier about that than Jodie Foster," Keith said, staring at the screen. "R.J., let's put 'bizarre' back in the lede. 'Waters's bizarre outburst.'"

R.J. half turned in his seat, arching a bushy eyebrow.

"You don't think a mass killer breaking into a Glen Campbell song and assaulting a marshal in court is bizarre on its face?" He put it back in, his fingers on the keyboard. "You think we got to explain that?"

They all looked at it.

"Never liked 'Galveston,' all that much, myself," Sully said, thinking it over. "Now, 'Gentle on My Mind,' that's your quality Glen Campbell."

"He sang 'Rhinestone Cowboy,'" R.J. said, "I'da shot him myself."

"Okay, you're right," Keith said. "Take it back out."

Eddie came out of the office, flipping the sheets on the story, not even looking up, coming to an abrupt stop at the side of R.J.'s desk. "Do we know who this 'Miriam' is that he was raving about?"

"No," Sully said. "That whole thing was off, you ask me. He was not anything like that, the times we talked."

Eddie shifted his feet, staring at the papers in front of him, deciphering his scribbled notations. "Maybe his meds wore off once he was in lockup. And look, there's nothing in the piece, no charges, about him shooting up La Loma, taking potshots at Sully."

"He's not charged with it," Keith said. "Yet."

"They arrested him at the scene with the gun in his hand."

"Right," Keith said, "but they are drowning in the paperwork, the filing, on the Capitol. They're wanting to get that straight."

"And then, what, they fit—"

"Eddie," R.J. cut in, softly. "The hour."

He looked up at them. Sully could see the irritation flare in the upper reaches of his face, the eyes, the forehead. It wasn't like Eddie didn't spend a good chunk of his life threatening or intimidating people himself. Man lived in a Georgetown mansion. Sully pitied the dude repointing the brickwork who didn't get it right the first time.

Eddie looked down at R.J., then at his Rolex. "Jesus. Alright. Do we know for certain where he, Waters, is at the moment?"

"Central detention facility," Sully said, "the cells beneath police HQ. They've got isolation cells. Or he's already at St. E's. Or in transport."

"And they'll put him in Canan Hall, same as Hinckley? That's c.q.? Even though he's pretrial?"

Keith nodded. "It's the building for the criminally insane, yeah, but, legally, it's a hospital ward. The question is danger to himself or others. It's like gen pop at D.C. Jail. You got guys waiting for trial, guys serving time. Like that."

"Gen pop?"

"General population."

"Okay," Eddie nodded. "Okay. Not bad work here. Not shabby at all. Any update on his physical condition? The marshals?"

"Nah," Sully said. "They shut down C-10 for the night after the dustup. Estes was plenty pissed, that sort of thing going down on his watch. Marshals are just saying bumps and bruises, a laceration to one guy's forehead. It might be worse, but they're not going to want to own it. Waters, for the record, had 'minor' injuries. They called it a 'scuffle.'"

R.J. snorted. "Bet it wasn't a scuffle once they got him back in the cell."

Eddie, playing the principal to the classroom, didn't smile. "This strategy from Miller, that's going to be the legal tangle. She's just predicting what the AUSA's office is going to do, but of course they're going to want to force-medicate him."

"She'll argue that his *medical* best interest, which would be to get treatment for a profound illness, is not in his *legal* best interest?" R.J. said, pushing his chair back, propping his feet on the desk.

"Yes," Sully said.

"If it wasn't a capital case, I don't think there'd be much of an issue," Keith said. "They'd be able to force-medicate. But here—"

"Keeping your client suffering but alive," R.J. cut in, hands crossed behind his head now. "In an insane asylum strong room for the rest of his godforsaken life, listening to voices coming from the light fixtures and picking lice out of his beard. I love lawyers."

"Beats being dead," Sully shrugged.

"Does it? It's the Vietnam argument of destroying the village to save it, if you'll pardon a reference from my generation. Maybe the jury would come back guilty, but not for execution. It's the District, after all. Or maybe not guilty by insanity like Hinckley, and he could wind up in exactly the same bed, on exactly the same floor, but medicated and in some semblance of existence."

Eddie nodded, done with the BS session. "In any event, her client might be crazy but she's not. It's a cogent argument, compelling. Well argued, this could go to the Supremes. So. R.J., be so kind as to punch the button and send it to the desk. It's at, what, fifty-seven inches, and we're budgeted for fifty, but I think layout will accommodate us."

R.J. sighed and pulled his feet down and put his hands back on the keyboard. Keith and Sully started to shuffle off. Eddie wasn't done.

"Keith. Any chance we'll have access to Waters over the next few days? Court appearance, anything at St. E's?"

"None. No chance. Estes made noise about a hearing in federal court next week, but I don't think so. We have no shot at access at St. E's. Canan Hall is the most forsaken of the godforsaken. Waters will be on lockdown, talking to a couple of shrinks for the next thirty days."

Eddie nodded. "Gossip query. I got asked this at poker the other night. Is Hinckley really dating that inmate up there, the woman who killed her kids?"

"I think you'd want to qualify 'date,'" Keith said, "but they've been seen together at some of the dances, the social functions they have up there for patients, yeah."

"A fly on the wall with those two," R.J. said. "'I shot the president, babe.' 'Ooooh. That makes me so hot. All I did was whack my children.'"

"Homicidal psychopaths need to get laid, too," Sully shrugged.

Eddie, cutting it off, pointing at Keith: "I want you all over Miller's idea, that she's going to refuse force-medication. Work the Rolodex, track down your experts on the golf course or at the beach tomorrow. See if you can turn a daily on this for Sunday."

Keith shrugged, nodded, yawned, headed for his desk.

"Sullivan," Eddie said, "walk with me."

He started back to his office, Sully falling in step beside him. The glass offices on the South Wall, the home of the brass, lay ahead, Eddie's the only one still alight. They were moving away from the copy desk, moving alone, a private conversation in what was usually a very public place.

"Exceptional work the other day at the Capitol," Eddie said, looking ahead, tapping the rolled-up printout on the palm of his hand, some jazzy little rhythm known only to him. "Truly special."

"Thanks, boss." Sully, hands in pockets, was ready to go home, have a late dinner with Alex and Josh, knock back some Basil's and sleep for a month.

"You okay? From last night?"

"I suppose. But I don't follow."

"I'm asking if you're okay. The shooting at the Capitol, the dead people, Waters trying to, for Christ's sake, shoot you and Alex. Are you mentally, emotionally solid? That's what I'm saying."

"It sort of sticks in memory," he said, slowing as Eddie did, keeping his face flat, voice steady, alert for the probes Eddie was sending. Not wanting to come off as defensive, or gung ho, and certainly not angry. Just normal. Why did that sound like an act?

"You know, it was kind of crazy there for a few minutes at La Loma. But I feel okay. The hands are steady."

"You need time off?"

"What? No. Eddie, don't even think about taking me off this."

"HR tells me you've been going to the therapy sessions, no problems."

"That's right."

"You back to the sauce?"

"Not a drop."

"Good. Then pack your bags. You're going to Oklahoma. We need to find out who this son of a bitch is. Boo Radley of the res, my ass."

"I thought we had Elaine, Richard, whoever out there."

"Had, yes. That's the operative phrase. They've finished their takeout. It's running tomorrow, but it doesn't tell us anything we don't already know. Now we've got a tropical storm, turning into a hurricane, in the Gulf. Richard's headed back to Texas in the morning. Elaine, she's in the middle of this piece on police brutality in Chicago. Besides, neither one of them, nor anybody else, has been able to get a goddamn thing on Waters. He's a ghost, a phantom, the fog, the mist. Get out there and remind us why you're the big swinging dick, the world-class parachute artist."

# SIXTEEN

"SO YOU'RE GOING?"

"If you can help me out with Josh, yeah."

"What does that mean, exactly?" Alexis asked in the dark, them in bed, the hour late, the ceiling fan turning. Light from the street outside filtered through the shutters. She sounded on guard, her head on the pillow, turned toward him. He couldn't see her features well enough to tell if she was being playful or offended.

"More or less staying at the house, babysitting, making sure he doesn't set anything on fire."

"What about while I'm at work?"

"That class at the Corcoran? He goes every day, all day. Kid's a phenom. Also, introverted and sort of nonverbal. His parents, that's my sister Lucinda and her husband Jerry, they're extreme Christians, so he's a little weird, you ask me. I let him hang out in the basement, watch all the horror movies he wants, drink some beer, ignore that he's watching porn on pay-per-view. Lucinda calls, you can skip that."

"My, but aren't we the funny uncle."

"Boy needs to be normal."

"Jerking off in the basement is normal?"

"He's fifteen."

"What does 'extreme Christian' mean?"

"Jim and Tammy Faye."

"What does he eat?"

"What do you mean, what does he eat? He's not a dog. Pizza. Cheese-burgers. Boy food."

"I don't know anything about boys."

"Think the grown version, only more gross."

"How much are you paying me again?"

"Scoot closer and I'll make a down payment."

"Not a chance."

"Well then. You can go with us to this cookout John and Elaine Parker are having tomorrow night, before I take off the next morning. He usually grills seafood. Man knows his charcoal."

"He's the homicide chief?"

"And his spouse, yes. Regular sorts. John, his momma is from Shreve-port. Ellen, she's from Myrtle Beach."

"Who else is going to be there? I mean, I don't want to go if—"

"Just us. I haven't been over there all summer. This isn't a D.C. func-tion. This is some Southern ex-pats eating proper food and drinking beer."

She yawned. "Okay. So I'll take the cultural excursion. I'll let you know your tab for Josh after I see how bad it is."

"Kid's a piece of cake."

"So long as I don't have to watch any porn."

"Wait, we've never actually discussed this. You don't like porn? You never struck me as a prude."

"I'm *not* a prude," she said, turning her head away from him, pulling up the covers. "But I already know what the inside of my hoo-ha looks like. I'm really not interested in looking at anybody else's."

\*        \*        \*

John and Elaine Parker had gotten married right out of college—they met at a mixer at Howard a million years ago—produced progeny nine months and fifteen minutes later, and now their boys were grown and settled in Seattle and San Diego. The couple had their two-stories-basement-and-an-attic American four-square stucco back to themselves. It was in Cathedral Heights, a leafy neighborhood in Northwest D.C., on Macomb, the south side of the street. Its back was to the trees and the open expanse of the Washington International School. They also had a small beach house on the Eastern Shore, which Sully sometimes rented in the off-season, and others rented in the high season. The couple spent two or three weeks a year there, the mortgage being covered by the rentals.

Alexis had agreed to house- and Josh-sitting, Sully suspected, half as an act of kindness, to help him get resettled after the shooting, and half as an act of going out of her mind in the microscopic studio apartment where the paper was putting her up during her trial run as editor.

She wore short cutoff blue jeans, sandals, and a spaghetti-strap top, a thing in gold and blue. The shorts were not quite Daisy Dukes but not far from it, either. They were ironic, what with her hundred-dollar Italian sunglasses, that's what they were. The go-to-hell self-confidence the woman possessed. It was what drew him to her the most.

Chez Parker faced the street, with a covered front porch, two gleaming white columns, rocking chairs, and petunias in hanging baskets. Homicide cops got paid only so much, but Elaine, who had gone into patent law, had worked her way up in a white-shoe firm downtown. She had made partner a decade ago. That the kids had gotten full-ride scholarships hadn't hurt.

Best, John had told Sully, they had been able to buy the lot beside them from an elderly neighbor whose children had moved him into an assisted living facility over on Connecticut Avenue. After a decent interval, they had demolished the one-story rancher in order to give themselves a comfortable, L-shaped back and side yard.

Elaine, being Elaine, had the entire property surrounded by a white picket fence. She came out onto the front porch while they were still parking, waving, smiling.

"Come on up here and let me hug your neck," she called out to Sully, as soon as they got out of the car, the Honda he kept in a neighbor's garage. "I hardly recognize you, driving anything but that crazy motorcycle."

"Hard to get three people on it," he called back.

Sully had dinner with them a couple of times a year at their place, and once or twice at his, ever since he'd come back from Bosnia. John had just made detective when Sully went abroad, and was running the homicide squad when he got back.

Work talk was verboten by unspoken agreement at social gatherings. Sully introduced Alexis and Josh and then they all retreated to the shaded back deck, where John was holding court. The grill was already going, sea bass and scallops above low flames. He was working on a beer from a frosted pilsner glass. Elaine, being Elaine, already had the outdoor table set up beneath a green-and-white-striped patio umbrella. A breeze came up, the heat breaking.

John came off the grill, grabbed a football on the deck, and playfully underhanded it to Alexis, with nothing but a quick "Hey now" as warning. She, having picked up a Corona on her way through the kitchen, nimbly shifted the bottle to her left hand and let the ball come to her, tucking it in against her right side.

"Whoa," John said. "Lady's got hands."

"And didn't spill the beer!" Alexis said. She set the Corona on the table, flicked her tongue across the middle fingers of her right hand, and took the ball by the laces. She patted it twice, shifted her left foot forward, and cocked her arm, the ball up by her ear.

"Gimme a look," she told Josh, flicking her chin up, toward the open expanse of the yard.

Josh looked over at Sully, who just nodded, smiling, knowing what was about to happen.

Josh, awkward as always, went down the steps to the yard, then half-trotted out in the grass, looking back at them all. Alexis zipped him a strike over the right shoulder, high and tight, a spiral that flew through his hands.

"Hey," he said, frowning, shaking out his fingers.

She laughed. "I thought you said, back there in the car, that you knew your football."

"I play," he said, defensive, color coming up in his cheeks. "I wasn't ready, that's all."

He came back, tossing it to her, wobbly. She caught it, then repeated the same motion, flicking the tongue, shifting her feet, but now bounced on her toes, knees bent, like she'd just come from under center. She snapped her right arm up, ball beside her ear, and slapped it twice with her left hand.

"Gimme a deep post."

Josh lit out, no kidding this time. She stepped into her throw, putting some air under it, a floating spiral that came down, down, down, right into his outstretched hands, five yards before the picket fence. Josh had to put a hand out for it, halting his momentum. He looked back, smiling, like he'd just snagged it in the back corner of the end zone.

"Nice grab, champ," she said, saluting him with a short, piercing whistle. "Now lemme finish my beer."

John stood with his hands on his hips, forgetting the scallops, eyebrows raised, looking over at Sully, who shrugged. Elaine made a show of dropping her chin, opening her eyes wide, and then closing them both. She used a paper towel to dab a film of perspiration from her forehead—the humidity, the heat from the fire—and said, turning to Alexis, "Where did—"

"I was the only boy," Alexis said, sitting down on the bench, crossing her legs, the show over, reaching for her beer, "that my father ever had."

*     *     *

By midnight, they were back at Sully's, the back-porch conversation with the Parkers having lingered over everything and anything but the shooting. *Gladiator*, which Alexis liked but said wasn't half the movie *Memento* was; the Saints, Sully's team; the Cowboys, John's ("They were the first to integrate. The Redskins, last. Old heads don't forget."); Tiger; the brushfires out west; the lingering bullshit over *Bush v. Gore*; Jesse Ventura as Minnesota governor (which drove Elaine to near distraction); land seizures in Zimbabwe.

Once home, Josh wanted to turn in without a shower. Sully was going to let him slide but Alexis, already in charge, said, "Absolutely not. Boys stink."

She frog-marched him to the basement door and gave a light push. "Wet. I want to see that hair *wet*. I want the smell of soap and shampoo. Don't try running the water for two minutes while you stand there with the door closed."

Sully went upstairs to pack, grabbing two pair of jeans, a pair of slacks, a sport coat, two dress shirts, two pullovers, some underwear and socks, and a pair of gym shorts to sleep in. Nobody on the road ever saw you more than twice, so nobody knew if you wore the same shirt three times in one week, and if they did, fuck 'em.

He was getting toiletries from the bathroom—razor, shaving cream, and toothbrush—and from that spot, there at the top of the stairs, he could hear that Josh had come back up from the basement to the kitchen. Alex was unpacking the dishwasher. Sully stopped, listening.

"So, here," he heard Josh say.

Footsteps and then a long, exaggerated sniff. "Aaaahhhhh," Alexis said. "Shampoo and clean hair. Girls dig that kind of thing."

"I know."

"Okay then. You good for the night? Need anything to drink? Water?"

"No. I'm good. Sully's got a baby refrigerator down there."

"You know they got the bad guy, right? That it's all okay?"

"Sure."

"Right then. Off to bed with you." She paused. "What are we doing after your classes tomorrow, after I get here from work?"

"I don't know. You like horror movies? We could watch horror movies."

"I'm a girl, so, no. But I'll give two of them a try to see if maybe I'm wrong. Tell you what. We'll go to Hawk and Dove—their veggie pizza *kills*—and then we'll swing by Blockbuster's on Eighth. You pick two horror flicks. If I like, we'll do it again Tuesday. If I don't, we'll go back and get two of my pick. Fair?"

"Fair. Sure. Fair."

The door to the basement squeaked on the hinges, then stopped. Josh, again, tentatively. "Hey. I ask you something? I mean, you mind?"

"No, you can't do tequila shots at the Hawk."

Josh laughed, soft, not forced. "No no, that's not what I was going to ask. See, no. I was going to ask—ah, I mean—do you like Sully?"

"Who wants to know?"

"Nobody. Well. I mean, well, like, you're staying here and so I just, not that it's any of my business, but I—"

"You're right," she said lightly. "It's none of your business. But yes. I like Sully. Most of the time. You?"

"Yeah," he said, his voice taking her tone, her inflection. "Most of the time."

There was a fluttering and then a pop, which Sully recognized as Alexis twirling the dish towel and then snapping it.

"Hey," Josh said.

"Think of a good movie," Alexis said, and the kitchen light clicked off.

Sully heard her feet moving and, gently, slowly, closed the bathroom door. He turned on the shower. Other voices, other people in the house. It was different. He liked it.

When he came out, fifteen minutes later, his waist wrapped in a towel, hair still wet, she was already in bed, the lights out. He padded down the hall and across the bedroom, the streetlight outside filtering through the heavy leaves of the cherry tree in front, the blinds, the curtain. The ceiling fan spun slowly, more a thought than an actual breeze. The bed, the furniture was outlined in shadow. He could have walked it in pitch-black darkness. But he liked the pale slats of light that fell in rows across the bed, over Alexis's stretched-out frame, lying on her side, her back toward the window, her face obscured. He dropped the towel from his waist and slipped into bed, pulling the sheets back up, scrunching up behind her, spooning. She adjusted her back, her legs, to fit into his.

He draped an arm over her side and stopped.

"Woman, what is—"

"One of your T-shirts."

"*T*-shirt? More like a muumuu. Since when did you—"

"There's a kid in the house."

He let that sit for a minute, there in the dark, then let a hand roam. "You know, he can't hear anything way down—"

"Absolutely not," she said. "No stuff for you."

"Oh, come on. I'm leaving tomorrow and—"

"Nope."

"You, you're serious."

"You may cuddle."

"Married people," he said, "I mean, people with kids, they have sex, you know, with the kid in the house. That's how people have two kids, three, like that."

"We're not married and we don't have kids. Cuddle or the couch."

A moment later she said, not even opening her eyes, "My ass doesn't need cuddling, thank you. Now. Go to sleep and keep your paws off my lady parts."

# SEVENTEEN

HE WAS OUT of the house before first light, not waking anyone, on the plane at National and gone, the plane turning west, away from the sunrise, him feeling light, clean, fast, like a real reporter again.

He leaned into his window seat, watching Appalachia disappear beneath him in the reddish purple light. Then he closed the blind and pulled from his backpack the manila folder of clips about Waters, the articles that the wire services and national and regional papers had filed about his roots. Laying them out on the empty seat next to him, they filled the space with everything but information.

Eddie hadn't been kidding. Nobody had gotten shit. Waters's picture from, what, middle school? Notices about his father's funeral the previous year. Quotes from tribal officials, testifying that Terry, long ago, had been a problematic and then violent child, clearly mentally ill, expelled for attacking a tenth-grade teacher with a knife.

The judge in the case—he was quoted in Elaine's story—had been inclined to send Terry to a home for troubled youth back then, a reform school, but the father had resisted. He'd said he would take care of it if the judge would release the boy, then sixteen, to him. The judge had reluctantly agreed. Terry had rarely been seen in the two decades since.

The old man, Russell Waters, was known as a hard drinker and an itinerant worker on oil platforms in Oklahoma and Texas. Lived far out on the edges of the res, Waters the elder made it clear that visitors weren't welcome. The place—a ramshackle brick affair in a picture in the *Times*—was described as down a state highway, then several miles down a gravel road, then south on a narrower gravel road, and, finally, down a half-mile drive, lined with scrub.

The old man had reportedly come into town now and again for groceries and hardware. Raised a few head of cattle. Sometimes he'd been spotted drinking at the new, sad-sack casino in Stroud. He'd once been arrested for drunk and disorderly in Tulsa. Sully couldn't blame him. Let him live his entire life in Stroud, Oklahoma? Drunk and disorderly woulda been his hobby.

Mom, the key to Terry's motive, was apparently long dead.

Nobody ever remembered seeing her, just that Terry was suddenly out there with his dad, hiring local women for help. The local rumor was that she'd died shortly after childbirth, that she was a hooker near one of the oilfields where the old man worked, that she was just a teen, that she was everything but the Virgin Mary. There were no records, no headstone, nothing, not even a name. No known siblings. People said they'd seen Terry in his father's Ford F-150 on shopping trips into town over the years, but no one was really sure. It might have been a sack of feed thrown into the shotgun seat.

Russell had been dead in the house for several days when his body had been discovered the previous fall, the livestock emaciated. When police showed up, Terry was long gone.

The plane bumped down in Tulsa a little after noon, jolting him from a nap, his papers scattering between his knees and on the floor. Outside the window, the dry plains lay waiting for him, sunny and scorching and rolling, the grass already going brown.

He blew the rental down I-44, taking the outskirts at eighty miles an hour, the cement factories and the cheap motels and gas stations and then the open pastures, the great void of rural America. Lunch was at the

Sonic Drive-In in Stroud, midafternoon, the car door open, the wind snapping across the prairie, talking to R.J. on the cell.

"I'm having the chicken and tater tots," he said. "You put enough ketchup on them, they're not bad."

"I'll never know," R.J. said.

"What did we have in the paper today?"

"The same thing as the *Times*, give or take. The bio piece Elaine and Richard had been working on. The house at the end of the road kind of stuff. Waters went mental in high school, or thereabouts, your typical teenage-onset depression, then voices, then things with knives—"

"I was reading that on a printout," Sully said. "The hell is that, things with knives?"

"Apparently he liked to cut things up, animals, birds, skin them, leave them around town. Guy quoted here, ran a motel, said he came to work one day, there were four squirrels and a coyote, decapitated and gutted in front of rooms number one through five."

"And they pegged it to Waters?"

"Not exactly, at least the sheriff here is quoted as saying, but he went out to have a talk with Terry and the old man. Things piped down for a while, then there was another incident with deer carcasses, this time at the res headquarters, and that got another visit, no fooling this time. The dad, that's Russell, he said he would take care of it. The last time anyone quoted saw Terry."

"How long is that?"

"Seven or eight years."

"Jesus."

"We quote, and the *Times* does as well, friends of Dad, if you can call them friends, saying they'd seen Terry when they had stopped by way back when, that Dad kept him either in a locked room or on a rope in the backyard."

"A *rope*? Didn't that like, sort of set off social welfare or something?"

"It's on the res, so it's Indian Country, and the res people say, basically, what do you want us to do? Where would we send him that's better?"

Sully ate a tater tot. "You put it like that."

"Dad was an ornery cuss himself, apparently. Dead for days before anybody found him."

"Was he gutted?"

"Your apparent garden variety heart attack, coroner says. Sixty-three. Found on the kitchen floor, facedown, by a neighbor who'd seen the lights on three, four nights in a row."

"And our boy Terry, long gone."

"Like the breeze."

"And, what, this was last year?"

"Last October, so what's that, ten months? Yes. Ten months."

"Terry then totally off the grid until he shows up at the door of the Capitol."

"The guys and girls in Investigative say there's nothing in the system on Waters. No driver's license record, no employment history, nothing."

"A ghost, a phantom, the mist, the fog," Sully said. "He worked with a gun at the Capitol, though, not a knife."

"You're forgetting the ice picks, champ. He got more refined."

Sully checked into the Corral Hotel, hard off the interstate, a two-story brick thing. His was a small room on the second floor, facing west, four walls of depression and low-end America that looked just right for hanging yourself from the shower rail. The afternoon and next morning he made the due diligence stops—the res administration, the sheriff's office, the feed store, the school. Twenty-four hours after he landed, he'd gotten the same pablum as everyone else. He'd tried even the casino the first night, the lowest rung of reporting, running a tab, trying to chat up the bartender, the waitress, the guy sitting down from him.

Nobody told him shit.

He didn't mind. He was the guy from out of town. No matter where you went on the planet, nobody who lived in little towns that had just risen to notoriety wanted to talk to the dipshits from out of town. Back home in Tula, if reporters from New York and D.C. and Chicago had shown up after his mother was murdered? Half the town would have beaten them senseless while the other half fetched torches for the bonfire.

That night he lay awake in the room, the clock ticking past one, then two, the vast, open landscape and the endless windswept vistas outside. It had broken him down enough earlier in the day that he had gotten a fifth of Maker's at the liquor store in town. This was, technically, a violation of the promise he'd made to Alexis, during his phone call back to her and Josh, that he would not drink on the trip. But good God, a man could have one, well, two, and possibly five if anyone had to count, when stuck in a bullshit hotel like this, the night long, the diversions nonexistent, the prairie outside infinite.

So late in the second day, another night and the other half of the bottle looming in front of him, he turned the car out of town, heading down Route 99, toward Prague, headed out to the Waters' old homestead.

The land here was wide open, trees not even close on the road, the pastures undulating to the horizon. Prefabricated tin warehouses, wooden country stores. There weren't many turnoffs. Still, he blew right by his turn. After stopping at a concrete-block country store three miles down the road, asking directions, he came back and turned onto an unmarked gravel road that the clerk had assured him was actually Spark Road, the one he was looking for. He turned left, heading west, and reset the odometer, red dust billowing up behind him.

Once you turn west on Spark, the clerk had told him, it was six or seven miles to his next turn, which would be a left, not long after he'd passed a little wooden church. From there, that gravel road would take him another few miles, across a creek, and the first right after that would be the Waters' driveway. It was in a clump of trees, lined with scrub, and there was no marker. You'll know it when you get there, she said, and Sully was country enough to understand that those were the best directions you were ever going to get.

Every now and then, tooling past the open pastures, he'd see a house, set back anywhere from fifty yards to half a mile off the road. The cattle outnumbered the houses ten to one. But that wasn't saying much, since there weren't much more than a dozen houses before he spotted the church, in a small grove of trees, a little cemetery by its side.

The left, he didn't even bother with the blinker, the rural habits of his youth coming back to him like cultural DNA.

Shortly before he got to the creek, he slowed, coming to a full stop. Dangling from a barbed-wire fence that ran alongside the road, corpses of two coyotes, hung upside down. Their snouts were at least a foot off the ground, their mouths gaping, their eyes open, the flies buzzing, the stench a thing to behold.

The Waters' driveway wasn't even gravel. Just two thin dirt tracks heading west, into the weeds. Grass had grown high in between the tracks. A sagging fence ran along either side. The tracks rose slightly from the road, over a small rise, then fell away.

The house lay in a low plain, visible shortly after he turned in the drive, open pasture around it, a concrete drive at the front of the house, leading to a shed that looked to be a one-car garage and storage space. The livestock barns were shabby wooden structures. One had a hayloft. A good wind would blow them into Kansas. A pond lay to the back and left. The tree line was maybe four hundred yards behind the house.

The house itself, now collapsing back into the earth with age and neglect, was the one-story redbrick rancher with a black slate roof that he'd seen in the photograph. It seemed to sag to the left. Two windows were broken. The weeds were knee high in the front.

Slowing as he approached, he tapped the horn twice, making sure he was announced, in case a real estate broker, or somebody else, was knocking around. No point getting shot for a lack of manners.

He parked the car a few yards in front of the house and got out. The only sound was the ticking of the motor and a light breeze, sighing through the grasses. The sun was in front of him, fading now, the first fingers of night stretching out.

"Hello," he called, repeating it after a moment. Nothing.

"Just a reporter, dropping by," he hollered, walking forward, notebook in hand, waving it. The house looked malignant, its black windows staring back at him, the open maw of the front door.

A screen door had fallen to the ground in front of the door. The door itself was rotting, fat with rainwater. It was half off the top hinge, giving it a drunken lean forward. Nothing inside made any noise. He slid past the door, not touching it, and stepped inside.

It was dark, darker than he expected, and he had to stop to let his eyes adjust. There was a deep stillness. He took in a full breath and let it out. The lives that had been lived inside these walls were erased and gone, just shadows and ghosts and faded voices left behind. If he stood there long enough, he would begin to hear them, the way he heard voices of the dead in the last, eyelid-fluttering moments before sleep. He'd been stunned when Eva Harris, the prosecutor back in D.C., told him she had the same thing, the voices of the homicide victims she represented sifting down into her mind in the darkness. He'd thought he was the only one. Whatever. He wasn't going to hang around in here long enough for it to happen to him. Terry Waters was long gone from this place.

"The physical," he whispered to himself. "Focus on the physical."

Rotting carpet. Bags of trash. Part of the ceiling had rotted and collapsed, spilling old insulation onto the floor. Buckets, two coffee cans. An overturned sofa. Three, five steps brought him to the kitchen, the front hall. The sink had been pulled out, the plumbing taken. A wet mattress in a bedroom, stinking like a dead thing, rat pellets everywhere, the closet door off its tracks, leaning over on the mattress. One bathroom. The toilet pulled out of the floor, the sink and the tub still there but going from brown to black with grime and dust. Bird feathers. The smell of piss and animal shit.

It closed in on him fast, the house a tomb. He walked through the kitchen and pulled open the back door, getting outside, wanting to get out of there, feel the breeze, see the last rays of light.

The backyard wasn't really worth the name. Packed earth and a fire pit. The old livestock pens lay twenty yards off to the west. There was a stand of trees farther out to the left, past the pond.

As he was turning back to the house, movement caught his eye. There, in the distance, a woman was coming out of the tree line to the far west. Some sort of checked shirt, jeans. She had long black hair and was walking head down, arms folded across her chest.

She came out of the woods, in the light now, walking toward the house, still a good quarter mile off. He started walking in her direction, an idea forming at the back of his mind.

When she raised her head, looking first up at the sky and then back down, Sully, still walking, smiled and waved. He was in the full light of the sun. He shaded his eyes with the notebook. No way she could miss him. He waved again, smiling, then calling out a long "Hellloooo," across the plain.

The woman stopped. Her head turned slightly and she caught sight of him. She did not acknowledge hearing him or make any movement at all.

She just turned and disappeared back into the shadow of the woods, leaving him there, standing, arm raised, waving at a ghost.

## EIGHTEEN

**HE WOULD NEVER** catch her. Running across the fields and into the woods, having no idea where she had gone, that was foolish. But he had to get to her, and fast. Just that quick, the idea had blossomed from the back to the front of his mind. He knew who she was.

Gimp-legging it around the side of the house at a half trot, he made it back through the weeds, to the concrete stretch in front of the house where the car was parked. Jiggling the keys out of his pocket, he dropped them, picked them up, and then slammed the door shut behind him. The car took him back down the driveway at a rattling clomp, shocks be damned. The gravel road came up on him quicker than he remembered and he slammed to a stop, the plume of dust catching back up with him, cascading over the car.

Left, back up to the road he came in on? Right?

"Fuck," he shouted, banging the steering wheel with a fist. The lady at the rental counter, she'd tried to persuade him to rent one of those GPS things. He'd scoffed—like he couldn't read a map—but now, here he was, time evaporating, stuck with pulling the folding map from the glove compartment.

Staring at it now, mashed flat on the seat beside him, he saw the county roads weren't exactly a grid, but they were close. The woman had come out of the woods to the west. That meant she had to be coming from somewhere directly behind the Waters' place. The properties, he was guessing, abutted, back to back. If true, that meant she would live on the next road to the west, and they would share a north-to-south property line. All he had to do was get there.

Where was he on the map, where was he . . . ? He folded the map to a quarter panel to narrow it down. Spark Road . . . the creek . . . here. He was here.

If he turned right, going more or less south, there was another county road, like Spark, heading due west. That would take him—he followed it with a finger—here. Gotdamn. He was right. There was another north-south road, just like the one he was on, maybe two miles west. Complete with Spark Road at the north, it formed a box.

He set his odometer and pulled out hard to the south, spraying gravel. The light was going, fading by degrees. It got dark, he'd be fucked. He'd never find her tonight, and tomorrow she'd be gone or never answer the door even if he knocked on the right one.

Two point three miles down, across the open fields, he could see the intersecting road at least a half mile in the distance. Hallelujah. No plume of dust rose from it, so no car coming, and he swung the rental hard to the right as soon as he got to the intersection, no more than a tap on the brakes before he floored it west, the car fishtailing. He was plowing past a cemetery, goosing it up to fifty, sixty miles an hour. The road was nearly a straight shot. Two miles down to the next intersection and at the next dirt road, he swung back north, again resetting the odometer.

Now he'd need to come back north the same distance—two point three miles—and he'd be more or less directly west of Waters's place.

Shadows falling, stretching across the road. Stars coming out above. He leaned forward over the steering wheel, willing the car forward, slowing when he got to the two-mile mark.

The land was still wide open, pastures with trees in clumps, the main tree line running far to the east from this perspective. A driveway up ahead led to a trailer built on a redwood platform. The windows were dark. He all but ran to the front door, catching his breath, then knocking. A dog barked from inside, a yapper. It came to the door on the other side, pissed off, jumping up against the door. Another knock. Nothing.

Back to the car, pulling out, shadows falling all the way across the road now. *Dark don't catch me here.*

A quarter mile up, two trailers sat in their packed-dirt-and-crabgrass lawns, maybe fifty yards apart, a couple of fruit trees between them, a pickup in front of one, an old Buick in front of the other. The windows were dark in both. He was at a crawl, debating whether to stop, when, in the back pasture, coming past a sturdy wooden barn, he could see a figure moving. It was a black-haired woman. She wore an open checked shirt. Jeans. She was headed for the trailer on the left, slowing, her head coming up, looking at his car.

"Gotcha," he breathed, throwing it into park right there at the side of the gravel road, not wanting to give her the chance to get inside.

By the time he was around the back of the car, she had reached the edge of the trailer. She had pulled out a pistol but was not walking any faster. She just came steadily toward him, past the trailer, into the scrubby front yard.

"Hi," he called out, stopping three steps past the car, pulling both hands away from his body, but not being so ridiculous as to raise them. She stopped, halfway to the drive, a dog barking from her own trailer now. She recognized him from before, he could tell. Her eyes flickered with it. She didn't speak. She didn't raise the pistol. She just kept it at her side. That she didn't raise it told him that she felt plenty capable of snapping it up, firing, and blowing him back into the gravel.

"Ma'am," he said, "my name's Sully Carter, and I work at a newspaper in Washington. I was looking for the person who discovered Russell Waters's body after he died last year. I'll drive all the way back into town to the liquor store, come back, and leave a bottle of bourbon in your mailbox if that's not you."

*    *    *

"You don't have to take your shoes off," she was saying, looking back over her shoulder, turning the lights on in the small front room. "Jasper. Sit. *Now.*"

Sully and the dog both did as they were told. The dog, a country mutt with a little pit bull to him, wasn't happy about it but settled by the couch.

Standing by the door, taking two steps inside, Sully saw that it was comfortable but basic. An upholstered couch with a faded throw neatly folded over the back. A recliner, television, newspapers and magazines in a rack. The paneled walls held family pictures, some art-fair-quality paintings of the prairie, buffalo in the distance. The kitchen and a dining nook were just past that. Sully, mindful of Jasper, asked if he could come to the dining nook.

"Yep," she said. She was in the kitchen. She'd put the pistol, an old-school six-shooter, on the countertop. He could hear cups being set down.

"I don't want to interrupt dinner if—"

"We call it 'supper' out here. I work overnight. Shift at the hospital starts at ten. You can eat with me or watch."

"Sure, I'll—"

"You can have spaghetti. If you don't like that, you can have spaghetti."

"I'll go with the spaghetti."

He pulled one of the hardback chairs out from the table and sat. His backpack, notebook, recorder, everything was still in the car. There was not a chance in hell he was going back out there to get it. He was *in*—for whatever reason—and he was not about to break the fragile spell that put him here. He looked at the dog. Jasper was losing interest.

"Hope I didn't spook you," he said. "I apologize, following you around to your property from the other place."

"I don't spook. It was reasonable tracking. You want water, coffee?" She looked at him, her black eyes steady. They didn't seem to take in any light at all. "Or whiskey, since you offered to fetch it."

"Ah, water would be great. Dry throat. And if you're having a splash of God's own, I'd be obliged."

She did not answer but turned back into the kitchen and busied herself. The kitchen was as narrow as a hallway. If she turned sideways, she could have one hand in the sink and the other in the fridge. He heard the *tick tick tick* of a gas stove, the *whoosh* of it catching, pans rattling. When the water was boiling, and he could hear (and smell) the sizzle of ground beef going into the skillet. She came back to the table with four glasses. Two were tall, brimming with ice and water. The other two were short, round, and empty. She retreated, reached to a shelf above the refrigerator, and pulled back a bottle of Knob Creek.

She poured two fingers for him and two for her, neat. "One and only one round," she said. "Like I say, I got work." She went back to the kitchen without touching hers.

"What do you do at the hospital?" he called out.

"What's it to you?" she called back.

He took a sip. "Whoa, look, I don't want to get—"

"R.N.," she said. "The name is Elaine Thornton. But you're not ever putting either one in your newspaper. Or anywhere else. Clear?"

"Yes, ma'am."

"Stop with the ma'am shit."

"Okay."

Time ticked on. A little air in the conversation wouldn't hurt. He sat back, sipping the bourbon. Cooking seemed to take up her attention and he contented himself to think for a second, taking in a breath down to his lungs and letting it out again. The best idea was always to be direct, to state the thing clearly. If it went screwy, then at least later you'd think it had gotten screwy for the reason that you came, not for some chatty bullshit you were trying to be clever about.

"So. Elaine. You, ah, you knew Mr. Waters? Russell?"

"All my life. Our properties are back-to-back. As you seem to have figured out. You grew up in the country to have sussed that out that quick."

"Did—I did, yes. Louisiana. By the river. And you were the neighbor who found him, called the police?"

"Nobody else would have found him for a month. And, no. I called the hospital to send the wagon. They called the police."

"Was Terry there at the time?"

"Nope."

"So, Terry, he just got loose when his father died? What happened to him after that?"

"Nothing."

"Well, I mean, I don't quite know what you mean by 'nothing.' He turned up at the Capitol last week, shooting—"

"When I said nothing, I meant nothing." She came back to the table, a spatula in hand, picked up her glass and took a shot. She leaned forward on the chair back, wagging the spatula for emphasis. "That's why I let you in, if you're wondering. I wanted to ask *you* a question. Namely, what in the hell is wrong with you dipshits in Washington? Terry Waters has been dead and in the ground for close on eight years now. Why do you people think he's shooting up the place?"

## NINETEEN

COUGHING OUT THE bourbon, putting his hand to his mouth to catch the spittle—"He was—"

"I helped put him in the dirt myself."

"—four days, I don't—"

"You really want to, you can see him yourself. You were standing not a hundred yards from his grave over there at the house."

He coughed, and coughed again, looking at her, sitting back in his chair. He coughed twice more. Felt his face going flush, the lack of oxygen. She turned and went back to the kitchen.

"I, I just don't understand. I saw the man. Terry. Talked to him."

The bubbling sound of water boiling, dimly, the simmering beef. A jar opened. She was putting in the sauce. *Ragu* bounced through his mind.

"You talked to somebody who *said* he was Terry," she said, not looking over at him. "Terry has been dead since early fall of, what was it, 1992. September. Russell came and got me. I was out back with the horses. Russell was drunk. How he walked all that way that plastered, I don't know. There's a trail there through the cut. Say what you will about the man but Russell could hold his liquor."

"And—"

"He told me Terry had died. That was all he said. 'Terry died.' The sum total. What do you do with that? So we walked back through the woods, the pasture, to his house. It's a long way. He didn't say anything. 'Terry died,' he said, me there with the horses and a bucket of feed, and he turned around and started walking back. So, the hell, I set the bucket down and followed him.

"We got to his house, it was more of a mess than usual. Furniture knocked over," she said, her voice flat, turning to the sink to drain the pasta, going on and on in that long, almost atonal delivery, looking out the window over the sink into the pasture, the land going full dark. "The walls, you know, it's that brown paneling, I'm guessing you saw it. Flimsy as it gets. There was a hole in it. Terry was in the hallway. He was on his back. He'd been shot with a shotgun. Blown up. You ever seen what a shotgun will do to people?"

Finished draining the pasta, she reached behind her, turned off the heat on the beef, looking over at him, gauging his response.

"Yes."

"How?"

"My mother."

"What about her?"

"She was killed. With a gun. Three shots. A pistol, not a shotgun. My girlfriend, I'd guess you call her, she was killed by shrapnel. To the head. In Bosnia."

She looked at him, her eyes moving over his scars, returning to his.

"It's a long story," he said.

She piled pasta, then spooned some ground beef in a thick red sauce over it, onto one plate, then another, set them both on the table, produced silverware, tore off paper towels and handed one to him, a napkin. She sat, a hand flicking her hair back over her shoulders.

"Then you know. He was a mess. I asked Russell what happened. He had, he had been taking care of Terry since forever. Marissa, that was the mother, she wasn't shit."

"Nobody else seems to know anything about her, even her name."

"I saw her. Twice, I think it was."

"Do you know what happened to her? Terry—this guy in D.C.—said somebody killed her."

"That's some happy horseshit. I don't know and Terry didn't neither. She lived down in Texas. She was white. Maybe from the panhandle. You can like the panhandle if you want but I say it ain't shit. Russell worked at an oil rig down there for a spell. Something was wrong with Terry from the get-go. Marissa cut bait when he wasn't but a pup. Russell brought him up here. By the first grade, second, he was clearly off. Schizophrenic, you ask me in my professional sense. People in Stroud, though, they've told you and the others about what he'd do to animals."

"Yes."

"So Russell brought him back home after all the trouble in town. What else could he do? Send him to the state? Abandon him? Cuss Russell, but the man wasn't a quitter. Blood was blood. He kept that boy, difficult as he was. People in town, they will tell you that Russell never brought Terry into town."

"I heard that."

She blew air through her nose, not quite a snort, twirling her fork around the spaghetti. "They won't tell you that they *told* him not to bring him into town, *warned* him. I don't know if it's better somewhere else, but people here, they're scared of mental sickness. Terry frightened people. People told stories. Kids. Legends. Anytime animals turned up dead, Terry was said to have done it. The talk, you wouldn't believe. He was a shape-shifter, he walked with the spirits, he drank human blood, he ran with the wolves."

"He was the Thing in the Dark."

She looked at him again, appraising. "Yes. The thing. The bogie man. The thing that moves in darkness. The terror of the night. So Russell wound up staying home with him. He'd take the odd day job every now and then. That's why he had the fence around the house, did you know that? He'd let Terry keep the door open and he could go out or not. He'd have me look in on him. I stayed over there a handful of times while Russell worked out of state. Can't imagine what it must have been like, the years going on like that, the two of them alone."

"There's a story," Sully said, forcing himself to eat, his mind reeling, trying to keep the story straight for later, "that Russell kept him tied up with a rope."

"Fairy tales," she said softly. "There wasn't no rope. There was that fence, a pen, attached to the back of the house."

"But medication," Sully said. "You said you thought it was schizophrenia. There's Thorazine, there's newer stuff. You're a nurse. You would have told him about that."

"Told isn't convincing. Russell didn't understand what was wrong with Terry any more than anyone else. I got a psychiatrist from the hospital to come out to the house one time. He prescribed him something, I don't know, and Terry took about three of them and went berserk and Russell dropped it."

Sully, carefully watching Elaine, was making sure to eat as much as she did, and at the same pace, more or less. People got touchy about hospitality.

"But, whatever it was that last day," she said, "Terry tried to stab Russell. He got a knife and came after him. Russell dodged him and knocked the knife out of his hand, or so he told me, standing there in the hallway of his house, Terry dead on the floor. They fought and rolled over and Russell got away from him to get the shotgun in the bedroom. He came out and Terry had the knife again and came at him. So he shot him."

She stopped talking, as abruptly as she'd started. She went back to her spaghetti. Sully was getting used to her conversational style, if that was the word. No wedding ring. He surmised that was one of her brothers' trailers next door. That led to an educated guess that she had never married rather than divorced. That would be one tough hombre if there had been a husband.

"Russell, he have any cuts on him, like that?"

She didn't look up. "You think Russell, he was lying? That he shot Terry to be rid of him?"

"It's not what I said."

"It's what you meant."

He hitched his shoulders slightly, letting the question hang.

She swallowed her bite of spaghetti and finished the rest of the bourbon. Ten seconds went by, fifteen. "Russell wasn't bleeding, if that's what you're asking, least not that I could tell. The house was so turned upside down and Russell so, so staggered that it didn't occur to me. Still don't. He didn't say Terry cut him and he didn't say he didn't. He said he came at him with a knife."

"Okay. That's okay. It's sort of beside the point."

"Russell was wore out. There was no end in sight. It was just going to go on forever until one of them died, then the other. He looked like he was about to fall over himself. I said, 'What you want to do, Russell? Call the police?' And he sat down and did not say anything for a long time. He just kept looking at Terry. And then he said, 'No.'"

"And I said, after a while, 'Okay.' I knew what he meant. I knew what he meant to do. They had a family plot there, in the narrow band of trees not far from the house. Mother. Father. Some others. I asked where the shovels were. I said I would help him dig but that I would not help him clean the house. He had only one shovel. I walked home and got mine and my older brother was here and I got him and we went back. Russell was already digging. The ground was not hard yet."

Sully nodded, sat back in the chair, looked at her, looked over at Jasper. After a while, she started talking again.

"A sheet. He brought him out and laid him on the ground in a sheet. He never said nothing. He laid Terry on the ground and hugged him. Held him for the longest. Almost laid on top of him to do it. Then we laid Terry in the grave. Russell got the shovels. We finished in a few minutes. It was getting dark. I remember it was getting dark.

"Usually, we sit up with our dead, all night. People cook, bring things. There is a hut for this, a ceremonial kind of shed, at the res. I don't know that he would have taken him there under any circumstance, people had exiled him so. But you sit up all night, that is the tradition. In the morning, when the sun rises, the spirit is thought to be free of the body. You take the body through the door that opens to the west. Then there is the burial. I think this bothered Russell, that Terry did not have this. I think he was in shock and buried him before he thought about it.

"My brother and I, we left after Terry was in the ground. Russell built a fire. He sat there with the boy, in the ground, by the fire, all night. I say that because when I came back the next morning, he was asleep on the ground, on top of the grave. He did this several times a year. I would go by to see him, bring him vegetables from our garden. And there would be a fire ring out by the plot. Sometimes smoke, sometimes not."

"Is there a tombstone, a marker?"

"A star. A copper, silver sort of star, like a sheriff's badge. It had no name on it. He nailed it to the nearest tree. I don't know why. Perhaps it meant something to the boy."

"So when Russell died last year, you were the one who found him."

She reached in her purse, found a pack of cigarettes, brought one out, and lit it, nodding. "Russell, he had always had a problem with drinking, but much more so after Terry. He went into town less and less. The house grew up around him, almost like it was swallowing him. He wasn't even throwing out the bottles by the end."

"So, there's not, like, a death certificate or anything for Terry."

She blew out smoke and looked at him.

"It's not really any of mine," he said, "but you didn't report it to the police because, because, it seemed to you punishment was already served. A father killing his son, those circumstances, out here, the isolation, Terry's illness."

Her silences were artful. The way she had of making her point by not making any at all, letting your statements or assumptions stand on their own. She asked for information when she needed it but not anything beyond.

"We buried him next to Terry." That was all she said.

"And, again, no marker?"

"It was just my brother and I. The res came up with enough for a pine box. We said we would do the burial there and they said okay." She took another long pull on the cigarette. "I nailed another star to the tree."

Sully considered all this for a second. "Might you have another shot of bourbon?"

She got up and poured it. He said thanks and sipped and sat back.

"So," he said, "I'll go with you on this. I'll say Terry isn't the shooter in Washington. That means there's somebody locked up in D.C. who has assumed his identity, for whatever reason, which means he had to know of Terry, his situation. He had to look at least something like him. So the res, I'm guessing, is going to know, or have an idea—"

"Terry did not look particularly like he was from Indian Country. His mother was white, like I said. Russell's father was half white. I have some whites in the woodpile, but not like that. Terry did not look like me. The man in the picture that I saw on television, in the paper, he looked like he was playing Indian to me."

"So, so why didn't anyone tell this to the feds, the police, the reporters?"

"Terry was, what did you call him? The Thing in the Dark? You could have shown people a picture of a werewolf and they would have said it was him. I was, as far as I know, the last person to see Terry alive, and that was nearly eight years ago. Some things are never known. The fate of Terry. The killer of your mother."

He leaned back from the table and polished off the drink—she had a light thumb—and picked up his plate and glasses. He went to the sink and washed his glass and put it in the rack to dry. The light in the kitchen was a bare bulb. It was harsh. It was dark outside now, the moon coming up, low and full.

"Did you tell the federals this, the police?"

"No one asked."

"But, I mean, they had to be throwing a pretty wide net. Even if they didn't come through the woods there, somebody had to be knocking on every door in—"

"I was not home when they came. Two FBIs. My brother was, next door. He spoke for me. He said we barely knew Russell, much less Terry."

"They believed him?"

"Why wouldn't they?"

"I was just asking."

"My brother, he is not one to ask a lot of questions."

"What about the locals, though, the sheriff?"

"They don't bother us. The sheriff, he and my brothers? Not a good combination."

"And you didn't go volunteering this because . . ." He hunched his shoulders, held up palms to the air, inviting a response, but not wanting to put words in her mouth.

She looked back at him. "Me and the federals, also not a good combination."

Sully sat back down at the kitchen table. Jasper roused himself, stretched, came over and leaned against Sully's leg. The dog's ears had been clipped.

"So the wolves can't get them?" he said, rubbing Jasper's head, scratching behind the ears.

"Coyotes."

"Which reminds me. I saw two of them, strung up from a fence by the heels, on the way out from town."

"That's Jim's place. He believes, like a lot of people around here, that the coyotes can smell their own dead and avoid them." She was looking in the refrigerator for something. The open door blocked his view of her. "He's got chickens. When he gets a coyote, he strings it up."

"You think it works?"

"I think Jim thinks it works."

"You know who he is, though," he said quietly. "The man in Washington. He stabbed the congressional rep from here in the eyes. Two knives. Well, ice picks. Like Terry, with the knives."

He said it looking out the window.

She didn't stir from the table, didn't look over her shoulder at him.

"There was a family," she said. "Whites. They lived several miles down this road, that you came up. County ten thirty-two. The house is just off the res. Kept to themselves, came, left, never stayed long. They had a boy, used to come up here with Terry in the summers. Terry and that boy, they'd be wading through the creek that runs through the woods there. They would come over and ask to ride the horses."

"Did they look alike?"

"Thirty years ago? Some? Kind of. Dark hair. Black. Like yours. Same sort of build." She shrugged. "I looked at the television, I thought about it."

"You remember his name? This other boy?" He came back to the table now.

She stubbed out the smoke. "Thirty years."

"Last? The family name?"

"Something with an H, maybe. Hill, Harris, Humphreys. Look, like I said."

Jesus. Something with an H. Or maybe not. Something that sounded something like that. The number of times he'd been through this, how many interviews in how many places. Jimenez. Faris. Phillips. This was the time to push. Before he could get his lips around a re-formed question, she was pushing back her chair.

A ragged smoker's cough and she was standing, not looking at him but across at the kitchen, the middle distance. "Well."

His lips froze, midthought. The invitation to leave, the conversational kick in the shins, the end of the time I got for you and your questions. *I gotta do these dishes, I gotta go to work, I gotta go see a man about a dog. . . .*

Maybe he should have made more of a show of eating, knocking back the bourbon. The spaghetti, it was only half finished on his plate, his fork sticking up in the middle like a palm tree on a desert island.

When he stood, the floor creaking underfoot, he was surprised, standing next to her. She was leaner than he'd thought. Her lined face was reserved, it wasn't harsh. Or maybe he was just reading that into it now. Maybe it had softened with the bourbon, on her face or in his eyes. Maybe, maybe he wasn't reading her so well. You couldn't, you know, turn your sensors on like a magic trick. People talking about their infallible bullshit meter, *that* was bullshit.

"Want me to help you with these?" Sweeping his right hand to the dishes, already reaching.

"No no. Jasper lives on leftovers. I'll put the plates in the sink for later."

She stepped back, indicating by doing so that he should go first.

He thanked her for the supper, the hospitality. She followed him and it seemed so quiet now, he was just becoming aware of that, every footfall drawing a response from the warped flooring. There had been no radio playing, and the hulking television in the living room, so old and so big he wouldn't be surprised to find vacuum tubes in the back, lay dark and blank, dust on the screen. The recliner in front of the television. He had to weave around that. The door creaked when it swung open and out.

Darkness had fallen. She flicked on the porch light. They walked out in the yard—people had yards out here, not lawns—Sully making a few last bits of small talk about Jasper and coyotes. There was a light on a utility pole by her brother's house. It had come on, an orange, sodium-vapor glow that cast shadows. He thanked her once more as Jasper trotted out to his car, lifted a leg on the rear wheel, then came back to him, expectant.

"It's like that now?" he said, shaking his head at the dog. "And here I was, thinking we were friends."

He had made it from the yard into the road, the gravel crunching under his feet, when he heard her voice.

"Mister," she called out.

He turned, looked. She was standing at the base of the steps.

"Don't come back. You," she waved her hands faintly, "you have a darkness to you. It is not my way. If you put my name in your newspaper? My brothers, they will come to Washington."

He nodded, raising a hand, believing it down to his bones. The lady didn't know bullshit existed. When he opened the car door, his right foot on the floorboard, the left one still on the gravel, he stopped.

He looked back—she was still watching, there beneath the porch light—and said, "I didn't tell you they, the guy, whoever shot my mother, wasn't caught. You said it wasn't known, though, who did it. How, how did you know that?"

She looked at him. For a moment, he thought she wasn't going to reply. Then she shrugged and turned to go inside. "You are here," she said.

# TWENTY

THE WATERS' DRIVEWAY seemed longer in the dark, the rutted tracks turning off the gravel, into the weeds, the headlights raking the high grass, the lone tree looking like a spectral apparition, its fingers clawing at something just out of reach. Once the car was over the small rise and he could see the way ahead—the grass was beaten down from when he'd come by earlier—he cut the lights and switched off the ignition. After a moment, when his eyes had adjusted, he took a small flashlight from his backpack and got out.

Terry Waters, dead and in the ground? Let's see. Let's just fucking see.

The full moon, brilliant and unbroken by clouds, loomed above. Houses lay dotted across the prairie, lights twinkling in the wind, three quarters of a mile or more distant. Three, maybe four places, far, far down the road. Still, if those houses could be spotted at this distance, that also meant his car lights could be seen. The last thing he wanted was a rancher seeing lights at the old Waters place and coming to check it out, shotgun in hand.

A breeze came up. Sully could feel it on his skin, hear it sighing, see it ruffling the long high grass that spread for miles in front of him. Ahead, the house at the end of the driveway, the old barns, appeared as dark lumps on a silver horizon.

He kept his steps on the car tracks from earlier. It wasn't that he didn't trust Elaine Thornton. It was that you couldn't trust anybody. You couldn't believe anything. Not even people's names, their identity. Look at the mess he was in now. People put on faces for the world to see. They lied about everything, all day and particularly at night. It was a descriptive of the species.

Shadows of the house and barns deepened and took shape as he drew closer. He looked up at the cloudless sky above and pictured it looking down at him, from hundreds, thousands of feet above: the land below vague, dark, moonlight glinting off the lakes, the streets. The trees and woods filled in as darker shadows. Little winking dots of yellow—the houses, the people inside leading lives that no one would really know about or remember, just some of the human beings who had come onto the face of the Earth after the invention of electricity. Before that, the world had fallen featureless in the darkness, only the glow of fire and torches.

Now, lights of cities and towns beat back the darkness on a massive scale, hot, bright spots that showed up in the low reaches of orbit. Then his mind's eye swept backward at some fantastic speed until the Earth was just a little blue ball bouncing in the blackness of space, receding until it was a just a pin dot of light in the sky, infinitesimal and insignificant.

*That is who we are and what we are*, he thought, walking through the grass.

Millions of lives teeming on the head of a pin, the universe neither concerned nor vindictive nor compassionate. It just went on and on and on because that was what it did. People—they were just one little self-regarding species on one planet. They died and the universe was indifferent. It didn't mean anything. It was like drowning in the ocean. The ocean wasn't trying to drown you. It was just being the ocean. You got out of the water, fine; you got eaten by sharks, fine; you drowned, fine. It didn't matter as far as the ocean went.

That was life on Earth. It killed you without thinking.

And now he brought his gaze down to the dark house in front of him, the breeze gusting, running invisible fingers through his hair.

The house was indifferent, too. It was indifferent to the hope and lives that had been lived and ended inside it. There would have been the warmth of the days when Terry had been born, the early years. Surely there had been some good times, some nights that darkness had settled over them all, Russell and Marissa in bed and their son in his crib, the plains quiet, dark, somnolent. Russell would have dreamed the great dream of peace and quiet nights and long days of the family, here, close, quiet, the star-specked canopy of darkness hovering above them. The long cold nights of silence and breathing, safe, together, a family, the future spilling out in front of them. Russell Waters, a man who would later shoot the beautiful child asleep in the crib, would have closed his eyes and drawn his breath slower, slower, until sleep overtook them all.

Sully stepped over the narrow concrete pavement and moved under the eaves. He moved from light to dark in the yawning maw of the door.

Silence. Not even the scurrying of rats. A pale light shone through the windows onto the warped linoleum. It fell over the kitchen sink. Shuffling his feet deeper into the darkness, the feeling came over him, rushing up his spine and over his scalp—the pulse and the feel and the rotting flesh of the place, the blast of the gun, dead voices landing in his ear, the desperate father and the deranged son, yelling, vicious, biting, trapped here for weeks and months and years. The great dream of peace, corrupted by the American nightmare of murder and blood. The comforting darkness melted into black despair.

The long hours of the night were the worst because they were exiled together in the house at the end of the road, each in his own isolation, nothing waiting for them, no hope, no wonder, no joy, no possibility of things getting better and brighter. There was only the slow augering into the earth, of waiting for the day when they would be lowered into the mud and dirt, left to decay among worms and sightless insects.

Did the gunshot that killed his son echo in Russell's head every time he walked in the house afterward? Did he see the grotesque obscenity of his beautiful son's body, blown open and seeping blood, lying in the hallway, every time he walked to the bedroom? Seeing his fingers trembling with their last flickers of life?

Amputees had phantom pain, arms and legs that were no longer there yet still itched. Russell Waters shot his child to death right here. Then he lived another seven years in the same house. The phantom pain of his child's death, the loss of his embrace, of his love, and of the possibilities of what he might have become—all this melted into a pool of gore and blood on the linoleum.

If Elaine Thornton was telling the truth, leaving the police out of it but leaving Russell here was, in its own way, a prison term and a death sentence. He would have had to clean up his son's flesh and tissue and fluids, mopping, soaking, disinfecting, then bury it all in a glop in the backyard.

Sully doubted there was a way back from that.

Outside, he watched his shadow as he walked, moving through the grass, his feet snapping stems. No need for the flashlight. Her directions had been approximate but there was so little out here in the way of landmarks that he should still be able to find the family plot.

The moonlight glittered on the pond. He walked past it, a good twenty yards off, the water flat, save for a snake making its way, the head the only thing visible above the surface, leaving a narrow ripple in its wake. Sully, skittish, looked behind himself, but there was no one, nothing. Just the wind. Just him.

By the time he reached the copse of trees, he was beginning to chide himself. Elaine, what, she put on her serious Indian Woman Face and gave him bollocks about native burial rituals and shotguns and dead sons. Hokum story for the White Man from Elsewhere. Selling it to him to see if he'd print it and then laugh her ass off the next day at work, *White folks will believe anything. How! Shoulda sold him dream catcher for big wampum.*

But when he walked into the trees, into the shadows, when he flicked on the flashlight, the fallen-to-the-side tombstones were in front of him in a small clearing just like she had said, granite stumps in a world of dirt and wood.

"Ah, man," he said, the voice escaping his lips.

He knelt in front of the first, then the second. The engraving had faded. Nothing, just gray and mottled and spots of moss. Switching the flashlight to his right hand, he opened his left hand like a fan, tracing all five fingers over the face of the marker, as if communing with the dead underneath. The rough touch of the stone, the lines and circles and dots that had been chiseled into it, gave themselves up to his fingertips, but not in any shape or pattern. Was that a "B"? An "8"? No way to tell. The names and dates and *Beloved*s were lost, gone, too faint to be read except perhaps by Braille, by etching on paper.

"Dust to dust," he said softly. "Granite be damned."

He swung the flashlight this way and that, slowly. Five, six headstones. None more than two feet high. One had cracked and was falling forward. The others canted backward, as if beseeching God above for a second chance, or sideways, as if they were in some slow-motion midstupor stumble.

Pushing himself up, he stood. Okay, stars. Copper stars, iron stars, some kind of metal stars, nailed onto tree trunks. Where were these? He flicked the light from trunk to trunk, up and down, too rapidly at first, but he was jumpy—standing on top of dead people gave him the creeps—and it took effort to slow it to a methodical search.

The wind stirred. It moved the leaves above him in a restless fluttering. They rose on the wind and then fell without it. His footsteps were loud. Then, without even looking, he caught a glint off to the right. He snapped the light back to it. There. The side of an oak.

Two steps and his left hand was on the rough edges of the bark. A five-pointed metal star, big as his palm, nailed deeply into the tree, waist high. He bent to look at it. The bark was growing over the edges, the metal mostly black and corroded, hard and rough under his fingers. No writing, nothing at all, at least that could be seen now. He looked down at his feet. Was one of them, father or son, buried just below? Couldn't be. The roots would have been too thick to dig through. But a few feet away? Yes. There was an opening between trees, almost in the clearing with the gravestones.

"Well, blow me sideways," he said softly, the wind taking the words away.

The second star. Now. Was there a second star?

Twisting the ring at the top end of the flashlight, he expanded the beam from narrow to wide. The clearing emerged in a slow arc, following the beam. The orb of light illuminated branches heavy with thick green leaves, scrubs trying to take hold. The clearing was roughly circular. When he finished the circuit, there was nothing. Back again. Then he started going trunk to trunk, skipping the undergrowth and the saplings, looking out for snakes at each step now, the wooded, grassy thatch at his feet.

"Come on, come on." The urgency was at the base of the neck, in his fingers. How long ago had he parked the car? He'd forgotten to check his watch, and now time seemed to be an amorphous thing. It could have been anything from twenty minutes to an hour. How long had he stood in the house, outside, looking—

Glinting, a small flash in the darkness.

—wait, take the light back—his fingers swept along the bark of another oak, not as big as the first but still sturdy, and here, at belt-buckle height, was another star. Not as deeply nailed in. Shinier. Not so rusted. Not as old. Hammered in last year, at Russell's death. His palm covered nearly all of it.

"Son of a bitch," he whispered. "Elaine, forgive me, for I have doubted."

The words had no more left his lips than footsteps came from deeper in the trees. The steps were light but hurried.

Adrenaline shot down his spine. He dropped to one knee and swept his arm forward, the beam going to the right, trees and limbs and bramble flashing across his vision and then two red glimmering dots appeared thirty feet to his right.

He swung the light back to it. He saw the snout and the laid-back ears of a coyote. The teeth were bared and the beast lowered its head toward the ground. The fur was matted and dense.

*Exhale, exhale*, he thought. Bulbs of sweat popped out of the pores along his scalp, his spine. He palmed his left hand across his forehead and down his face.

"Fucking asshole," he said, then shouted "HA!"

He leapt forward. Before the word was out of his mouth the animal flicked to his left and was gone, through the woods and across the open field, sprinting, its back bunching and elongating with each gathered and released stride, galloping until it was just another shadow moving across the grass.

Sully clicked off the light. He leaned over, putting both hands on his knees. Pulling on his lungs for a full breath, heart trip-hammering. His hands shook now that it was over. *Goddamn. Goddamn.*

"Nerves," he said. "Got to do something with the nerves." The image of his half-empty fifth back at the hotel danced across his mind. Time to go. Time to get the fuck out of here.

He came out of the stand of trees and looked back toward the house and there was the car, a hundred yards beyond. Moonlight reflected off the hood. Its low curves and confident mechanics looked modern, polished, secure, like civilization, and not at all like dead bodies buried beneath bronze-age metal stars nailed into trees. He started walking that way. He put a quicker hitch in his giddyup, trying not to break into a run, but feeling some desperation to get away from the bodies of Terry and Russell Waters sleeping their eternal sleep beneath the plains of their ancestors.

While he was walking, he looked up at the sky once more. *If we are all so insignificant,* he thought, *why did settling the accounts of the dead matter so much?*

## TWENTY-ONE

"YOU WANT ME to go dig up Terry and the old man?" Sully, flat on his back in the hotel, tossing his pillow up in the air and catching it, the lights off but not the television, a bourbon on ice next to him on the nightstand. His second. Could be the third. "I mean, you think she made it up on the spot? That's a hell of a story to dream up when you see a white man pull up in front of your country-ass house."

R.J. was taking the call at home, flat-footed. Elwood, his partner, was talking in the background. Sully couldn't tell if it was on another line or if there was someone else there. A little after eleven on his clock, a little after midnight in D.C.

"But why," R.J. harrumphed, "why would some psycho pretend to be a paranoid schizophrenic Indian from the plains?"

The pillow came down and he caught it.

"I don't have to know that. Because he's crazy, too? He's Bruce Wayne, he's Batman, he's concealing his true identity. We don't have to know *why*. We just have to *know*."

"So she, this trailer-park broad, this Oracle of the Plains, she didn't have any idea who Waters's friend was, that kid was from way back when?"

"Not other than maybe some white folks who used to live down the road, maybe with a last name starting with H."

"Jesus. So how did Waters, I mean that Waters out there, how did *his* mother die?"

"Unknown, but she was unknown, too. Well. Marissa. Her name. Our total bio at this point is that she was some hustler the old man knocked up while working at an oil rig down in, I think, Odessa. We poke around, I'm giving eight-to-five we're going to find they were never married. She came up to play house with Daddy Waters once or twice, cut out for good when it appeared little Terry wasn't going to be breaking any of Jim Thorpe's old records."

"This is incredibly fucked up, I want to tell you."

"I had put that together all by myself."

Sitting up now, a sip of the bourbon, rattling in a plastic cup from the bathroom. Baseball highlights on the screen, the sound off. He was in boxers and a wifebeater. He ran a finger along one of the long, hairless scars on his right knee, not so much purple anymore as just discolored. It itched. Scars itched. Nobody told you scars itched.

"We can't even correct our story," R.J. was saying. "What would we write, 'According to one unnamed source who didn't offer a shred of evidence, other than two metal stars nailed into two oak trees, in the middle of Bumfuck, Oklahoma, we now retract everything we've written about Terry Running Waters being a psychopathic, eye-stabbing Capitol Hill killer. Mr. Waters is, in fact, dead, and has been the entire Clinton administration. The paper regrets the error. The multiple errors. Pardon as we pick up our dick.'"

"Like I say, we can go dig 'em up, you want. Apparently we can buy the place out of probate on the cheap."

"But now, you see this? We have major, *major* problems going forward using the name Terry Waters as the perp. I mean, we have serious reason to believe that's false, but it doesn't rise to a level of fact we can print."

"Knowledge is a burden. I think that's what God was trying to tell Adam."

"You're drinking, aren't you?"

"No."

"You're rattling the ice in your cup. You always do. I just heard it."

"It's Coke."

"Mixed with what, Jim Beam?"

"None but a savage pours Coke into bourbon. I won't say what type of individual drinks Beam."

"That's a nondenial denial."

"Are you worried about me or the shooter?"

"Okay, so okay. I got to call Eddie. I can only imagine his joy."

Sully stood, batting the pillow to the side of the bed. "Am I the bearer of bad news? I'm turning the nation's number one news story on its head in a mind-numbing exclusive. A thank you, a little bonus, that'd be nice to hear about."

"Get all the tater tots at Sonic you want."

"Holy cow."

"Look," R.J. said, "this may pan out, but right now it's just a giant pain in the ass. So what's the plan? What do I tell Eddie you're doing?"

Sully flopped back on the bed, looking back at the ceiling and its water stains. The best news in his life: the NFL preseason was underway. Maybe he could get Alexis to the Dome for a Saints game this year. Stay in Uptown for a few days. October was always a good time to go. He was, he realized, starving. He never ate enough. The spaghetti, he should have done more than pick at it.

"When the doors open in the morning, I'll be at the county land records office, maybe the tax assessor's," he said, then yawned loudly in R.J.'s ear, just for that tater-tots bit. "Wherever they keep the real estate records around here. Those, we get those, that'll show land ownership, past and present. People tend to have acreage out this way. So likely not that big of a list. I mean, this lady, Elaine, she pointed down the road. Can't be that many farms in that direction, the next several miles, whatever the last name. I look for something with an H and we see what we get."

"Then what? Let me blue-sky this. Let's say you find a guy with an H. How do we know *that* paleface is the shooter locked up in St. E's?"

"We don't. But, Christ, whoever the Capitol Killer is, he knows Terry Waters. *That* we know. And he knows something else nobody around here does, and that's that Terry Waters has been worm food for a long time. How big is that universe of people? I'm thinking five or six, tops."

"The lady you just talked to said both she and her brother knew."

"They're not homicidal maniacs, so I don't know they count."

"Apparently her brother might be."

"If it was her brother doing the killing," Sully said, "I'd be in the dirt next to Terry right about now. These people don't fuck around."

R.J. thought about it. "That's actually true, Sullivan. You irritate almost everyone."

"The county records, then school records, yearbooks, maybe the Census, that's what I hit. The Census, if the family answered it, would be spectacular. But we're looking for a white guy, possibly last name H, who would now be roughly forty years old. That would put him in middle or high school, what, twenty-five years ago. That's a graduation date in the late nineteen seventies, a DOB 'round about nineteen sixtyish."

There was a long quiet.

"Sullivan."

"Yes, boss?"

"I'm going to prolong all of our lives and tell Eddie that this won't take you more than a day or two. Because the longer we keep printing 'Terry Waters,' the more moronic we look with each usage if you're actually right about this."

"Not as much as the other guys, when we break this."

"*If*," R.J. said. "*If*, not 'when.' Your enthusiasm is as touching as it isn't contagious."

Sully signed off, standing there in his boxers, turning the television off. There was stubble on his cheeks—he had forgotten to shave. Hadn't taken a shower before heading out this morning. This might be a good time for that. He started the water, decided to make it a bath so he could soak and sip, then sat on the edge of the tub. He called his house, popping his neck, then leaned over, stretching out his back, looking down at his bare toes while the phone rang.

"Hello, stranger," Alexis said, her voice warm, a little sleepy. "How's life on the investigative trail?"

He sat back upright, rattling the ice in the cup. "You ain't gonna believe this shit."

"You're drinking," she said. "Don't even try to bullshit me."

# TWENTY-TWO

THE HANGOVER WAS a thing of beauty. The headache banged on the front edge of his skull. Rolling to his right in the bed—it took him a moment to place the anonymous curtains, the pale white walls, the lone painting of a prairie sunset . . . where was—and then he lay back in the sheets.

Reassuring, that's what it almost felt like, rubbing a palm over his forehead, his closed eyes, yawing. Familiar. Something he knew.

A rat's-ass cup of coffee from the lobby downstairs and a complimentary doughnut, plus twenty minutes of driving around in the early light (behind sunglasses) brought him the realization that the county seat was in Chandler, a dozen or so miles west.

He banged on the steering wheel the entire way. Didn't Stroud at least have the pride to be the county seat? This drive necessitated a stop at a way-too-brightly-lit gas station for two bottles of water, and he was walking along the narrow aisle, gum, chocolate, cough drops, little frosted white doughnuts, motor oil, cold medicine . . . where was the Goody's? Didn't they have a Goody's for a man's headache? He asked and the clerk said "What?" and he said never mind, grabbing a tiny plastic bottle of ibuprofen. Fucking apostates.

He popped three in his mouth while he was paying and then chugged them back with one of the water bottles, nearly draining it, standing bolt upright at the counter, nobody behind him. Had to beat back the dry mouth, the dehydration that was shrinking his skull.

The Lincoln County Courthouse turned out to be a one-story thing, set in the middle of a way-too-wide-open square, far back from the street. Half hidden by a gaggle of trees, it looked like the low bid on a contract nobody wanted.

The main drag of town, Manvel, was part of old Route 66. The charm, if there was any left, was lost on Sully, him scuffing across both lanes, looking left and then right, still blinking in the early light, looking along the storefronts for an honest-to-God coffee shop. . . . Bail bondsman, flooring center, bank, hardware store, an old movie theater . . . no diner. Maybe on the far side of the blockwide square, but he couldn't see over there for the courthouse, and it was too far to walk just to see. Every town square had to have a café, a diner, some half-assed place to eat, didn't it?

He decided Oklahoma wasn't shit.

The sidewalk took him up to the courthouse. Inside, down a lusterless hallway, set against a wall, there was a framed rectangular guide to offices, the kind where you could move the individual lettering and kids were immediately drawn or dared to rearrange the letters to form "dick" or "ass" or whatever.

County assessor's office, county tax office, commissioners . . . following the directions, Sully walked on and made a left and found himself at the county records office.

It was bathed in a dim, windowless, fluorescent glow, rows of files extending into the back, where the light was dimmer. The tiniest wave of claustrophobia swept over his spine. This wasn't going to help the hangover. Besides, what if these deeds went all the way back to the land rush days? His enthusiasm, so bright and so bold and confident last night, had burned down to a dim little bulb in a dark room.

A clerk set him up at a desk, bringing out several of the plats books. Each was the size of a Chevrolet. Air-conditioning thrummed through the vents. It was as quiet as church. By a quarter of eleven, he had nothing to show. He flipped the last fat book shut and lugged it back to the counter dividing the public space from the clerks' work area. He set it down with a plop and a sigh.

"Didn't find what you were looking for?" beamed the clerk, coming forward to the counter, way too goddamn cheerful. She looked up at him eagerly. Hangovers and cheerful people. This was an ugly mix, worse than ginger ale in bourbon.

"No, ma'am, I didn't," he said, working up one edge of his mouth in an effort he hoped would come across as wry good humor. "But you were lovely to let me look around so long. Is the tax assessor's room down the hall there? You think they might have land records?"

She looked back at him through her goggle-eyed glasses and considered the matter at hand, like her day turned on it.

"You lookin' for the same thing, what you told me earlier? People in the south end of the county, twenty, thirty years back?"

"Yes, ma'am."

"They relatives of yours? This a court case?"

"Neither, ma'am. Actually."

She looked at Sully. He looked at her. The clock ticked.

"I'm a reporter at a newspaper back east," he finally whispered, so no one else could hear. He hoped this might inspire a sense of confidentiality, adding a conspiratorial glance around the room. "I'm looking for a family that might have known the Waters family. You know, *that* Waters? Socially, sort of. Last name, I think it started with an H."

She sighed, taking her weight from one foot to the other. "Those are country people out there, you don't mind me saying."

"I'm from Tula, Louisiana, ma'am. You don't got to tell me."

She raised an eyebrow.

"How many people live in Tula?"

"No more than have to."

A peal of laughter, bouncing through the recycled air. Two of her coworkers turned to look, then went back to their computers.

"Sounds like here," she whispered. "Being a reporter, is that a good job?"

"Beats shoveling cow shit," he whispered back, "which I have also done for cash money."

"Hunh. This right here? Sitting in the same office all day, same people, same music on the radio. Did you notice we don't even got windows?"

"It's not so bad," Sully said, looking around the dropped-down ceilings, the cubicles somewhere between lifeless and soul killing. "But I bet Tulsa, Oklahoma City? Those would be okay, too. You know, maybe move up there."

She shrugged. Her pale shoulders were bare. Sully was surprised they weren't blue. The AC had to be turning her into an ice cube. "You know the FBI was in here, the courthouse, for days, looking at the Waters' family everything," she said. "But it just weren't nothing."

"I guess not."

She started to pick the book up and stopped and said, "But you, you ain't interested in the Waters."

"Not really," Sully said. "I'm trying to find out a family who owned land to the south of them. White folks, maybe."

"Hunh."

"Like I said, maybe with an H."

"You know Quapaw Creek Reservoir? Site 6?"

"No, ma'am."

"You know where sixty-two is, coming out of Prague?" She pronounced in the local manner, "Pray-gue."

"Sure," he lied, but knowing enough about little towns to fake it. "You just take that right."

She nodded, her bangs bouncing. "They call it Main Street, but it's just sixty-two coming through town. Now, from here? You get yourself back over to Stroud. Get on ninety-nine, go down—this is south—past the res. Go way on. Now you get in Prague, such as it is—and I mean, don't blink—you go past that Jim Thorpe mural over on your left. You'll see a gas station, an old gas station, it's painted sort of pink, it doesn't work anymore, it's on your left. But you, you wanna turn right on sixty-two. You with me?"

"Riding shotgun." With a nod, to keep her going.

She flushed, smiled. "Now. You take that right, you go past the bank, the Sonic, you just keep on going. You get out of town—that don't take but a minute—and you're gonna pass a church. Now you want to slow on down. On your right, you're gonna come up on a gravel road. You'll know it because it makes a quick little S turn right off. You take that one, you hear? You go a mile, maybe two, the reservoir'll be on your right. It's real fat for a bit, you know, you can see it, and then it turns into a finger."

"Now. North of that, just a little bit, you'll see a gravel drive to your right. You take that, you go back maybe a quarter mile. You can't see it from a road. There's an old house. Nobody's lived there since God was a baby. But they did back then."

She stopped, looking at him, nodding. It took a second before he realized she was finished.

"And who's that?" he asked.

"Who's what?"

"The people who lived in the old house."

"The Harpers, of course. Isn't that what we were talking about?"

Sully felt the hairs on the back of his neck rise.

"Harpers?"

"I do. They been gone for years and years. William, that was the husband? He had money in oil or cattle or something in Texas? He wasn't here that much. They just used that place out there on the reservoir as a weekend sort of place. They'd be out there a lot in the summer. They're all dead now. Far as I know."

"So, okay, so what's the name of that road they're on, my turn off sixty-two?"

"If it's got a name, I never heard it. On the maps, its county road

ONLY THE HUNTED RUN    161

thirty-four eighty, but nobody ever calls it that. It's just the road that goes by the reservoir. Hardly nobody lives out that way."

"Hunh. I didn't see any Harpers listed in there, the land records."

"I would imagine William had it under the company name he ran. Tex, Texa-something."

"Tex-Oil?"

"That sounds right. Way yonder." She fluttered a hand out toward the parking lot and beyond, south.

"Yes, ma'am. That was listed . . . wait." He flipped the big plat book back open, going through the pages. "Jesus, I just had it."

"Language," she said, frowning.

"Sorry. I got home trainin', I just forgot it. Here now. Tex-Oil. That sounds like an impressive company. This property right here, though, it's small. Couple dozen acres."

"It was just a weekend place. It wasn't his oil operation or nothing."

"Hunh. You remember the family?"

"I wasn't but a tadpole. All I remember was the story that went around."

"The story."

"Yep."

He waited. "Which one was that?"

The clerk leaned forward, dropped her whisper even more. "Mrs. Harper, she committed suicide. Slit her throat with a butcher knife one morning, right there in the bathroom just off the kitchen."

"Good God."

"Everybody talked about it for *years*."

Sully blinked. "Slit her own throat?"

She nodded, chin bobbing. "I think she really didn't want to be with us no more."

"You don't say."

"I don't know if the house is still out there or not. The family, they left right after the suicide, you know. The scandal and all?"

He nodded. The lady was gold. "Sure, sure."

"I don't remember ever seeing them again."

Sully was looking at the pages open before him, the map, spelling out the plat as clear as day. The Harpers had frontage on the lake. He flipped the book shut.

"Ma'am, we got started to talking, I didn't even get your name."

"Jo-Ellen." She looked at his scars, her eyes flicked just that quick, then back at him. She was trying to decide if she should bat her eyelashes, he could tell, wondering if his question had been personal or professional. But no, the issue was decided: too many scars. She eased back from him ever so slightly. Half an inch.

"Jo-Ellen," he said, "thank you for the help. I might miss the driveway the first time, but I'll find it. If I pull into the wrong one, somebody'll just run me off with a round of buckshot."

"Hon," she said, "there ain't no more than three driveways out there to pull up into, and I don't think any of 'em got a pot to piss in or a window to throw it out of, much less a shotgun."

"Okay."

"But there's a crooked tree just before you get there. The lake, the tree, the driveway. When my daddy used to drive by there, he'd tell us that's where the ghost of the crazy lady lived, that she'd come get us in the dark if we weren't good."


The house, by the time he found it, was an abandoned shell baking in the heat.

Open fields, pasture, the lake to the south. A narrow grove of oaks set along the long, unpaved drive. The prairie grass rustled against the front bumper as he eased ahead. The driveway was more of a memory than an actual thing.

The house lay in front of him like a ruination from Faulkner. It was a crumbling two-story brick farmhouse, two columns out front, the whole thing falling in on itself. Shutters had long since faded beside the windows and were now just dried out slats of brown wood. Half a dozen windows were broken out.

As he pulled up to the front, a squirrel squatted on a window ledge upstairs. It ducked back inside when he killed the engine. He got out. Nothing but the wind moved. It was nicer than the Russell Waters place, he guessed, but its sense of decay was heightened by the pretensions to grandeur. It didn't even look back at him. It just sat there, hulking, stupid, dead.

"Too bad for you," he said, to the house, as he was getting out of the car, "I don't believe in haints."

Sweat was already starting to roll down his forehead when he pushed open the front door. The architects had been going for the classic Southern mansion. A center hallway. What would have been the library to the left, the main dining room to the right. Kitchen to the rear right, through a narrow door from the dining room. He stood, listening. Nothing. He pulled his shirt out, untucking it to try to keep the sweat from soaking it, unbuttoning the top button. Trash and leaves in a corner, an empty bottle of Jack Daniels. A broken ceramic cup.

Taking the circular stairway upstairs, he kept to the outside of the steps, avoiding the rotten spots in the middle. The steps, like the flooring, had saddled in, buckling from water damage. The walls, all bare, were ruined with water and seepage and mildew, the paint long since cracked and peeling. Rat pellets were everywhere, mixed with dust and dirt. Bird nestings. He didn't spot the squirrel, but there was scratching in the attic. Looking out the back window of the master bedroom, he saw the cracked and faded pool in the backyard. It was now a stagnant pond of brown water.

That's when he heard the sound of a car approaching from out front.

He walked to the front room, careful to stay out of the line of sight. A sheriff's patrol car, white in the middle, black at the hood and trunk, pulled to a stop behind his car. The deputy—or sheriff, hell, he couldn't see—waited in the air-conditioned car. Sully could make out only his outline, but guessed the man was calling in his plates.

Not moving, barely breathing, he waited, looking.

Then the driver's side door swung open, the cop got out, surveyed the area, and plopped his hat on his head. The man was beefy, leaning toward fat, lumbering stiff-kneed toward the house. He was wearing a flak jacket underneath the uniform. Seriously? There was that much bang-bang in Lincoln County?

Sully cursed under his breath. Then he went to the window. He called out, "Helllooo, Officer? Hey? I'm just looking around. Here's my hands." He held them out. "Just me. Nobody else."

The deputy looked up, brought his lumbering to a halt, and put his hands on his hips. He said, not putting much into it, "Don't suppose you're the absentee owner."

The cop leaned over and spat a black line of tobacco juice. He seemed pained, as if walking from the car had taxed him and now he was pissed about it and going to make somebody grieve for it. "Come on down, then, and tell me the hell you doing. Jo-Ellen said I'd find you out here, like as not."

The cop was coming up to the porch by the time Sully reached the front door. "Jo-Ellen, she said a reporter fella was interested in the place," the deputy said, putting a hand on a rotting front porch rail. "That'd be you."

"It would," Sully said. "I didn't know I was that much an item of concern."

"You ain't. I just saw her there at the Arby's. Lunchtime. I asked after how her day was. She mentioned you. I drove out."

"Sully Carter, Officer, good meeting you." He stepped over a rotting board on the porch to shake the man's hand, look him in the eye. This was a deputy, not the sheriff, but he walked up onto the porch, into the shade, like he owned the house himself.

"You mind my asking your interest in the old Harper place here?" he said. "Not to be particular, but you are trespassing. If we were to get technical about it."

"Do we want to get technical?"

"Why don't you tell me what we're doing and we'll see."

Sully nodded. "I'n leave, no problem. I's just looking around, nothing in particular." He waved his arms around, demonstrating a lack of focus, a lack of knowledge. "I'm a reporter, like Jo-Ellen told you. You know, that Waters business? Casting a wide net. Imagine you guys been flooded with feds."

He fished a card out of his wallet. The deputy barely looked at it, tucked it into his shirt pocket and ignored the opportunity to piss and moan about federal law enforcement.

"Casting a wide net for what?'

"A story. A feature. The Wicker Man. Anything. Jo-Ellen, she said the Harpers, they had an incident back in the day. There ain't nothing else going on, so I came out here. You always want to show the home office movement, that you're doing something. This is just local color."

"We're kinda local-colored out at the moment," the deputy said. "Reporters from Japan to Germany, all of last week."

"I bet."

"Who's the Wicker Man?"

"Nobody," Sully said. "Well. An old horror movie. Locals in this little town had a weird cult, built a big wicker model of a man, put this guy inside it and burned him alive. Orgies and naked chicks. It's sort of the idea that strange things are happening in little places that look normal. If that makes any sense."

The deputy did not appear that amused. "It doesn't. I was up there at Russell's place just now," he said. "Fresh tire tracks. That you?"

"It was. Late yesterday."

"Most reporter types, even the ones from Japan, they came out last week, gone home. You sorta runnin' late, ain't ya?"

Sully smiled, recognizing the jibe for what it was. Man pronounced it "jap-ann."

"The first wave, deputy, they come and they go. Then you get the second wave, the magazine writers, long deadlines."

"So, the Harpers," the deputy said again. He'd never offered his name, not at the beginning and not in return when Sully handed him his card. Sully couldn't make out the name on the little silver bar on his chest and didn't want to peer. Extending an arm from his side, putting a palm on one of the columns, the deputy leaned into it heavily, taking a load off, letting out a sigh. He was half looking at Sully, half squinting over the prairie, like he was expecting somebody on horseback to come galloping over the horizon. Sully put his age at maybe thirty-five.

"You want to know about the old lady's suicide," the deputy said. "Seems sorta women's gossip, you ask me."

"But I'm not asking," Sully said. "I'm just interested in knowing what happened."

"We're not taking notes here, are we?"

"Not unless we say so."

"We don't."

"Okay."

"This place, it's been abandoned since I was a kid," the deputy said, and spit again, rolling the chaw over to the left side of his jaw. "The local haunted house. Your Wicker Man, you want that. Me, I was always thinking it was like, that place, you ever hear tell of the little town in Kansas where that family got killed and that little gay guy what wrote a book about it?"

"The Clutter family," Sully said. "Capote. *In Cold Blood*. Holcomb, that's the town."

"That's the one. Liked that movie. Don't know why they made it in black and white. But what I'm saying, everybody talked about that. It got to be famous. This suicide here? It wasn't like that. You a kid here, you didn't want to ask your folks, your teachers. It was something you were supposed to whisper about, at least when the adults were around. Maybe because it was suicide, which out here, for the churchgoing, means you going to Hell. Everybody's churchgoing out here. I don't know. Anyhow. It got to be a thing kids would tell at campfires, spooky story nights, at the drive-in. If and when you got drunk, you'd dare somebody to come out here at midnight. I did it and had it done to me."

"Everyplace you go," Sully said, keeping him talking, his antennae picking up now, "there's a spot like that."

"I imagine. But this place here," here the deputy leaned back to rap on the column with his knuckles, to look at the house behind them, "would scare the shit out of you. Off the road, in the dark, at night, wind coming up, coyote or a coon or something in the house, scratching around? It'd shrivel your pair right up tight, I can tell you that. Particularly if you're fifteen and drunk."

"I bet."

"It's a million versions of the story, but the way I'm going to tell it to you, I heard from Sheriff Lewis, he was the law at the time, and he was the one what came out here that day. So that's the only firsthand account I know.

"And the way he'd tell it, this was seventy-two, seventy-three, right along in there. The Harpers, they weren't here that much. The old man worked oil in the panhandle. They'd come here on your weekends, your holidays. Older couple. You'd see 'em out on the boat on the reservoir, people said. But they kept off to theyselves.

"So this one day, mid-July, the phone rings down to the sheriff's. It's Mr. and Mrs. Harper's grandson. He's powerful upset. Says his grandma hurt herself and the granddad's been gone for two days down to Texas. Sheriff Lewis says, 'Well, how you mean, hurt herself?' Boy says, 'With a knife.' Sheriff says, 'What, in the kitchen?' Boy says, 'No, she went in the bathroom, locked the door, and cut herself open.' Sheriff says, 'Well, how you know if the door's locked?' Who believes kids? Boy says, ''Cause there's blood running out from under the door and she's screaming.' *That* lit a fire under the sheriff. He jumped up fast like, telling the boy to sit still and he was a-coming. He tells Bo—that was the deputy then, Bo Thompson—to call the hospital and he come out here, lights and siren blazing, ninety miles an hour. He comes running up these steps, right where we standing, barges in the door. And there's the boy, right there in the hallway, slumped up against the door right behind you, right outside the kitchen."

"You mean that washroom, the half bath?"

"I do. Boy was sitting there. Pool of blood. A lake and getting bigger by the minute. Boy looks up and says, 'She's dead.' That's the full business of it, whole and entire. 'She's dead.'

"The sheriff asks, like any man would, what, you looked in on her? Boy shakes his head. 'She stopped screaming,' he said. Well, the sheriff has to move the boy outta the way. He calls out to the missus a couple of times and then tries to shoulder the door open. But this is when they made things that lasted, and the door wasn't no joke. Besides, the floor was too slick with blood to get any sort of head start. He tried to lean back and kick it open and damn near busted his ass. So he pulls out his gun and tells the boy to look the other way and cover his eyes, and he shoots the handle, blew it right apart.

"Now. The door swings open, he pushes it back. There's Missus Harper. She's sitting on the toilet seat, but with the lid down, it wasn't like she was using the thing. Slumped up against the wall, right below the window ledge. Blood everywhere. Her right hand, it was still at her throat, the fingers up under the skin. The knife was still in her left hand. This butcher knife from the kitchen. Silver and sharp as shit. She had a death grip sort of thing on it. She'd been slicing at her neck, little cuts, like she was working up the nerve to go for the gusher. She'd finally hit it, though. Front of her dress was drenched, it had sprayed over on the wall, run down on the floor, a river right out into the hall."

"Good God," Sully said.

"But look here—she ain't dead yet. Sheriff shoots the lock out, bang, door bounces, all that brings her back to. She, swear to Christ, opens her eyes at the sheriff, sort of waves the knife around in a little circle, but she can't raise it up. And then—this is the goddamndest thing—she pulls her right hand off her throat and pulls her dress back down below her knees. It had gotten pushed up, what with all the thrashing, I reckon, and it was high up on her hips. So she pulled it back down. That's what was on her mind. Her knees. She didn't want the sheriff to see her knees. 'Course, she pulled her hand away from her throat? All this blood comes gushing. She makes this weird little noise, like she's gargling, waves that knife around in a little circle at the sheriff, like, go away. So he comes over, real careful like, and gets the knife away from her, then, there ain't a towel or nothing, so he takes off his shirt real quick, whips off his T-shirt and gets that placed up against her neck. Pulls his shirt halfway back on, grabs her up, trying to keep her head from lolling back, and carries her out to the car, drives like hell for the hospital. She died on the way. DOA."

Sully looked at him. The day had gone hot, stifling, airless. Sweat poured down him. He felt it mass on his stomach, pool in his crotch.

"The thing of it all was," the deputy said, with another brown jet of juice, "that's not the hell of it. The hell of it was the boy."

"The grandson?"

"Yeah. See, the ambulance had never gotten out there by then, and the sheriff, he had to decide whether to leave the boy by hisself or bring him. A helluva thing either way. But he lays Missus Harper in the back-seat, stands back, and there's the boy, standing there with the butcher knife. Sheriff said he damn near jumped outta his skin. 'I thought you might need this,' the boy says. Holds it out. Just covered in blood. Well, good God, the sheriff gets it away from him. The boy commences to caterwauling and jumps in the backseat with his grandma before the sheriff can stop him and he's all but laying on top of her, screaming 'Granny, Granny,' and the sheriff, he ain't got the time, he just slams the door and takes off. Boy sat in the backseat, blood everywhere, laying up against his grandma, holding her hand, the sheriff hollering into the radio, the whole entire way. It was a helluva thing. Helluva thing."

"You don't remember the boy's name," Sully asked, all but holding his breath, closing his eyes against the heat. "By any chance."

"I do. George. Sheriff said he had to keep hollering, 'George, is she with us? George, is she with us?' the whole way to the hospital. It was something stuck in his mind ever after that."

## TWENTY-THREE

OF COURSE THERE was no cell coverage. None. He was driving north on the gravel road just up from the house, barely moving, holding the phone outside the window, upside down, sideways. He even stopped, making sure the deputy hadn't doubled back from the highway to follow him, and stood on top of the rental, holding the phone as high as he could. Not a single bar.

"Piece of shit," he said. He looked around from his car-top perch. Nothing. Just a few trees in the distance, dying of loneliness.

Susan in News Research, that's who he needed. Someone with her skills digging through the computerized databases, LexisNexis, Accurint, Accutrack, tracking down Tex-Oil, Willliam Harper and his grandson George, the family or business in Texas. People didn't walk off the face of the Earth. They left traces, fingerprints, property, financial transactions. What had Faulkner called it? A scratch mark on the face of oblivion?

Somewhere out there, Harper's family had left their scratch mark. Somewhere out there, there was some record, some document, somebody, that could tell him what happened to the boy in the back of the car. Somewhere out there, there was something that would confirm in print what he already knew to the deep recesses of his marrow: George in the back of the sheriff's car was the killer on Capitol Hill.

The problem was finding those traces, his mind spinning, stuck out here, nowheresville, on a gravel road, in the place where they strung up coyotes by their feet. Who would have pieces of them, where? He was looking for people who had left here twenty-five, nearly thirty years ago. What time was it . . . ? Coming up on two. That gave him three hours till the county offices closed at five, and he was a good twenty or thirty minutes away. The schools, that would be good. Maybe young George had gone to school for a year or two up here. The land records for who owned it now. Didn't the deputy say something about an absentee landlord? Christ, why hadn't he thought to ask him that while he was standing there?

In the car, he put his foot to the floor and the rear end spun, fishtailing until he got it straightened out. Muttering under his breath now, "C'mon, c'mon."

The next driveway turned out to be a mile up the road. He pulled in, a trailer on blocks and a dog in the yard. One truck parked beside it. Clothes on the line, a barn thirty yards behind the trailer but no livestock to be seen. The dog, a country mutt, was loud but not fierce. "Hey dog," Sully said, loping out of the car, walking to the wooden steps leading to the door. The dog, following, head lowered, sniffing, but he wasn't growling.

"Helllooo," Sully called out, then rapped on the door gently. "Not a salesman, just a reporter." He stepped back and leaned against the railing, holding his notebook in one hand, a pen in the other, as nonthreatening a stance as he could manage. He looked down at his shoes, in case anyone was eyeing him through the door, so that they couldn't see his scars right away. No cars came by. There was no sound from inside. He was broiling, wide swatches of sweat dampening his light blue shirt, turning it navy in irregular blots. Rapping again, five knocks this time, he fished his press ID out of his pocket and slung the lanyard around his neck, letting the badge dangle. It couldn't hurt. You wanted people to think you were a reporter nebbish, look like one.

He was halfway back to the car, holding his shirt by the top button, flapping it away from his chest, when he heard the door open behind him. A woman, wearing a pale T-shirt and brown yoga pants, bed head, her eyes puffy, looked out through the narrow opening. The dog went beside her into the house. She looked out, not saying anything, yawning. Sully, staying put, introduced himself, said he was just looking for anyone who might know the Harpers, who had lived next door a long time ago.

The woman pinched the bridge between her eyes, then sneezed. It made her hair flop over her forehead. "We ain't been living here but two years," she said.

"The people who had it before you, they—"

"They went off to Florida."

"Okay. Any other neighbors what might be long timers?"

She just shook her head, brushing the brown hair back from her eyes, now holding a palm flat out from her forehead, a temporary visor from the sun.

"And ma'am, just in case there might be an owner who's been around awhile, do you own this land out here, or do y'all rent?"

"Own," she said. "Two years now. Thank you."

She latched the screen door before closing the other. Even in the yard, Sully could hear the bolt turn.

When he got into town, things didn't get any better.

Jo-Ellen had left for the day, and the lady at the clerk's office, about fifteen minutes from retirement, harrumphed and hawed and heaved out a records book or two and confirmed the place had gone into probate, been divided up and sold off by the county in chunks. A man named Mitchell, Ross Mitchell, in San Francisco, he owned the Harper house and surrounding five acres. He'd been buying up derelict property around the county for ages, nobody really knew why. He paid the taxes by check and that was all he had to do, so. There wasn't a phone number for him. She closed the book and looked at Sully.

He nodded, stealing a glance at the clock on the wall behind her before she could. Twenty till five.

"Ma'am," he said, "not to hurry you any at all, but could you tell me the name of the funeral home in town?"

"You're asking a mean thing," Mr. Larrington was saying, looking down at Sully's business card, the air in the room as dead as the clientele.

"Yes, sir, I know it."

"But what on Earth for? A reporter from a fancy newspaper in D.C. shows up just before closing time, asking about a client we had nearly thirty years ago. This doesn't happen a lot out here . . . Mr. Carter." He said this, looking down at the card in his hand.

"I suppose not." Sully, wearing down some now, fighting to keep the momentum, his eyes adjusting from the glare outside to the gloom here. The amber lighting in the office was professional, he realized, not happenstance. The darkest day in January, the brightest July afternoon, a client would be comforted by the dim yellow air falling over their skin, not casting too harsh a glare on their grief-ravaged faces. If they wept, there were tissues and shadows. The management of grief. You were Mr. Larrington, you needed to manage that grief into the $6,345 Eternal Comfort package, versus the velvet-lined $3,995 Peaceful Slumbers. It made Sully wonder, briefly, what his father had chosen for his mother. Or, for that matter, what his aunt had chosen for his father. Nadia, there weren't options. They were burying people in modified bookcases in Sarajevo by then.

"I came out here on this Waters thing, like everybody else," he said. Mr. Larrington, the man with the fleshy jowls and the kind face, looking back across the walnut desk at him. Not a single paper on the desk.

Nothing but full attention for the client. "And then I came across this, this family tragedy. It's just a feature story, about the county, when Terry Waters was growing up out here. The places that form people, that sort of thing. I wonder if George, the Harpers' boy, knew Terry."

Mr. Larrington cleared his throat and tapped Sully's card on the well-carved edge of the desk. Sully had the idea Mr. Larrington cleared his throat every time before he spoke to clients in this room, to make sure he had just the right baritone edge.

"I wouldn't know, of course. I was in my early thirties then. My father, he was aging out of the business. Things were quite busy. You wouldn't think it, coming from where you do, but they were. We don't rush things out this way, particularly the passing of loved ones." He paused, to give the observation the proper gravitas. "But of course I remember the day they brought Mrs. Harper in. No one would forget that. I remember Sheriff had to put a new backseat in the patrol car. There just wasn't nothing else for it."

"The boy, with her that day. Helluva thing." Stealing the deputy's line.

"Of course. I remember the day, but little of him. This is a funeral home, not a hospital. He was a sprite of a thing. Sat with his grandfather the next morning when arrangements were made. My father, he was handling the transaction, but wanted me to witness it, to learn how to handle death in trauma."

"The boy's mother didn't come to fetch him? His father?"

"I have no idea. But not by the next day, apparently. The father, I remember being told, was not in the picture, and the mother wasn't available."

Sully looked up from his notebook, and Mr. Larrington was already holding up a hand. "I don't know what 'not available' means, either. The mother, she was the Harpers' daughter. For all I know, she was on vacation in Niagara Falls. Or in a dry-out tank in Los Angeles. Families in grief are odd things. It's not our business to question."

"Of course."

"The boy, carrying her name, and not the father's, suggested they were never married."

"Of course."

"Still, it was odd. The grandfather and the little boy, selecting a burial package for a wife, grandmother, and a suicide. The overwhelming impression I have of the time, however, is not the boy, but the grandfather. Mr. Harper. Sternest, most humorless man you'd want to meet. Does it carry weight that an undertaker says a man is humorless, void of feelings, possessed of a robotic presence? Yes or no, well then. I see many a decent people at their worst, penny-pinching moment in life—'Do I spend the extra three thousand for mother's coffin that no one will ever see, or do I take the wife to Hawaii for a week?'—and Mr. Harper was not a decent person."

"I see."

"He said he worked outside, on rigs and in the fields, but was pale as a ghost. Denim jeans, denim jacket. Looked like he had donated two quarts of blood and had a hangover besides. Touched the brim of his hat to my father. Didn't speak to the boy at all, who sat there on the floor, back against the wall, as his grandfather sought to spend the least amount of money possible to put his beloved wife in the eternal dirt."

Sully shifted in his seat. "So, not a lot of negotiations there."

Mr. Larrington bristled. "I would say not. It's not that we negotiate. He kept asking about the most economical thing we had, and my father, he really couldn't believe it, that this man would so dishonor his wife this way. So my father kept asking, 'Economical how?' as if he understood Mr. Harper to be talking about a minimalist casket, something about the design, until Mr. Harper grew impatient and said, 'I mean the cheapest.' Which is pretty much a pine box. There's lots of poor people around here and there's a lot of people who have little in the way of book learning and there isn't any reason to pretend there isn't. But Mr. Harper wasn't either of the two. Pardon my French, but it was just a sorry goddamn thing to witness. Mr. Harper, he arranged to have his wife buried in the city cemetery and did not stay for the services."

Sully, scribbling in his notebook, the pen scratching the page, stopped and looked up to see Mr. Larrington looking at him. "He didn't attend his own wife's funeral?"

Mr. Larrington shook his head, pleased his point had been received. "Paid cash money for the site, picked out the granite. Just a flat dash marker."

"I'm sorry. A 'dash marker'?"

"Yes. The year of birth, year of death, and the dash in between. Your entire life, distilled to a horizontal blip between eight numbers."

"Ah."

"He didn't so much as spring for 'beloved.' "

"Well, that's just common."

"He picked out a spot in the cemetery and told us to do it at the first opportunity. Gave my father half up front and said he'd send us the rest when we sent him a picture. And he stood up, put his hat back on, touched the brim again to my father, and was gone, with the boy in the truck."

The words floated out in the room like one of the eulogies spoken in the adjacent chapel, the final summing up, the last echo fading away.

"Did you ever see him, the boy, again?"

"No. There was no funeral. The interment was just me and the pastor. The grounds staff was a few yards off, leaning on shovels, waiting for us to finish up."

"Hunh." Sully was back to writing in his notebook, more to give himself time to think than to record every word, and, without looking up, said, "Did Mr. Harper pay the rest? And any chance you might still have that address where you mailed the picture?"

Mr. Larrington shook his head, no, no. "It was a quiet scandal. No one really knew them. My father, he didn't even mail the photograph to trigger the second payment. The insult he had been given, that we could not be trusted without photographic evidence. Outrageous. No, she was interred and that was all. Much more known in death than in life. My missus, she didn't even know Mrs. Harper's first name until she read in the obituary in the newspaper."

Sully, starting to look up, to fire a final question or two, stopped, blinked. The obit. What kind of sorry reporter came to town looking for dead people and didn't look up the obit?

# TWENTY-FOUR

THE *LINCOLN CITIZEN* was an eight-page weekly, doing business in a tired one-story redbrick building between a hardware store and a card shop. It had a long storefront, most of it plateglass windows, and most of them had a sepia tone to them. When Sully was parking, he thought they were tinted, to keep the sun at bay. When he got on the cracked sidewalk, he could see that they were just old and had been dusty for so long that no amount of cleaning would make a good goddamn. The dirt, the dust, the grime had long since baked in.

The glass double doors were locked, but the interior lights were on. A heavyset man with a white dress shirt half untucked appeared in the hallway a moment after Sully knocked, then came to the door. His hair was disheveled and he looked like the worst Rotarian in town.

"Help you?" he said, opening the door halfway.

Sully, one hand buried in his pocket, straightened his shoulders, introducing himself and his employer, the name of the paper getting a raised eyebrow and a step back from the door, an unspoken invitation. Sully came inside, the air-conditioning turned up to the beef-hanging stage, thank God, the sweat-dampened shirt instantly going cold against his flesh. The man fell in beside him, pointing the way to his office, from which he'd just emerged, with a collegial flick of his thick wrist, the watch on it the size of a dinner plate. "We go to the printer's tomorrow morning," he said, "so this is my one late night of the week. John Edgar Jenkins. Everybody calls me John Ed. Family's owned the *Citizen* since my dad bought it in '57. Here, sit down and let me get you a card."

Half an hour and two shots each from the Buffalo Trace bottle in John Ed's drawer later, Sully felt like he'd returned to the land of the living. He was set up in the paper's morgue, actually just the dimly lit back storeroom. It was a large open space, a concrete floor, with lots of boxes and barrels lined up along the walls and long rows of metal shelves covering the open area. On them were stacks and stacks of papers, going back to World War II, a double handful of each week's edition, side by side and shelf by shelf. It was a fire hazard of breathless potential.

"We sell the back copies every now and again," John Ed said. "Five dollars. People are forever wanting something from sometime about one of their people."

John Ed said he'd been going through them since he was a teen, tracking down old copies for customers. So it didn't take him any time at all to skim along the row of papers from the summers of 1972 and 1973, taking one copy of each, then plunking them down on a sagging wooden table in the corner of the room, setting off a small cloud of dust. Flapping open the first of the papers, he pointed out that the obits ran on page six, right across from the comics on page seven. He said they didn't report suicides, even now, so he doubted there would be a news story from the Harper incident, but there might be an obituary.

"Holler, you need me," he said, heading back to his office, running his hand through his hair, slouching from the shoulders down. "We ain't ready when the printers come, we got to pay extra."

There was a little triangular rubber wedge on the floor, and he scooted it around with his foot until it was under the door frame. It propped open the door to the main newsroom, such as it was, and, with a small screech of the door grating on the concrete, Sully was alone with the research.

*    *    *

The smell came over him, unfolding one paper, then another, turning the pages, the must and the sense of passing of time in still rooms. They were oddly addictive, old newspapers, especially in little towns. They felt and read like diaries from another time, something secret that you had stumbled across in your grandfather's closet after the funeral. The stories were kind and decent, fuzzed by familiarity and not bothered by the news of the larger world. There were no major investigative pieces, or small ones, either. Everybody knew everybody anyway, and nobody really wanted anybody fired from City Hall, not really, unless they were just drunks and incompetents and still that just meant people would pray for them all the harder in Sunday School, or just say, "Bless his heart," and go on to something else. You certainly didn't hang the dirty laundry out on the front page of the weekly for God and everybody to read.

Week by week, and page by page, he flipped through the journalistic record of Lincoln County, the pages brittle and going brown. He didn't expect to find anything in particular, but this was the one newspaper of record where Terry Waters and George Harper had lived when they were boys, before they were trying to hide anything. Maybe Mrs. Harper had been at one of the ladies' functions. Maybe the old man made a local business deal or turned up at the Rotary lunch on the first Monday.

"No Rain for Three Weeks," ran a 1-A headline from late summer of '72. "County Commission Votes on Sewer Rates." "Governor to Speak at Cattleman's BBQ." He went through them, a page at a time, from May to the first week of September, and there was nothing in the summer of any note, except that the boys' football team had made it to the state playoffs the previous year and hopes were high for this year's team, which was starting two-a-days the next week. Nothing in '73, either.

He put them back, calling out to John Ed that it must be '71 or '74, and John Ed hollered back to make himself at home.

It was near the end of going through the papers from '71 when he turned to page six and felt a jolt buzz up his spine. "Mrs. William Harper," ran the small headline at the bottom left of the obit page, one of three that week. He didn't breathe, swallowing it as much as reading it.

> *Mrs. William Harper passed away last week at her home in Lincoln County, just west of Prague on the Old Schoolhouse Road, Sheriff Bobby Lewis said.*
>
> *Mr. and Mrs. Harper have been part-time residents of the county for a few years. Mr. Harper is in the oil business near Wichita Falls, the sheriff said, and the family has a place on the reservoir.*
>
> *Mrs. Harper, Miriam to her friends, was known to be quiet and devout, and seldom went out without her husband. She died suddenly, the sheriff said.*
>
> *The Harpers' grandson, George, often spent summers here with them. They had a daughter, Frances, who lives in Washington, D.C., the sheriff said.*
>
> *Mrs. Harper was sixty-eight. She is to be interred at Lincoln Memorial Cemetery in a private service. There was no word from the family about donations or memorials.*

That was it, five homey paragraphs, all attributed to the sheriff, but the words glowed like burning coals. *George. Miriam. Frances, who had been living in Washington, D.C.*

"Shit," he said, standing up and flipping the paper shut. What had Terry Waters brayed in court? *Miriam.*

But he couldn't go. He couldn't run for the plane. Instead, he was staring at the sports page, the back of the paper, that now lay open in front of him.

Summer-league baseball had wrapped up and there were the pictures of each of the local teams, each posed on a dusty field with scrubby grass and a half-ass wooden dugout in the background. Eight teams. The lay-out was such that the pictures took up the entire page.

The seventh picture, in the bottom left corner, was the team photo for People's Bank. The boys were in two lines, kneeling in front, standing in back, just ten of them. Dark-colored shirts, hats askew. Two of them wore jeans. Some wore shorts. In the back row, a name flickered across his vision.

Terry Waters.

He looked up at the image, frozen, to see a skinny boy with black hair, his cap jammed down on his head, the brim obscuring the top half of his face, biting his lower lip to try to keep from laughing. Leaning into Waters's right shoulder was a slender, black-haired kid with three bats slung over his shoulder, no hat on his head, the slugger with a touch of preadolescent swag.

"George Harper," read the caption.

Sully leaned forward, not breathing, staring at the image until it dissolved into a million tiny gray dots. The man shooting in the Capitol, lying on Mass Ave., singing in Superior Court. There was no doubt.

"I ain't got a lot," he whispered to the picture, tapping it with his index finger, "but, sweet pea, I got *you*."

Still staring, he hollered out loud. "Hey, John Ed?"

"Whoo."

"You know when the last flight from Tulsa goes wheels up, brother?"

## TWENTY-FIVE

"WE ABSOLUTELY CAN'T print it, and even if we could, I don't know that we should," Eddie was saying, leaning over his desk, looking down at the brittle broadsheet laid out in front of him. "It's not enough. Not yet. I'll give you strong facial similarities, I'll give you circumstantial."

"Agreed," Sully said.

"But I can't give you, and no one would, beyond a reasonable doubt."

"Miriam," said Sully.

Eddie, still leaning forward, said, "That comes pretty close. I'll give that to you, too. But we're still fucked."

"No argument here."

"This woman in the house, Elaine, the Waters' neighbor. Do you see any way to verify her story?"

"None that I didn't already do," Sully said. "But for what it's worth, I absolutely believed her. Can't see a motive for her to lie. Like I said to R.J., on the phone out there, coming up with that story on the fly? I just don't see it."

Nine fifteen in the morning, Sully, bleary-eyed, sipping on black coffee with a ton of sugar, Eddie, R.J., Paul, and Melissa in Eddie's glass-walled office, the door closed but the newsroom yet to populate for the day.

R.J. shifted in his chair, his pants up over his ankle-high socks, showing pale calf, not caring, weighing in again. "No, but we don't have to know why. Maybe she didn't like you. Or palefaces in general. Maybe she was drunk. Maybe she's really Terry Waters's aunt. Who knows. She won't even put her name on it."

"But," said Eddie, "what this does do is screw us over, in at least the short term. We're supposed to, on one hand, keep calling this guy 'Terry Waters' in print, while we're thinking that's wrong? It's not journalistic malpractice, but it's . . . troublesome."

And then R.J. was talking about good faith, glancing over at Sully, that the paper was working in good faith, we had a lead on a story of interest and we were checking it out, as any responsible news-gathering outfit would do, verifying it before publication, the lines of due diligence being laid out, getting some air, everyone nodding.

"Okay," Eddie said. "Okay. If, *if* this guy in jail is *not* Terry Waters but *is* this putz George Harper, why doesn't law enforcement know? Wouldn't fingerprints iron that out?"

"You don't get fingerprinted," Sully said, "unless you're arrested. There's no record Terry Waters was ever arrested."

"What about Harper?"

"Susan, over in research, I called her last night on the way to the airport in Tulsa, and got her started on the Harper family. LexisNexis, Accurint, Accutrack. Granddad, that's William, is probably going to be our best bet since he was in business somewhere in north Texas and was living life aboveboard. From there, we should be able to get George, his mother, other relatives, neighbors."

Eddie let out a sigh at that and sat down. "Jesus. This guy pretends to be a dead Native American and says his dead grandmother is going to kill a D.C. Superior Court magistrate." It was just an observation, not meant to prompt any response, but it hung over the room. Sully fighting back a headache, the lack of sleep catching up with him.

R.J., his face pinched, took his glasses off and rubbed his eyes, suddenly looking old. Paul, one of those guys at the gym at 6:15 five days a week, reading the *Times* on the stationary bike, looked like a million. He was writing on his legal pad, no doubt sketching out assignments for his National staff. Melissa was, for once, looking like this was something they should pursue rather than trying to convince Eddie that Sully had gone off the deep end. She sensed that Eddie was thinking, thus offering a break in the conversation for a lower editor to chip in.

"Frances, the mom?" she said. "Were you able to get anything else on her? Can we get how she died? Isn't that what this guy is pissed about? Maybe that's the link to Representative Edmonds."

Sully held his hands up, hey, don't shoot. "No. No time. I mean, I left that office out there and drove like hell for Tulsa. Left everything at the hotel. Last flight heading east was to Detroit. That connected to Minneapolis. That got me into Dulles this morning about an hour after midnight. I gave the name, though, to Susan, with George's. She's working it."

"Any word on the dad?"

"None."

She nodded. "You mind letting us in Metro chase that end? Keith is really good with records, the courts. Any leads, he'll call them in to me. He'll run down Frances, or, if there's multiple possibilities, I can assign a warm body to each one. Anything to pass on, we will."

This politeness from her, this jumping in on the effort, what did you even do with that? Whatever. The sleep deprivation was making everything blurry around the edges. "Keith's great, sure," he said. "This thing has too many tentacles anyhow. George, that baseball picture I came across? He was in the ten- to twelve-year-old league. That would put him born in 1959 to 1961. Frances, she could have been anywhere from eighteen to what, maybe forty when he was born?"

"Which would make her sixty-something now. Maybe seventy, seventy-five."

"Possibly still alive," Eddie said.

"Sure," R.J. said, "and if living here, might have provided home and shelter to sonny boy. This thing could be right the hell under us."

"He certainly wasn't living under an overpass," Melissa said. "I've had half the staff in every homeless shelter and soup kitchen in town."

Paul finally looked up from his notebook, that shark-glint to the eyes. "Eddie, for National? The best line of inquiry here is the old one: the man's ties to Edmonds. We were looking for Terry Waters before. Nobody was looking for a George Harper. Maybe Frances Harper. Maybe we were looking in the right place with the wrong name."

"Yes," Eddie said.

"We know, at least we think we know, that there were no threatening calls, or letters, or what have you, to the congressman's office from anyone, no matter the name," Paul said, looking back down at his legal pad; he'd made summarized notes. "He wasn't getting any extra security, his staff didn't know of anything. His schedule was public knowledge, on his Web site. So it wouldn't have been all that difficult to know, at least in a general way, to know he was meeting with the Speaker's staff that afternoon."

"What about his family?"

Paul shrugged. "Closed off. No statements, no interviews. The funeral, it was just accolades and sorrow. That's been the only time his wife, the daughter, have been in public."

Eddie unclasped and clasped the band of his Rolex, looking around the room at each of them. "All that's great. Do it. Full bore. But that's not job number one. Job number one is who the hell is the individual being eval'ed over at St. E's right now, and what do we call him in the paper. Now. How do we find that out?"

It sat in the air like dead weight.

"Easy," Sully said, finally. "Walk up behind him, say, 'Hey George,' and see if he jumps."

Eddie folded his arms across his chest and tucked his chin down and tilted his head slightly to the side, irritation rising across his face.

"Our boy is currently being held in the heavily secured grounds of one of the most notorious mental hospitals in the United States. He is, further, in the most secured building on that godforsaken campus, on the lockdown ward of the hall for the criminally insane. How, exactly, do you plan to just walk up to him and say, 'Hey, George?'"

Sully had seen this coming since he'd pulled out of the motel in Stroud the night before, blowing the rental up Interstate 44. It had come to him in its simple brilliance.

He nodded, more to himself than Eddie. "I got a guy for that," he said.

## TWENTY-SIX

SLY HASTINGS SAID he had two words for the idea, then, wait, no, it was three: "Oh, *hell* no."

"You always telling me you go up to St. E's all the time," Sully said, "that your mom used to take you to see her brother, dear old Uncle Reggie—"

"You the one needs to be locked up in there."

"—and you still go, look in on him and all, 'cause your momma made you promise."

"You going to do a lot better in life, you don't mention my momma to me," Sly said. He fiddled with a toothpick. "The thing about that place, it's not hard to get *in*, never has been. But it always used to fuck with me, being a kid, you know, getting back *out*. They close them gates and shit, who's to say they won't call you as crazy as the rest of 'em?"

They were sitting at the usual meet-up, Kenny's BBQ Smokehouse on Eighth and Maryland Avenue on Capitol Hill, just a few blocks from Sully's house. They sat at a steel table with an umbrella in the shade. It was muggy, overcast, a few hours after he'd left the meeting at the paper. Felt like rain. Sully had been working on Sly with the idea since three in the afternoon, and now it was coming up on five.

"So I just don't see the reason, if it's so easy to walk in there, why it's a big deal to bring one lousy visitor with you one time."

"Why you want to talk to this man if he crazy?"

"He tried to kill me."

"Maybe he's not crazy."

"Why is Reggie up in there, anyhow? Canan Hall, right? The baddest of the bad?"

"Why is Uncle Reggie in St. E's," Sly said, leaning back in the chair, pausing to watch a lady walk her dog past the restaurant, then cross Maryland Avenue, heading for the corner store. It was a weird little dog, all the hair poofed up around its neck, the rest of him looking like he'd been skinned. "Used to not see white people 'round here at all. Now you got girlfriend here, walking the dog. My grandfather, he got himself killed just after the riots in Red Summer, 1919, you know about that?"

Sully nodded.

"He, his name was Lester, Lester Hastings. Sold life insurance to the black folks. Did real well at it, had been to Howard. A race man. He knew Du Bois, I mean, for real. The Talented Tenth. Then he got hisself killed and we wasn't the talented shit."

"What happened?"

"Got pulled off a streetcar. Year after the riots. Crackers beat him like a dog in an alley. Left him there. He crawls out, some brother sees him, take him home, he dies two days later. Intestinal, no, internal bleeding. Septicemia. Blood poisoning. Not a good way to go. They had their own house, over in Anacostia. He died and Grandma went broke in ten minutes. Get this. He sold life insurance? But he didn't have any hisself. Just, I mean, Jesus. House repossessed, the family went to boarding houses, back rooms, public housing.

"Grandma's a drunk by then, you know? Worked at a saloon, gave it up for extra cash, to pay the rent, whatever. Reggie, he got born in '35, not even after a year after my mother got born. Different fathers, so my mom always said. Who knows. Reggie wasn't ever right in the head. Got sent up to St. E's in 1981, I think it was. Drunk or high or crazy or all three all the time. Got through fifth, maybe sixth grade. Stabbed two niggers and shot another, was doing life on the installment plan at Lorton. So one day they send him up to St. E's for evaluation."

"And been there ever since," Sully said.

"And been there ever since. But, look, the real story, you want it straight up, is that we couldn't take him back, hear? He's family, but you know what a pain in the ass crazy people are? Tearing shit up, yelling at three in the morning, eating the neighbor's flowers, barking at they dog, getting a gun and shooting up the house, pistol-whipping other crazies in the parking lot of that whore hotel on New York Ave.? My mother, she had her own shit to deal with, me and a drug habit, both. She passed, there wasn't nobody left *for* him."

"Except you."

"Except me."

"How often you go see him?"

"Once a month. Sometimes twice."

"For how long?"

"Since 1981, the year he went in."

Sully sat back. That was nineteen years, nineteen times twelve visits a year, that was, what, a little short of two hundred and forty visits. Well, exempting the times Sly had been in lockup himself.

"I didn't know this."

Sly looked over at him. "Why would you?"

"I'm, I'm just saying. That's a hard thing."

"You, you, don't know the half of it. I . . . it'll . . . eat you alive, that place. I won't lie to you. Uncle Reggie is my one tie to all that came before me, my family, my history, my people. Last of that generation. And he's in there, that shithole. He ain't ever coming out."

He sat there, looking across the street. Sully had not seen Sly this way. It was a raw nerve, as deep as it was unexpected.

"I—"

"Shouldn't come out," Sly said, softly.

"Shouldn't?"

"You don't know the man. You don't know the place." He looked up at Sully. "There's places worse than prison."

Sully let it sit.

"That'll work on you, brother," Sly said, "the last of your people living that way, you let it sit in your head."

"Does he know who you are? I mean, is he on this planet?"

"Depends. Half the time they got him on lockdown for trying to fuck somebody up in there. You know they don't call them inmates, right? It's *patients*. Motherfucker in a locked ward and ain't ever leaving, he's a *patient*. My black ass."

"So, how you get a visit?"

"You family, they got days. You call ahead."

"Do family members have to sign their name, state a relationship?"

"They know me. They don't know you. You don't look like family."

"I'm the cousin you don't talk about."

"And why is it you think," Sly said, "once I get you in, that I can fix it for you to get in a room with this ice-pick motherfucker?"

"You just said they know you."

He let that hang in the air. Nobody who knew who Sly Hastings was and what he did and what he could do to them with a flick of his finger was going to get in his way, particularly not anyone whose best job in life was emptying piss pots at the crazy house.

Sly looked back across the street. "It ain't for free. I mean, I got to take care of some people. You'n pay for this? I thought you guys couldn't pay for news, like that."

"We can't."

"Then you shit out of luck, brother."

Sully took a deep breath.

"Noel," he said, softly as a whisper in the dark.

A car pulled up to the traffic light and stopped. Birds flapped around in the tree above. Far above, a plane left ice trails across the sky. Sly's face did not move, not an eyebrow. He just kept looking at the corner market across the way, the door clanging open, like he was waiting for the lady with the crazy-looking dog to emerge. "Noel who?" he said.

"Don't play."

Sly let it hang.

"That's the transaction?"

Sully nodded and now Sly looked over at him, his eyes black, tight. "One more. I do you one more solid on this and we're good. We clear? We do this thing, I don't hear that name again."

Sully's mouth was dry, he could feel it at the corner of his lips, a little cracked piece of skin. This was vile. He thought of Lorena, Noel's sister, and wondered why he'd never stopped back up by her house to, you know, say hello, see if she'd ask him inside to have another drink on her back porch. It shouldn't have to be this way. A feeling in his chest, like a rock descending in deep water. When he couldn't feel it anymore, he licked his lips and let go of the last hope of justice that Noel Pittman's murder likely would ever have.

"Yeah," he said.

"Suit yourself," Sly said. "Visiting's tomorrow. Me 'n Lionel'll pick you up right here, ten in the morning."

Sully nodding, standing up, wanting to get this over with, changing subjects. "How's George these days, things in Frenchman's Bend?"

Sly stayed seated but waved his hand over his head and Sully heard Lionel crank up Sly's Camaro, where he had been parked on the street, the boss's righthand bodyguard, and saw the car pull up to the curb. "They all over his ass down there, the cops. Can't move so much as a ki. I been up at the apartments most of the summer, getting them ready to rent out. Good time to work. You can get them Hispanic brothers, man, they work all day and half the night. Might have to put George to work up there, things don't pick up."

He put tuna steaks on the grill that night, some shrimp that had marinated in a tequila and lime sauce of his own mixing. Alexis made the salad. Josh played disc jockey, putting on a bunch of crap Sully hadn't heard before but didn't mind, the more he listened to it. Something, anything, to take his mind off tomorrow, the number of ways that it could go wrong. Bourbon could be your friend, times like this. The Blanton's, half empty—Josh or Alexis had found it—was in the cabinet. He uncorked the pewter stopper and poured two fingers over some chunky ice cubes in a crystal tumbler, loving the gurgle.

Rattling it around, he wandered up to the front bay window, looking out, the light traffic, the streetlights winking on. Three people staying in the house. Hunh. Things happen you don't see coming. Somebody walking by out front on Sixth Street, getting the waft of the grill smoke, the music, Alexis and Josh bantering in the backyard, darkness descending? They could mistake it for domesticity.

They ate on the back patio. The table wobbled on the uneven bricks. Sully got two books of matches to prop up the short leg. The heat had given way to a breeze. It swirled up the alley and through the branches of the cherry tree, tracing over them, a delicate-fingered, invisible thing.

"Is that the first touch of fall?" Alexis wondered aloud.

She had her hair down, home from work, getting used to the pace of editing in the office, then coming home on time. She said she was liking it.

"You coulda stayed gone a couple more days," she said.

"Yeah," Josh said, looking over at her. "We were fine."

Alexis wore shorts and a sleeveless blouse the color of sand. It set off her olive-brown skin. Josh, infatuated in the way only teenage boys can be, was turning her into his personal pinup, following her around with a sketch pad and a charcoal pencil, getting lines down even while she was doing the dishes, for God's sake.

"You want to tell me what this plan is you've got to see the mystery man?" she said. "How exactly it is you're going to get in St. E's?"

"You don't even want to know."

Josh put six, seven sketches beside him on the table. Sully wiped his hands and flipped through them, leaning back in his chair. All were of Alexis. In thoughtful repose. Smiling, looking off to the right. Walking out the door to work, hurried, lines blurred.

"Landscapes," Sully said, putting a bite of tuna in his mouth, letting it dissolve on his tongue, it was that thin, that good. "I thought the class, what you were working on, was landscapes."

Josh, not worried about it: "Random other assignments are good."

"Yeah," Alexis said, mock defensive. "Fresh eyes. Gotta have fresh eyes."

After the dishes, in the basement—which Josh was turning into his own apartment, his sketches now tacked to the wall, making plans to come back for Thanksgiving, Christmas, Spring Break, anything other than the endless oppression of Sunday School and Bible study in Phoenix—he had them watch *Alien*.

"It's the third time," Alexis complained.

"But that thing on his *face*," Josh kept saying.

The boy was asleep by midnight. They left him on the couch and went up the steps, tiptoeing to the top floor, Sully with two or three bourbons in the bloodstream and Alexis with at least three glasses of wine in hers. They tumbled into the bed in a giggling rush, him tugging off her blouse and shorts, pulling the thong to the side, just enough, and her gasping, slow down, slow down.

"Thought you said you wouldn't with a kid in the house," he whispered.

"You want me to stop?" she whispered back.

The darkness unfolded and he felt himself losing himself in it. Things moved in his chest, his conscious mind fading from him, giving way to a deep well of lust and need and fury and fear and she was whispering in his ear again.

"With me, baby," she was saying, her hips still moving, her left hand on his shoulder but her right on his chest, "with me. Not to me."

## TWENTY-SEVEN

ST. ELIZABETHS, NO apostrophe, thank you, was not a happy place, and neither was its home in Southeast, the poorest, roughest quadrant of D.C. Almost entirely separated from the rest of town by the Anacostia, Southeast was its own world. It was a place that the majority of the population in, say, Northwest—the wealthiest, whitest part of town—had never been and had no intention of going.

Lionel took the Camaro uphill from the eastern banks of the river, the car thrumming alongside the brick boundary wall of St. E's. Martin Luther King Jr. Avenue, the main drag through this part of the city, split the asylum grounds in two, on a roughly north-to-south basis, dividing the east campus from the west. The original brick boundary wall lined the streetfront of the west campus, the oldest part of the hospital. It was high, imposing and solid.

It always stunned Sully, the few times he'd been up here, the size of the place. More than three hundred acres at its peak, seven thousand patients and who knows how many staff, back in its early twentieth-century glory days. The idea then that the mentally disturbed needed peace and quiet and sunshine, thus the working farm and huge grounds, removed from and across the river from the stresses and bad humors of Washington proper. It had been rural then.

The west campus, situated on a ridge line above the river, offered one of the most dramatic views in America—the U.S. Capitol across the river, the federal city swaddled by the Anacostia and the Potomac, the Washington Monument, the sun fading to the west, over the wide sweep of the continent—and it was the sole property of the insane.

It sort of explained Washington, in a way.

"You know, my hometown, it was maybe two thousand people," Sully said, looking out the window, the boundary wall looking back at him, "and this place, it used to have two, three times that many crazy people, all behind that wall."

"I thought everybody in Mississippi was crazy," Sly said, drawing a snort of laughter from Lionel.

"Louisiana, hayseed. I'm from Louisiana. The other side of the river. It's different."

"You say so."

Sully, feeling butterflies in his gut, moved around on the backseat. How Sly came up here to see his crazy-ass uncle mystified him. The place had given him bad vibes the few times he'd set foot inside. Ghosts and lunatics, the long halls of madness. The nights in there. Jesus, what it must have sounded and smelled like back in the day. The howls. The stench.

Lionel pulled the Camaro into the main entrance and stopped alongside the security booth, letting the window down. The guard looked at him, leaned over to look in at Sly, who just looked straight ahead, tapping his right hand on his knee, and glanced at Sully, who looked out of the opposite window.

The guard did not speak. He leaned back in the booth. The gate swung open.

Unfolding before them, as Lionel slowly pulled into the property, was the wide sweep of dozens of seen-better-days brick buildings with red tile roofs. Most of them were a century old and looked like it, their façades dotted by white-brick or cement inlays arched above the doors. Windows on upper floors looked to be set in crooked frames. The doors seemed to hang on hinges gone askew. Gargoyles, their eroded stone faces more impressionistic than detailed, looked like they were about to fall off the edifices they enhanced.

Oaks and elms and fruit trees stood withering in the heat. The grass was dry, uneven, and patchy. The feds, downsizing mental health facilities after Thorazine ended the warehousing of the mentally ill, had dumped the white elephant of St. E's on the overburdened city government decades ago, to the benefit of no one but federal taxpayers. Misery, a hopeless lack of funding, mismanagement, the exodus of talented medical staff, finger-pointing and exposés followed. Receivership, lawsuits about conditions. The patient load went from mostly well-to-do whites from across the country to impoverished blacks from D.C. Then the feds blamed the District for the horror show they had dumped in their lap . . . or, really, just another day in how the federal city worked.

Directly in front of them was the main administrative building. The white rectangular clock tower was perched neatly atop the center of the roof, just above the double row of white round columns. It was possible to believe it was a college admissions building on a small Southern campus, gone slightly to seed. Hitchcock Hall, the graceful old theater building, enhanced the effect: two stories, red brick and white trim, a black slate roof, the arched stone front over the door with 1908 at the top of the frame. Paned windows, set in an arch, were above that, and at the very top, the smiling face of a satyr. Two round, porthole-like windows were on the upper floor, left and right, like a set of eyes, white woodwork framing each.

Lionel idled through the grounds at the speed of a golf cart. There were only two people to be seen, both men in suits walking out of the administration building. He pulled down the ridge line to the left, the wards spreading out in wings from the center building, the windows a series of blank, unseeing eyes. They eased forward on the narrow ribbon of asphalt, the streets named for trees on the grounds: Plum, Cedar, Birch, Redwood.

And then, bringing his eyes forward, Sully saw the hulking redbrick mass of Canan Hall. It loomed directly in front of them. The building was three stories. It lay on the grounds, heavy and squat, a faceless hulk that took human beings in and never let them out. It was more than a century old. It seemed to have absorbed all the pain and violence and madness into its bricks, into the rotting wood of the fascia that lay discolored and dark at the roof line, into the peeling white paint of the eaves and ledges and doors. The windows looked like cataracts, blind and unseeing. It looked like it could take an artillery hit. It had presence. Like movie stars. Like monsters.

Lionel parked in the shade of the only tree and cut the engine. Sly didn't move.

"Well," Sully said.

"Hate this place," Sly said.

A beat passed and then he opened his door, stepping out, already walking by the time Sully freed himself from the back.

"Okay," Sly said, not slowing, "one, you got to remember is that this ain't D.C. Jail. These *patients*, they got rights. They walk right up on you, too. Sniff. Put they hand on your dick."

Sully, squinting in the harsh light. "You skeered, Sly?"

"This one dude, he come up to me one time I'm up here, he looked alright," Sly said. "And so I say, 'Hey, nigger what you doing today?' You know, passing the time, waiting on Uncle Reggie to come out his room. And this dude, he says, just like a regular motherfucker, 'I been in hell most of the day. They's Christians and Jews. Lots of Jews. All the Negroes are burned to toast, and many people speak Chinese. The hell god says, 'Suck my balls.' And he goes on like that till they come get him up off me."

"That would—"

"So I ask the orderly—guard, nurse, you can't tell—'What'd he do?'"

"Yeah?"

"Killed his family. Every last one. Said that they were 'servants of Satan.'"

"Shit," Sully said. It was starting to feel like a roller coaster ride: it looked fun from a distance. Then you got up on the thing and started thinking, hey, wait, this shit is crazy.

A pause, then he couldn't help but ask: "That dude still in here?"

"Where else he got to go?"

"I was hoping maybe he died."

"That'd be news. But if he did, he's still here. The ones ain't got no money? Bury 'em right there."

Down the hill, far over, a small forest of tombstones on the slope, in the trees. "Talk about your life sentence," he said.

Sly said, "Everybody up in here, it's a life sentence, 'cause there *ain't* no sentence. Your 'indefinite hold.' But it's definite alright."

They were coming up on the building before Sly spoke again, this time in the instructional. "Okay, look, going through here, signing in, all that? You make like you put your ID in the slot, but you don't. That's for the camera in the corner. You go past all these niggers, you don't say shit. You walk right with me, we go up in the ward, through the control room thing they got, they buzz us in, you sit in the chair right next to me in the big TV room and you don't say shit to nobody till I tell you. You hear?"

"Just out of curiosity, who's your connection in here?"

"I got connections, in what you call the plural," Sly said, "wherever I need to be. If I don't got connections, I don't go. You want to talk to the freak, right?"

"I do."

"Then listen. They ain't even gonna bring him out his room. We gonna go in there, sit and talk to Reggie. This orderly, he's gonna walk down the hall to boyfriend's door. You watch him. He's going to go in and secure him. That ain't going to be but a minute. When he steps out the door, you step in. You got two minutes to chat. The orderly's going to wait right outside the door. Then he comes back in, party's over, you come out. Clear?"

Sully felt the adrenaline surge through his veins. *Hold it steady, champ*, he thought, *hold it steady.* "Yeah. I mean, sure."


Doors and locks, people saying no, hey, you're not on the list, you can't go in there, that's a secure area, no access, back up before I make you back up, permit denied—that's what getting past guards was. That was the deal.

And that was how you made your money in this gig: getting past the guards. What kind of reporter stayed outside the tape with the rest of the proletariat? How could you find out anything there? You had to get *in*.

They were coming up on the front door, frosted glass, a tiny black receptor to the right for your magnetic ID. If you didn't have one, you had to hit the button and wait for them to buzz you in. Sly—wearing slacks, a light blue-gray shirt, sleeves artfully rolled up, sunglasses propped on his head—pressed the buzzer. There was a pause and then the door clicked, Sly pulling it open.

Lock one, cleared.

The guard station, a box of bulletproof Plexiglas, was set into a long wall with a door on either side. It was a standard jail or prison two-lock process: Once they pressed the buzzer to unlock the first door, you walked in, stopped, and it locked behind you. You were then in a locked chamber adjacent to the guard station. Then a guard at the second level pressed the buzzer to open the second door to let you inside. The second door could not be opened unless the first door had locked behind it.

Sly walked to the Plexiglas, said hello to the guard behind it, put his driver's license in the tray that ran under the window. Then he said his name and Uncle Reggie's, and with a jerk of his head back at Sully, "This my cousin. I told Vinny he was coming today."

At the mention of "Vinny," the guard, a heavyset black guy wearing a dark blue uniform, looked up from Sly's ID. He looked at Sly, then at Sully. He kept his eyes on Sully and said something to someone else in the booth. Another guard materialized behind him and then the security door clicked open on the right. Sly walked in, it shut behind him, the far door opened, and he was in.

Sully, not making eye contact with the guard, pulled out his wallet and his driver's license. He put his hand in the slot, but did not actually put his ID in it. The guard, looking over his head and not at him, pressed the button. The door clicked, he stepped into the lock box, and as soon as the door behind him clicked so did the one in front.

He pushed it open, the air stale and flat and a hundred years old. It smelled like the doors hadn't been opened since the Eisenhower administration. Sly was standing there, talking to one of the guards like they were best friends, Sly twirling his sunglasses around by one of the stems, smiling. "Hey, I already signed you in. Jamal here is gonna take us upstairs."

Lock two.

The third lock was to get into the day room of the ward, and that was easy. Jamal put his badge to the buzzer and swung it open. He nodded to them both, said he'd get one of the orderlies to go get Reggie. Sully and Sly walked into the room. The door swung back behind them. From the other side, they could hear Jamal rattle it to make sure the lock had engaged.

"Hate that sound," Sly muttered.

Sully started to razz him, to say, "I guess not," but dropped it. The room, what did you want to say, did not invite levity.

You would not know it was a day room for the criminally insane if you saw it in a picture. You needed the smell, the tang, for that. Large, airy, light-filled, some worn carpets by the window, some by the couches, which had no cushions. There were two televisions, both high on the wall, out of reach. Maybe the lobby of a cheap hotel, it looked about like that.

The smell was something like Pine-Sol poured over vomit and mopped up and left to dry.

Three patients were in the room. Two were watching television. One was staring out the floor-to-ceiling window. The two watching television turned to look at them, the new fish in the aquarium, then over at the control booth. After a minute, they went back to looking at the television. The third one, Sully didn't think that guy had moved since this morning, so he walked over and looked out the window, too. The view was over the grounds, the old cemetery, the bluff falling away toward 295, the Potomac way down there. A maintenance guy was mowing the yard, but without a grass catcher attached, just spewing the dead dry grass out of the blower.

He was about to turn and make a comment to Sly about the inmates—sorry, the patients'—multimillion-dollar view, when he heard Sly's raised voice behind him.

"Uncle REG-GIE," Sly was saying, walking toward the couches. A burly man with a thick gray beard and matted hair coming up on him, swallowing Sly in a bear hug. "I mean, hey, brother. Look at you."

Sully came over from the window and, keeping Sly between him and Uncle Reggie, joined them as they sat on the couches, taking a seat where he could see down the hallway toward the patients' rooms. As soon as he sat, Reggie stopped looking at Sly and looked at him. "Who this motherfucker here?"

Sly looked over at him, like he'd just noticed Sully. "Friend of the family," he said.

"Not mine," Reggie said, lumbering to stand back up. "Not this family. The fuck's with his face? Talk to me, boy." Sully scratched the back of his neck and looked down. Sly pulled on Reggie's sleeve and said,

"Calm down, Unc. He was a friend to momma back in the day. He straight."

Reggie sat, still confused but glaring, scratching at his neck, just like Sully was. Behind him Sully could see an orderly walk by in his white sneakers and sky-blue scrubs. He went to a door halfway down the corridor on the left, stopped and looked back at Sully. He pressed his magnetic stripe to the keypad, it buzzed, and he went in.

"Okay," Sully said. "Go."

Sully pressed down on the balls of his feet and stood, his heartbeat coming up harder in his chest.

"Now where he going?" Reggie said.

"You talk to me," Sully said. "You tell me about why this skinny white motherfucker, Hinckley, is getting some ass up in here and you just wearing out your left hand."

" 'Cause I eat with my right," Reggie said, throwing back his head to laugh, half his teeth gone, Sully moving past him, smiling, walking like he wasn't in a hurry to the door.

He had worn hard-soled shoes and now he regretted it, the clicking on the tile. Everything seemed loud, the television, Uncle Reggie, the muttered conversation of the other two patients, the click of the locks. The security cameras, they had to be up on a wall someplace, tracking him, and he fought the urge to look up and find them. Act like you been here before. Act like this is routine.

When he got to the door—it had only the number 237 on it—he rapped it, three times, softly. The hallway back to Sly looked a mile long. In the chest pocket of his sport coat was his recorder. Fumbling with it, he clicked it and saw the tiny red recording light go on.

The door in front of him swung open a moment later. The attendant walked past and did not speak or make eye contact. Sully stepped inside and the door hissed shut behind him and he heard the bolt click back into its slot.

Nine feet away, staring at him with cloudy, heavily-lidded eyes—

hazel, green and brown, swirling—was the killer he'd seen in the Capitol, on the street on Massachusetts Avenue.

He was seated on the side of a bed, his wrists handcuffed in front of
him. The cuffs were part of a padded chain that ran around his waist and
then to a bolt in the floor. His ankles were bound and these restraints
were also connected to the bolt. Wispy black hair fell to his shoulders.

Sully put his hands behind him, his palms against the door, and
leaned back against it. He smiled, just a bit at the corners of his mouth,
looking at the raptor-like edges of the man's teeth—had he never gone
to the dentist?— the lowered chin, the slightly opened mouth, then said
what he'd come to say.

"Hi, George," he said. "Pity about your grandma."

## TWENTY-EIGHT

IT CONFUSED HIM, you could tell. The gaping mouth, opening and closing, a fish on the bottom of the boat.

He was ragged-headed, unshaven, raccoon pouches beneath the eyes, the cheeks puffy, the shoulders sagging under the restraints. The white jumpsuit was a size too big, billowing out like a balloon, making him appear small and lost beneath it. His knees rattled back and forth, his fingers reached and plucked under the cuffed restraints, as if he were playing an invisible accordion. It wasn't clear if the movement was voluntary.

Silence, breathing. Silence, breathing.

"Wait, wait," he said thickly, his tongue slow and lugubrious. "Sully?"

"We got to go a little quicker," Sully said. "I only got two minutes."

The man tried to rub his eyes, bringing a sharp rattle when his wrists hit the limit of their chains, startling him. He'd just woken up, they had him laced on some sedative, something.

"How'd you, how'd the fuck you get in here?"

"Introductions," Sully said, ignoring him. "You know who I am, George. But you seem to be telling everybody you're Terry Waters, your schizoid elementary-school buddy from Oklahoma, though you haven't seen him in donkey's years. You've been back by there, though, haven't you? You went to see them, Terry and his dad. You drove right up there to the door. Did his dad tell you Terry was dead, buried out there in the woods by the creek, or did you figure that out all by yourself?"

The man coughed, cleared his throat. "Okay, no, wait."

He blinked, the eyes still cloudy. Sully tried to set the man's features in his mind's eye. It was difficult to get a fix, the man sitting down, wrapped up. His hair and bronzed features the only color in the all-white room.

"Didn't just happen to kill Dad, too, did you," Sully said, "so that then you'd have Terry's identity to yourself? I mean, the man had been dead three days when he was found. You choked him out, you know, I don't know there'd be a lot of evidence of that."

This time, the man in the jumpsuit reared back, regarded Sully as from a great distance, as if he'd been speaking to him through a long, dark tunnel, and only now could he make out the words. The eyes gained focus. For the life of him, Sully would swear he'd just offended the man.

"You, what you got to understand is, see, Sully, you don't know everything," he said, voice still thick, but clearing up now. "Sully. Sully. Look. This has gotten sort of fucked around. We got a bond, see, our mothers. I got a story to tell, you got stories to, to write. Us. Injustice. There are larger—"

"You tried to *shoot* me," Sully said, voice rising. "Bond, my lily-white ass."

"—themes to what we're, no, see, no." A deep breath, pulling it from the base of the lungs, like he'd learned it in yoga and he was restoring his balance here. Another deep one. "I'da wanted to kill you, I would have. Had the drop. I just wanted to get your attention. I wanted to get—" he stopped. "I shot some glasses on your table. I wanted us to meet, before they found me. See, what came to me," another rumbling cough rattled his chest, "seeing all that shit on TV? They wanted to kill me. They did not want to take me alive. Or they wouldn't be able to, just some trigger-happy asshole with no training, blam blam and too bad for me. So it dawns on me, what I needed to do is make sure that I'm safe. Make sure that they arrest me and not shoot me like a dog. I needed a *witness*, somebody to make sure they didn't blow my head off and then put a pistol in my hand and call it self-defense. And who better a witness? Who better to keep them honest? Who better to tell the tale?"

He gestured forward, palms up, hands open, extended fingers, a wan smile. "You."

Sully looked at him. "George?"

"Why do you keep calling me that?"

"That is bullshit."

Waving the hands, no-no-no. Warming up to it now. "It isn't. It really isn't. You were there at the beginning, with Edmonds. You saw. *Only* you. Only *you* will understand. Can understand."

"Understand what."

"The nightmare."

"Okay, look, let's cut the crazy-man, mystical bullshit. Superior Court, fucking Glen Campbell. I'm not here for the circus. I'm here—" and, on instinct, on the fly, he changed. He'd been about to demand an explanation, or what passed for an explanation, on the murder of Edmonds. That was why George was here, that was the linchpin upon which the rest of this all revolved. But he saw playing the hard-ass wasn't the right option, not now.

"I'm here," Sully said, making himself slow down, his voice softer now, sliding to the floor, sitting cross-legged, back against the door, keeping eye contact, looking as deeply into the man as he dared.

"I'm here," he repeated, faintly now, bringing it down to imitate an intimate conversation, "to hear about what happened to your grandmother. Miriam. The knife."

"Miriam, the knife? Isn't it supposed to be 'Mack'? You know, the song?'"

Gently, again. The word had popped into his mind, *gentle*, and your instincts were there for a reason. Sully curled his fingernails in against his palms. The man in front of him, he wasn't the killer in the Capitol.

He was the boy in the back of the patrol car. He was the boy bathed in blood. The horror this man's life had been. Gentle. Nobody had been gentle with him in, what, how long? Sully had a flash vision of George leading prostitutes into hotel rooms, rough sex, taking them from behind, handcuffs and blindfolds, sex doubling as hostility.

And it slipped into his mind, as natural as the Mississippi running into the Gulf, Alexis whispering in the dark *with me not to me*, the way he had needed to take Dusty on her knees, the hands cuffed behind her, the others he couldn't remember, the ones who had loved and encouraged it and the ones who had complained, the way he tended to black out afterward, not just fall asleep.

We have a bond our mothers only you the nightmares. . . .

And George, having read about his mother, not even Nadia, had him pegged to the marrow.

"Miriam," Sully forced himself to say out loud, to snap back to the urgency of now. What did he have remaining, sixty seconds? Less? "You said her name in court the other day, George. In C-10. You slipped, brother. You were doing your crazy-man rant, and you shouted 'Miriam,' at the judge. Party's over. Miriam Harper was your grandmother. You're not Terry Waters, that was a kid you played baseball with. Rode horses. Your grandmother, Miriam, she slit her throat in a two-story country house outside of Stroud, Oklahoma. You called the sheriff. She bled out on you in the back of the patrol car. Miriam. It wasn't your fault, George. But you got stuck with it. A terrible goddamn thing."

The man staring at him, the accordion playing forgotten, his hands frozen in place. Stammering, the balloon of self-confidence punctured, all the air escaping. "You, you, are so off the, what is it, the—"

"Your granddad took you to the funeral home," Sully said, quietly, as if someone might overhear. "William. He didn't take you to the funeral because there wasn't one."

Softly as the benediction now: "It's over, George. I know. I was there. The old house. Your old room. Tell me about her. Miriam."

Nothing but emptiness, the eyes gone vacant, hollow, a canyon, still locked onto his.

"Tell me about what Barry Edmonds did that you had to kill him. Tell me about your mother. Frances. I can help. We got this bond, George. It's only me. Only you. Tell me about Frances, George. Tell me who killed your mother."

George Harper stared at him. A single tear, shiny as a diamond, seeped from the inside corner of his right eye. And then, in a sudden flash of movement, he was barking, bellowing, weeping, shouting, and crying all at once, yanking on his chains, stomping on the floor, spittle flecking from his mouth, howling, the sound tremendous in the room, the man losing his balance, nearly falling, careening into the wall.

The door behind Sully burst into his back, the orderly shoving it in, knocking Sully to his side, stepping in over him. Before Sully could roll over, another orderly—larger, beefier—stormed in behind him. Sully seeing them from the floor, the pair of them looking fifteen feet tall, outlined in grotesque proportions against the all-white environment.

"Shut up! Shut up! SHUT UP!" the second orderly was bellowing, and George was bellowing back at him, spewing obscenities and slurs and now the first orderly was yelling down at Sully, into his face, "What did you do? What did you do to him?"

Hands were on him, pulling him upright. He shuffled his feet, slipped, went down, was pulled back up. "I didn't do shit," he shouted above the din, "I didn't do shit! I didn't do shit!"

They were dragging him out of the room, his feet sliding. He could see Sly and Uncle Reggie and the rest of them down the hall, staring. Now George, looking straight at him from the back of his cell, bellowing over the shoulders of the orderly, "Ice picks! Ice picks! Freeman! Ice picks!!"

## TWENTY-NINE

HE PLAYED THE tape, and replayed it, and replayed it, leaning forward from the backseat in the car so that Sly and Lionel could hear. They were driving out of the place, the gate swinging up, and they were back in the land of the relatively sane, heading down the hill. The sun was too bright. They were merging into midday traffic. Sully's head was killing him.

"Shit," said Lionel. Which, for him, constituted a soliloquy.

Sly didn't even turn around. "I told you. Crazy people. What did I tell you about crazy people."

"The sound and the fury," Sully muttered, rewinding the tape yet again, like the man was going to say something different this time.

"Sound of bullshit, you mean."

"Look, what does he say there? Everybody's yelling like the place is on fire. 'Free ice picks'? 'Free, man, ice picks'? 'Freeman's ice picks'? I can't hear shit. You roll that window up?"

Sly gave a half glare back over the seat, leaned forward to roll his window up and then turned up the AC.

"Can't hear with that thing blowing, either."

This time, the full glare, Sly turning in the seat to look back at him, leaving the AC just where it was. "I ain't one to tell a man how to run his business? But you know how close you came to getting busted up in there? Setting off shit like that?"

"Thought you said you had contacts," Sully said, still holding the recorder to his ear, squinting, like narrowing his eyes would improve his hearing, "in the plural."

"Didn't say I *ran* the place. Staff. I got contacts on staff, the help. Not with the shrinks and shit. There's what you call protocols, that ward there in particular. That fucker is celebrity of the week. Jamal had to get back to the booth to keep them from hitting the button to call the medicals. They were halfway to getting Lantigua down there."

"Who's Lantigua."

"The man what runs the place. Him, you do not fuck with. They got protocols, I'm telling you. Anything funky with psycho boy there, anything with any of them in Canan, they get Lantigua on a rope."

"You didn't mention that."

"Didn't think I *needed* to."

The tape. Stop, rewind, pause, play. Again, pressing the tiny speaker to his ear. "Freeman? I think he said Freeman."

"Lantigua'd come down there, you'd been in deep shit."

"Me? What about you?"

"You who, Kemo Sabe? I'm a devoted nephew, visiting Unc. You, you're—"

"The unethical hack who snuck in the place."

"Exactly."

Sully sat back in the seat. His shirt was half untucked, his jacket rumpled. He was lucky it didn't get torn in that clusterfuck. Six, seven orderlies by the end, shoving him against the wall, Jamal yelling at Sly to get him out get him out get him out, the fuck was this even about.

Lionel took them down 295, across the river, bringing them the back way onto Capitol Hill on Pennsylvania Avenue. The Capitol lay up ahead, the neighborhood around them sagging two- and three-story town houses, gloomy child-care centers, check-cashing joints, a thrift store. They were, he realized dully, taking him back to his house. Josh would be there. Or would he? Didn't he say they had some sort of field trip? National Cathedral?

But home, no, he didn't want to be there. The office, no, you got to be kidding, sit in there and look at people looking at him. Alexis? And tell her what, he'd just snuck into the city's hellhole of an insane asylum with a drug dealer and killer? No, no, no. Big boys held their water.

Restless, he punched numbers into the phone, the paper's Research desk. Susan, picking it up, sounding jumpy when he said hey. She said she was all over the family research, okay, and he jumped in, knowing he was just going to make it worse.

"Look, I hear you. I hear you. Do me a solid, though, one more? You in front of your computer? Great, that's great. Okay, look up the name Freeman, like free man, and ice picks. You get any hits on that?" She went on for a minute until he said, "Yes, I mean, for real."

He waited, looking out at the city, until she picked the phone back up and said, "Jesus, Sully, what is wrong with you?"

"Lots. What do you mean?"

"The pictures."

He waited, but she didn't elaborate. He could hear the keyboard clacking somewhere in the background, pictured her at her desk, the far back right of the newsroom, lost in a corner, a shot glass with Hershey's kisses in them, pictures of her dog, Frank.

Finally, he said, "What pictures we talking about here?"

"I don't even . . . okay, I can't look at this."

"Susan, hey? I got no idea what you're talking about."

"Lobotomies. Walter Jackson Freeman II, M.D., pioneer of."

"I don't get this."

Clicking on the keyboard, silence. "He was the research director at St. E's."

Sully rocked forward in his backseat, leaning forward from the hips, his forearms coming down on his knees, forehead nearly hitting the back of Lionel's bucket seat. "You're saying some lobotomy lunatic worked in *Washington?*"

"Yeah," she said, still reading. "Look at this. His papers are at George Washington University, just up the street."

## THIRTY

"YOU WANT TO see the pictures?"

He was halfway sitting down in the chair and Jerry, the grad student manning the special collections library in the G.W. archives, was setting out the brown boxes of Walter J. Freeman's catalogued papers on a table in front of him.

He'd had to convince Lionel and Sly to bring him across town, Sly bitching the whole way that if he had wanted to get over to Foggy Bottom, he shoulda said so. They could have taken 395 around to Maine Avenue, come up past the monuments, by the Watergate, like that. But now, Sully being disorganized as shit, now they were slogging through town, red light, red light, red light, and Lionel going hey, where exactly *is* the G.W. Library.

"Just, like, Twenty-first or Twenty-second, I'll find it from there."

"Twenty-first or Twenty-second and *what*?" Lionel said

"I don't know. H, I, somewhere. Just go up Pennsylvania."

"Did you see a taxi sign on the top of my car?" Sly said.

"You don't want me to cut down Constitution?" Lionel said.

Like that, the whole way.

Then, it turned out, the Freeman stuff wasn't in the library. It was in the medical archives, which was upstairs, which you needed a pass for, which he had to stand in line to get. His headache was a good solid throb by then. Once upstairs, an August afternoon, school not started, he was the only customer in the shoe-box-sized reception area.

Now he sat at his small wooden table, like he was back in fourth grade. The instructions for handling archival material and the rate sheet for copies were at his right. His notebook on the left. Good God. He just needed a lunch box and a cubby.

Standing in front of him was Jerry, the only employee in sight, sporting a playful smile, hamming it up, still on about pictures this, pictures that. Sully guessed Jerry here was probably giddy just to have another living humanoid to yammer at. Stuck in here all day in a windowless reception room on the eleventh floor, nothing but rows of shelves with medical records behind you.

"We're talking about the transorbital things? The transorbital lobotomy?" Sully said, cocking an eyebrow. "I think I'm good just—"

"No, no. Man, not those. Those, you can see on the Internet. I'm talking about *the* pictures."

"Okay, okay," Sully said.

"The autopsy ones," Jerry said brightly. Kid was all but bouncing on the balls of his feet. "Everybody always does."

"Everybody?"

"Look here," and Jerry was standing beside him, Mr. Super Helpful, pulling open a file box, knowing right where to look. "Freeman, he was sort of a genius, kind of P. T. Barnum. Absolutely into studying the insane. Research director at St. E's back in the twenties. He was thinking phrenology at the time, like measuring people's heads, bumps on them, and it would tell you about their mentality."

"Is this going to involve bleeding people with leeches?"

Jerry, ignoring him. "But you don't know *how* he measured them."

"I'm guessing this is the point in the story where you show me."

Jerry pulled out a folder, flipped through it and then slipped a glossy in front of him. At first Sully thought he'd handed him the wrong picture. These were not corpses because they were standing upright. Then his eyes focused and saw they were dead. Naked. Dangling from what appeared to be meat hooks.

"What—"

"Freeman wanted to measure them, but you don't get violently insane people to sit still, right? So, autopsies. For whatever reason, he wanted to do it with them standing up. So he would get an assistant and they'd put clamps in their ears, like ice tongs? Then they hooked the tongs to a steel cable. That ran on a hydraulic lift to the top of the room. Then they'd turn on the crank and haul them up in the air, like carcasses at the slaughterhouse. They'd swing them over to the wall, see here, where they had this grid, for measurement."

Sully blinked and looked at the picture again. He took the folder from Jerry, spreading the photographs, dozens of them, across the table. Men and women, white and black. The bodies were misshapen, bloated, twisted from sclerosis, nearly skeletal, arms limp. They hung like puppets. Greasy hair and long beards, thick body hair, sagging breasts, floating penises, spines hunched or legs splayed. But it was the faces that drew him in. Mouths open, eyes finally closed to a lifetime of mental agony, jaws pulled to one side or another as if trying to speak some lost syllable from the land of beyond, gaps in the teeth or missing altogether, the cheeks hollow, tongues lolling. Their ears flattened and pulled up to grotesque angles by the metal clamps.

"I don't even, what, are all these lobotomies?"

Jerry perched on the edge of the table, already looking in another box, pulling out more files. "No, no. Lobotomies were later. But Freeman? He still loved him some pictures. Here."

These were eight-by-ten portraits of men and women looking into the camera. Black-and-white images, some of them smiling, some not, some blank and seemingly unaware they were being photographed.

"These, now, are the before and after lobotomy portraits. The man did his documentation."

"He worked here, that's how you guys wound up with his stuff?"

"Yes. No. He had his own clinic in town. He was a researcher at St. E's. Later on, he was an adjunct or an associate here at G.W. I never can remember. Freeman and his partner, a surgeon, did the first lobotomy in the United States, right here at G.W. Then everybody did. Yale. Johns Hopkins."

"Yale did lobotomies?"

"Sure. This was cutting-edge stuff, man. This was the nineteen forties, the early fifties. Before Thorazine? The best you could do with paranoid schizophrenics, the catatonically depressed—and I mean, for, like, all of recorded history—was warehouse them. This was a big step up from demonic possession. Doctors back then, they fell over themselves, congratulating each other on being so humane. St. Elizabeths was its own village. People stayed for twenty years, forty. Hydrotherapy, wrap them in warm towels, let 'em play in the dirt. Then, shazam, the lobotomy! Schizophrenics calmed down. The violent became manageable. Well, some of them. A lot went home as drooling vegetables. A lot of them died."

"This, this is . . . I don't even know." He was still looking at the portraits.

Jerry bounced a pencil on the desk, off the eraser, and caught it. "Is it? What do we do with brain cancer patients today? Targeted radiation. Destroy part of the brain in the hope of saving the rest of it. Patients know that radiation, chemo, is going to make their hair fall out and make them spew vomit like Linda Blair, and they'll pay for the privilege. It's the best thing money can buy. It's the best science can offer. And if you don't? You die right now. So it's not that much different, you think about it."

Sully shook his head. "I guess. I mean—"

"The prefrontal lobotomy, the guy who thought of that? Awarded the Nobel Prize. It was very dramatic, very invasive. They partially shaved the head, drilled the skull open in several places. That's your prefrontal lobotomy. But Freeman, our boy Walter? He knew that the skull was weakest right at the top of the eye socket. You could get through that by hitting an ice pick with a hammer, then—don't look at me like that— then waggle it back and forth, and cut the nerves. He could do in ten minutes, in his office. Knocked you out with a jolt of electroshock, wham wham, and you were done. No more shaved head, full anesthesia, power drills."

Sully sat up, tapping the desk. "Wait wait—you said 'ice pick.'"

"Sure. That was the transorbital. His big contribution to science. It was like a fad. You know, like when Prozac first came out and everybody you knew started taking it?"

"Ice picks."

"Look, no disrespect, you don't seem to be getting this. Some lobotomized patients left the asylum, went back to work, their families. A little diminished, a little flat, but they were home. This hadn't happened before. Like, in recorded history. Astounding. The miracle cure. It was on the cover of magazines, of science journals. Even JFK's sister was lobotomized."

"The ice pick is—"

"Rosemary. I thought everybody knew this story. She had some mild mental disability. It got worse when she was at a convent school, here in Washington. She was sneaking out, as I recall, and there was some concern she'd wind up pregnant. Joe, the old man, thought Freeman was a genius. Lots of people did. So Joe sent her over to Freeman for a transorbital, there in his Connecticut Avenue office. It went bad. Rosemary was mentally destroyed."

"You're saying the sister of a sitting president of the United States had a doctor drive an ice pick into her brain and people were surprised it didn't turn out well."

"John, he wasn't president then. This was in the early 1940s. I think. But yes. Freeman went in above the eyeball, under the eyelid. See?" He leaned forward, pushing his eyelid up to display the fleshy strip above it, then let go, blinking. "He was trying to sever the connections between the medial thalamus and the ventromedial part of the frontal lobes. Cut the cords and voilà! No more crazy emotions! Just a quick tap up through the eye sockets. That was how you could recognize the recently lobotomized—they had huge black eyes. The way people with chemo now go bald, like that. He would give them sunglasses. A parting gift."

"I got this headache, man. I think I'm going to throw up."

"People often did, watching the procedure."

"You seem to know a lot about this."

"If one is interested in mental illness in America, one does. Freeman made lobotomy trips across the country. He'd show up at a state's mental hospital and do twenty in an afternoon. He'd do the nervous housewives of the well-to-do."

Sully, looking up now. "Oklahoma? He go through Oklahoma?"

Jerry shrugged. "Possibly. In the summers—by then, he was teaching here at G.W.—he'd barnstorm from here to California. A real evangelist. People would be stuck out there in small-town America with their depressed relatives—and then the great Dr. Freeman would come to town! He was a big name. People would bring their spouses, kids."

"You are not going to sit there and tell me he drove an ice pick into the brains of children."

"As young as eight. But see these pictures? No, the other ones. Those. They're from South Dakota. That's from the state hospital. He wasn't happy with what the superintendents brought him."

The photographs spread in front of him were grim. Faces of men, bent, gnarly as a tree root, pale, near hairless, twisted into a state so severe that Sully suddenly saw them on their own death tables, the undertaker having to break the legs to make them fit in the coffin.

"The superintendents would tend to bring him wards of the state, over sixty-five, all of them lifers, so if it was a disaster, who, really, was going to complain? Freeman wanted younger patients. Those on whom he could demonstrate improvement. So he took their portrait before the lobotomy and, when he caught up with them later, on his trip the next year or whatever, he'd take it again."

"You're going to tell me this guy wound up with an endowed chair."

"Nah. Thorazine came along, like I said. People could take a pill and be better, live at home. It was the beginning of the end for warehousing the mentally ill, for lobotomies. Everybody else eventually stopped doing them. Freeman didn't. License eventually jerked. Died in disgrace. More or less."

Sully asked, "So I'm interested in Oklahoma. How would I find that out?"

"Gimme a minute." Jerry slid off the table and disappeared into the back.

Sully rolled up his sleeves and walked from his table to the next, looking at the pictures Jerry had spread out. The dull faces, the heavy eyebrows, the lightless orbs in the sockets. What hellish world, he wondered, did they see, looking out? What voices echoed in the empty chambers of their minds? How did they see their keepers, as saviors or multiheaded monsters? The worlds of Lovecraft brought to life, an endless existence of mausoleum shadow and molten darkness?

Looking down into the boxes, opening one, then another, a tingling sensation crept over his shoulders and spread up his neck.

In the bottom of one lay two slender black-leather cases. Both had "Dr. Walter Freeman" embossed on the front, one in green, the other in gold. They looked like they had been expensive. They were both about a foot long and each was held closed by a pair of metal snaps, like an old eyeglass case. He reached down to pick them up, finding them heavier than he'd expected.

Jerry materialized at his shoulder.

"Here we go. The photographs from the trips, they're categorized a couple of different ways, but mostly they're kept in a box by state. Then the inside folders are kept by the institution, and then the patients are in alphabetical." He paused. "I see you found the Holy Grail."

Sully looked down at the leather case in his hand.

"This?"

"Open it."

He popped open the snaps and pulled the cover back. Clasped to a felt backing by elastic bands was a steel ice pick, dull silver with gray to black spots. Below it was a similar-looking steel rod with a curved top that tapered to a needle-sharp point.

"You can pull them out," Jerry said.

He did. The ice pick had, on the four sides of its slender handle, "Yolland Ice & Fuel Company." It was heavy.

"The very first one," Jerry said. "He thought it was like history, like Edison's first lightbulb. When he donated his papers here, he mentioned these at the ceremony."

The second case held two thicker but similar metal picks, with notches at the top and calibrations in millimeters. Each handle was engraved with FREEMAN.

"Those, he had machined specifically for the transorbitals. The notches there are centimeters. He thought that seven centimeters was the right depth for the first lobotomy. God only knows how he came up with that; he should have known from measuring all those corpses that there are differences in facial structure."

"You said 'the first lobotomy,'" Sully said, with a dull sense of horror.

"Yeah. You went home, you weren't acting right, they'd bring you back and he'd knock it up to eight centimeters. Some people he lobotomized three times. The ice picks, he thought they weren't quite sturdy enough. They could bend after you used them a couple of times. The leucotomes, though, as you can see, were just plain steel rods."

"Leucotomes?"

"His word. He coined it. The instrument of lobotomies."

Sully sat back down at his little table, heavy, looking at the paperwork, the narrow rods of glimmering steel in front of him. Jerry, taking the cue, said no rush, take your time, he was going to catch up on his filing.

Freeman had typed up the histories of each patient, usually three or four pages, stapled it, then paper-clipped them to the photographs, and dropped that in a manila folder with the patient's name across the top. Failing that, he scribbled notes on the back of the photographs themselves. Notations about their age, profession, weight, relationships, sexual habits. The ones that did not do well, Sully was soon able to identify almost on sight—they were marked by only a few notes. Freeman, pitchman that he was, was far more interested in documenting his relative successes.

Miriam Harper, it turned out, was not all that hard to find.

Freeman had worked his way west on—what else—Route 66. That would have brought him right through Lincoln, on the very same road Sully had been on. He would have come in the summer, when the Harpers were at their place outside of town. Had Sully known to look, no doubt he would have found front-page notice of Freeman's visit in the musty files of the *Citizen*.

William Harper, taciturn, humorless, would have opened the paper to see the news and taken the chance on the procedure more out of exasperation than love. What had Sly told him? That the family had not wanted Uncle Reggie back anymore? Maybe it was the same out there in the house by the lake. Maybe William Harper looked up from his paper, saw his delusional wife, and figured he had nothing to lose.

Miriam had been lobotomized at a doctor's office in Lincoln, on June 15, 1961, Freeman's file noted. In the first picture, taken before the procedure, she had a high forehead, cheekbones, dark hair pulled back into a severe bun. It would have been the day of her lobotomy—how could it not have been?—and she stood outside, on a sidewalk, the asphalt street and parked cars behind her. She looked at the photographer beyond the camera. She looked like she was staring at eternity. The attached notes had descriptions of her symptoms—agitation, outbursts, delusions, insomnia, violence.

The second photograph and attached note was from four years later. Miriam Harper, haggard, hair scattered, lopsided smile, Freeman taking the picture from five feet away.

This, then, was the grandmother George Harper grew up with. Haunted, empty eyes, vacant stare, errant hair, no makeup, sagging features.

*This* was the ghoul that Harper had burst out in court was coming to kill the judge, living in the diseased mind of her grandson. Miriam Harper, lobotomized and brain destroyed, had cut her throat and then bled out on him and the blood never left. It had soaked into the boy's skin. His mind. His dreams.

The eyes of Miriam, the supposed windows of the soul, held nothing in this photograph but reflected light. They had no spark of their own. It had be to terrifying, coming home to this every day as a child. The smell, it came across him, unbidden and unwanted, the musty old-woman smell that George would have inhaled when he embraced her, stale sweat and talcum powder.

There were very few notations on the sheet attached to this photograph. She was "better" and "much improved, husband reports." At the bottom was a one-line scrawl: "Suicide, 1971."

He turned the photograph over before flipping the folder shut, and there was another line of handwriting that froze him to his schoolboy's chair.

"Lobotomized daughter, Frances Harper, 4/16/67. D.C. office. Last session."


It took Jerry twenty minutes of digging in the stacks, but he eventually returned with the Frances Harper folder. While he was gone, Sully worked out the knots in his mind. The mom "off in Washington," they'd said out there in Oklahoma. Christ. Schizophrenia. It ran in families.

The father, seeing the traits of the mom blossoming in their only child, sent her for a cure before it could get worse. To Washington, to the great lobotomist himelf, the patron saint of lost causes.

Jerry set the folder on the table. There were only two photographs inside.

The first one, the day of the lobotomy: an attractive young woman, maybe thirty, fair features, full lips, shoulder-length blond hair that she had tucked behind her ear on one side. But her face was drawn, nervous. She wore a turtleneck sweater, arms folded across her chest, eyes bright, frightened, like a small animal in the grip of something more powerful.

Jerry, though, wasn't looking at that at all. He was focused on the date, tapping it with his finger.

"Wow. Dude. Remember I told you Freeman died in disgrace? That's because he kept doing the transorbitals in his office, long after everyone else had quit, after it was considered malpractice. The last session he did were two women. One died the day after. The other, it went bad. There was an investigation. That's why his license got pulled. Manslaughter charges were considered. This chick here, she had to be the second lobotomy that day. She's the very last lobotomy he ever did."

The other photograph in the folder was the "after." Sully pulled it out.

"Holy shit," Jerry said.

Frances Harper lay on her back in a single bed, wearing nothing but a white smock. Her eyes were lidded, heavy, the eyes rolled up. The mouth gaped. The skin on her face was sallow, barely clinging to the underlying bone. The once blond hair was white, listless, cut boy short. The only note on the back was, "St. E's, January 1970."

Sully looked down in the folder, pulling out a small scrap of paper. It was a copy of a hospital ledger entry. "Harper, Frances, DOD, 11/26/1993. Plot seven, row seventy-two, grave nine."

"You mean," Sully said, "she lived another twenty-three *years* like that?'

And then it came to him, the nightmare he was supposed to under-stand. George Harper had known St. E's nearly all his life. Freeman had destroyed his grandmother. His mother was sent to St. E's and destroyed by Freeman, too. George Harper would have visited her for two decades, washing her face, her feet, brushing her hair, a mindless lump of flesh that wouldn't die. And then she did, buried there still.

Who had killed his mother? It wasn't a who. It was a what.

St. Elizabeths.

## THIRTY-ONE

WHEN HE CAME gimp-legging it out of the library, he was stunned to see it was after five, lines of cars pulling out of parking garages, the quad empty. The light was muted and diffuse overhead, thick gray clouds piling in. When he turned his cell back on, the messages were stacked up.

Clicking into the voicemails as he walked, he noticed, to his great exasperation, that the G.W. library at this time of year wasn't a haven for taxis. Not a one. Not even in the distance. He started up H, past the quad, then hooked left on Twenty-first, realizing too late that it was a one-way running south, and now he was going to have to hoof it up to Pennsylvania Avenue before he'd be able to flag one.

The first two messages were from Josh, wondering if maybe he and Sully and Alexis could take the boat out this weekend, because he was flying home next weekend, and really, no kidding, it would be great if Alexis could come. The second message, five minutes after the first, was also from Josh, this one accentuating his fine record of emptying the dishwasher and throwing out the trash and cleaning even the counter-tops as meritorious conduct, fully deserving, if he hadn't mentioned it in the first message, of letting him drive the boat. With Alexis there.

The shit started with the third voicemail.

"Sully Carter. Hey. Janice Miller, over at PDS. I need to know, like yesterday, why my client, I'm going to repeat that, *my* client, is going ape shit. Says he wants to make some sort of statement today at St. E's—but if and only if *you* are there. Says he has a 'bond' with you. This is what I need to know. Why and how does *my* client have a *bond* with *you*. The fuck, Sully. Call me."

He pulled it away from his ear, fumbling at the buttons to make it play the message again—holy shit, had George ratted him out? That he'd been in the asylum? He patted his pockets, his shirt, like a pen and paper was going to materialize, before he stopped and got one out of his backpack, writing on the back of his notes from the library.

The next message wasn't any better.

"Mr. Carter. This is Eduardo Lantigua. I am the director of St. Elizabeths Hospital. For many years. I have a most unusual request from a pretrial inmate. His name is Terry Waters. He says he will end his case, of which you are acutely aware, this very evening. It is based upon the condition that you are present. He has become very agitated. This is a very unusual request. Please call to discuss."

The fourth call, he could have predicted.

"Sullivan," R.J.'s voice boomed. "One, where are you? Two, Special Agent Gill, that lovely woman from the FBI? She just crawled up my ass so far she could tickle my tonsils. She wants to know why Waters, or Harper, or who the fuck ever, is demanding you be at St. E's tonight. Three, and savvy reporter that you are, you'll already know this: Call me. Right. Fucking. Now."

He leaned his head into a palm. George was playing some fucking cards, leading him by the nose after his visit. And there was nothing to do about it but go, take the bait, see what it was, and then make a decision about what to do with it. George was going to tell them all—the FBI, Janice, Lantigua, the U.S. attorney's office—that he'd been there.

How could he do that and keep his job? He couldn't.

No, wait, turning to look for a cab, Jesus, anywhere. *Just hold your water*, he thought to himself. This would still work. On the inside, the staff? Who was going to back George and say that they'd seen Sully in the place, that there had been a huge altercation this afternoon?

No contact of Sly Hastings who wanted to keep breathing, much less keep his job, that's who. None of Sly's sources were going to cross him. Nor were any of their colleagues, once it was explained exactly who it was they were about to cross. Most of the staff lived in Southeast, anyway. They would know the name of Sly Hastings, and they would know they did not ever, ever want to see the man up close.

A deep breath now. Right, right. Tell them all he had no idea what the delusional Terry Waters was talking about. Skip the meeting at St. E's. Write his story exposing George Harper that night for tomorrow's paper. The resulting shit storm would so advance the story that the soap opera of today would be forgotten, lost in the confusion. That wasn't bad.

*But*, he thought, coming up on Pennsylvania now, *no, wait. Turning down an interview in the nuthouse with the Capitol Hill killer?* That *would be insane.* He could still deny it all there. He could sell that. He could make that play. All he had to do was play it straight for, what, half an hour? So he'd go, okay, sure. But the party was over, like he'd told George—the exposé had to run tomorrow. He had to set it in motion now, before he went up to St. E's for the sit-down.

There was one more voicemail, this one from Susan, in news research, saying to call her back as soon as he got this.

By now, he was making Pennsylvania and, there, the first taxi he saw, an old beat-up Chevrolet Caprice with a wobbling yellow TAXI sign on top and faded lettering on the side, pulled to the curb for him.

Ducking into the backseat, telling the driver, a disaffected Sikh in a turban, the guy's eyes not even rising to look at him in the rearview, to head for the paper. Susan picked up on the fourth ring.

"So," she said, "the name you gave me? This George Harper, his granddad, William Harper?"

"Yes."

"I've run it fifteen ways to Sunday. You got something to get this down?"

"On the way in, but gimme the highlights now. I can scribble."

"Okay. Look, he bounced around, but mostly he ran an oil drilling supply business out of Odessa, Texas. Made things called g-force hammers, drill bits, diverter boxes. The business editor from the *American*, the newspaper in Odessa—I called—remembered the company. Said the old man was a hard-ass."

"I'm with you."

"LexisNexis is showing he was a landowner, too. Not sure if it was mining, livestock, timber, what. The place you found in Oklahoma. Land in Arizona, outside Houston, and a good chunk of property, a couple hundred acres, in Wyoming. Two hundred acres in Georgia, an hour west of Athens. You're going to rack up some frequent flier miles."

"What happened to the business, the oil-drilling supplier?"

"Shuttered in 1991. Nine years ago. That's the year after he died."

"The family cashed out?"

"I would guess."

"Who inherited the estate?"

"Not clear. He was a widower, you already got that. Appears to have had one child."

"A daughter named Frances." The taxi, making good time in the light August traffic. It was like the city had been turned upside down and emptied.

"Correct. Looks like she was born in Odessa. Grew up there, mostly. She also had one child, no father listed."

"This is going to be our boy."

"Yep. George Hudson Harper, born in Odessa, September 30, 1962. But look, Frances, she all but disappears after 1970. It's like she fell off the Earth or—"

"I got that. She got committed to St. E's that year. I been in the G.W.

library all afternoon. Freeman, he lobotomized her, she got left in St. E's, a vegetable, died in, what was it, 1993."

She started off again, but then stopped. "Wait, ninety-three?"

"Yes."

"Can't be."

"Why not?"

"Because she's shown here opening an electrical maintenance business in the District last year."

"Not possible. Saw a picture of her on the ward. Trust me."

"It's right here, FKH Electrical. Down in Southeast. It's her initials. Frances Kelly Harper."

His phone started buzzing at his ear. He lowered his hand to look at it. The caller ID showed R.J.'s cell. His Bat Line, the no-bullshit-pick-this-up signal.

"Okay, look, quick," he said back into the phone. "I gotta get this. Gimme the address of that electrical place. Then call Melissa and get her to tell Keith to get to that place right now, beat on the door."

"FKH Electrical, 3964 Xenia SE, the District. That's deep Southeast, off King, up on the bluffs, overlooking the river. Call it a mile from St. E's."

He repeated it back to her. R.J.'s waiting call stopped, then, ten seconds later, started right back. "Okay, look, what about good old George Hudson Harper? He show up in LexisNexis?"

"I pulled it, but it's a common name. Lots of hits, all over the country."

"That land his grandad owned," Sully said. "He could have been living out there, with the money from the business. All but off the grid."

"In D.C. and surrounding, there are four George Harpers between the ages of thirty-eight and forty, which would be in the range of our boy's birthday. Two are African American. One of the Anglos lives in Chevy Chase, the other one in D.C. at . . ." she paused, "at 3964 Xenia."

"Bingo," Sully said. "Tell Keith I'll meet him there in twenty minutes."

He clicked off that line, then fumbled with the thing, trying to see how to click over to R.J. and tell the driver, at the same time, to switch directions, to bolt down to Southeast, for Xenia.

Into the phone, talking to R.J., he said, preemptively, "I got no idea, so don't be asking me."

"Sullivan? What?"

"I got no idea why the man wants me to show up tonight, what the hell this is about."

"Bullshit," R.J. said. "You leave here, saying you got a way to get in to see him, then, blam, he wants a meeting with you, PDS, what's his name, the prosecutor."

"Wesley."

"Yeah, well, that guy's an asshole. He was just on the phone, lighting up Eddie. Trying to light up Eddie."

"About what?"

"Misconduct, your end, something. Says you'll taint whatever it is the man wants to say, you're there. So, what, did you get in to see him? You didn't do anything stupid, did you?"

Sully thought about this for a second, the driver's eyes now searching his, mutely asking which way to go, Sully repeating the address.

"I'm not taking you there," the driver said.

"3964 Xenia," Sully repeated. "Come on, man, go go go." To R.J., he said, "No. Didn't get in."

"I thought you said you had a guy."

"I did, but it didn't work out right."

The driver pulled the cab to the curb, put it in park, turned on his flashers. "No."

"What?" Sully said. "What are you doing?"

"Who are you talking to?" R.J. said.

"Buy your own drugs," the driver said.

R.J.: "Wait, drugs? What the hell is going on?"

Sully, ready to punch somebody: "Pipe down, R.J., hold on. You, look, drive, goddammit. This ain't a drug run. I'm a fucking reporter."

The driver, unmoved, motioning to the door.

Sully reached into his back pocket, tugged out the wallet. "Look. What, I got forty, fifty dollars, there's seventy . . . okay. Seventy-three. That's all I got." He handed it over the seat. "I can't be buying drugs with money I don't have. You got it." His ID was there, so he handed that over, too. "See? A reporter."

The driver, hesitating now, looking at the rumpled clump of bills. "Reporters, you people do drugs, too."

"Not this one," Sully said, "I drink. Now would you please drive?"

Still not liking it, looking at the curb, the oncoming traffic, the driver clicked off the blinkers and pulled back into traffic, shaking his head.

Sully pulled the phone off his lap, talking into it now, "Okay, R.J. No, we didn't get in. I'm guessing, what, I don't know, maybe Waters heard I was trying and he spooked."

"Couldn't you give me a heads-up, for Christ's sake? I'm sitting here at the desk, Agent Gill calls, she's in my ear before I even know what she's talking about."

"Just found out about it myself," he said. "Apparently this went down this afternoon, while I was at the G.W. library."

"The what?"

"It's the key that turns the lock. Ask Susan, she's got it solid. I don't got time now. But, I mean, look, tell Eddie we're going with this tonight for tomorrow's paper. We got it cold, the whole thing. Save me fifty inches on the front. Tell Alexis to get herself or another shooter up there for fresh art of St. E's, before it gets dark. This guy, he's going to make a statement, a confession, something."

"They're saying this thing is at seven. You going to have time to write?"

"Keith will be coming back to the office before me. He can get the b-matter in, the background, the stuff Susan's got, and I'll come in and top it off."

"It's going to be tight," R.J. said. "And we still don't know what this meet-up is going to amount to, if anything. If there's news, we write. If not, we sit on it for twenty-four hours."

"Tonight, R.J. We can't get beat on this. Not now."

"Just calm down. Look. Go to this thing, sit there, take notes. Don't say anything and don't make any promises. You are there entirely as an observer. They going to let you use a recorder?"

"I haven't worked it out with them yet, but of course. No deal without it."

"Call me when it's over. The instant. We'll hold space on 1-A."

The taxi had been working its way across town, across the Frederick Douglass Bridge into Southeast D.C., the Anacostia below, drops of rain spotting the windshield. Then they were on South Capital, the windows halfway down, the wind blowing his hair, hooking a right onto Xenia, the brick face of Covenant Baptist at the corner.

They were getting close, and Sully, after thinking about it, made one more call.

As they went up the hill, he talked into the phone. The mean little row of brick houses that lined the streets here tended to have additions tacked onto the back—weathered aluminum siding, decks cantering off to the side—giving them a weird, unsettled look. A faded deuce and a quarter sat in the backyard of one, listing like a battleship that had taken a torpedo to the hull.

He listened to the response for a while, then said, "I don't care if there ain't no visiting hours. You *got* to get there this evening."

He paused to listen again.

"Because Noel, Sly. Noel. That was our deal. I let you walk on Noel, you get me in and out of St. E's. We didn't say one time only. You be in that patient area and keep your head on a gotdamn swivel."

He hung up and rapped on the seat in front of him and got out before the man could stop.

"We're here," he said. "You'n wait just a minute, right?"

The house was a simple two-story brick construction with a black slate roof and a driveway on the side. It was typical post–World War II housing. A window on each side of the front door, dormer windows on the second. A rusting-out dark blue panel van, a ladder tied on the roof rack, sat in the driveway. Worn-out shrubs going brown in the front. Weeds, not grass, in the yard.

All of the houses on Xenia sat on the east side of the street. On the west side, there was a strip of grass and then trees and wild growth on the edge of the bluff. The Blue Plains water treatment facility and Bolling Air Force Base lay far below, across I-295, and then there was the river and National Airport due west, the Capitol to the northwest.

Still, despite the vista, the neighborhood had long been abandoned to the descendants of the slaves who had once worked farms on these same acres. The spot to shop down here wasn't Mazza Galleria, like you had in moneyed Northwest D.C., but the Eastover Shopping Center, where you had the Get-a-Lot Grocery Store, the When You Need It check-cashing joint, empty storefronts, the Hot Pink Nail Palace, the Maximum You beauty salon and a third-rate florist shop so tired it didn't even have a name. That was this place. And people wondered why the locals tended to have an attitude.

"Sully, hey, hey. Sully."

The voice made him jump, coming back from his right. It was Keith, in jacket and tie, stepping out of one of the paper's nondescript sedans, crossing the sidewalk, popping open an umbrella. "I was up in Chevy Chase, checking that George Harper up there, when Melissa called. The number for this place," he said, nodding toward the house, "is disconnected. Nobody answers the door."

Sully, glad to have the help, especially from Keith, turned and looked at the house. There were no lights on, and if someone was inside, they were being decidedly tolerant about two strangers standing at the front step.

"You tried front and back, right?"

Keith nodded, then added, with a smile. "Both locked."

"Ha. Looked in the windows?"

Keith shrugged and Sully walked over, pushed his way through the thick green shrubs, and cupped his hands against the glass. The curtains were drawn but he peeked through the gap. Bare hardwood floors, the edge of a chair. The other room offered the same slice of domestic nothingness—the back of a cheap couch and some pizza boxes on a table in the far room.

"Nobody's home next door on either side," Keith said. "People still at work, maybe. I was chilling in the car waiting for folks to come home. Might go down on South Cap and get a burger, wait till it starts getting dark, come back. If this is our guy, somebody would have had to notice him."

Sully nodded, looking at the upstairs windows, walking around the side of the house, coming back. "Seems like they would have called it in, though."

Keith was over at the van. The "FKH Electrical" on the side was peeling. Closer inspection showed it had been done freehand, not with a stencil. It was ragged, done a long time ago, on the cheap, somebody with a can of paint and an artist's brush.

"The dust," Keith said, wiping a finger across the windshield.

The rain, picking up into a spatter, hit like small artillery in the caked dust, streaking it downward in rivulets. The taxi driver across the street put his window up, the movement catching Sully's eye. The distraction made him check his watch. Fifteen till seven. Shit. Showtime. Walking backward toward the taxi, he said, "I'm getting to St. E's. Hang out here, you like, looking for a neighbor. But, no shit, we got to file tonight.

Check with Susan, soon as you get back to the mothership. She's got the dope."

"You sure you want to do this tonight?"

"Have to," Sully said, now in the street. "Too many ways for this to leak after this meeting, too many people are going to know."

Keith, calling out across the street: "Know what?"

## THIRTY-TWO

LANTIGUA HAD THEM all meet in his office in the administration building. Sully; Janice, the head of PDS; Wesley Johnston, the AUSA; and the attorney for St. E's, a fleshy man with sweaty palms who introduced himself as Eli Ezekiel, a man so pale it looked as if they kept him in the basement.

The office was a strange, musky space, breathing St. E's Victorian-to-modern history. The heavy paneled walls, the magnificent mahogany door, the arched windows, the Queen Anne settee, the unironic scrolled writing desk with the scuffed edges in the corner, the well-worn Persian rug with the tear in the corner—all looking like stately ambassadors of another age, when Teddy Roosevelt was president and it was the nation's most prestigious mental hospital. The dented metal filing cabinets, the sorry telephone receivers, the grime on the windows, the air-conditioning unit that was sealed with duct tape—all those testifying to the down-on-the-heels run of more recent decades, when it was a white elephant waiting for extinction.

Lantigua, standing behind an oaken writing desk that might have been as ancient as the rest—you couldn't tell, the papers stacked on it might have dated to Roosevelt, too—talked them through the procedure for the "the statement," as he kept calling it. They would walk from here to Canan Hall (there were umbrellas for them all, he said primly, not to worry about the rain). They would meet Waters in a secured conference room in the ward.

The ward doors would lock behind them, as would the ones in the conference room. Waters would already be there when they arrived. There would be chairs and a long table, with Waters seated at the end of the table. Lantigua would tell him to start, Waters would say what he had to say. If anyone had any questions—and by this he meant only for clarity's sake about what had been said—they could write or whisper them to Lantigua, and he would or would not ask Waters, as he deemed medically appropriate.

"Legal advice," Janice said, looking at Lantigua.

"Yes, yes, of course," he said. "I just meant, ah—"

"That you don't want me asking him a damn thing," Sully said.

"Not to put too fine a point on it," Lantigua said.

The air in the office grew close and tense and unpleasant. The dampness, the humidity, from outside wormed its way into this inner chamber. Everyone sat with their legs crossed, wishing they were somewhere else.

"I would just like to say again, for the record, that I object to the media presence," Wesley said. "Carter here, he's the colorful sort, and while that's good for selling papers, it can't be allowed to jeopardize the judicial process."

"Agreed," Lantigua said. "Ms. Miller, is there not a way to call this off? Can you talk to your client again? The media here gives this an air of . . . the circus."

He didn't look at Sully as he said it, but letting him know where on the food chain he sat.

"It is my client's wish that we are here to begin with," she said, sounding resigned. "I spoke with him by phone at length this afternoon. I have just finished speaking with him, not thirty minutes ago. He says he has a statement he wants the public to hear. He would not tell me what it was, but said Sully would understand, which is why he wants him here."

Lantigua looked nonplussed.

"Mr. Carter? Could you enlighten us?"

Sully looked over at him, arching his eyebrows as if surprised by the question.

"No," he said.

"See what I mean," Wesley muttered.

"Sully," Janice said, impatiently.

Sully leaned forward at the table, uncrossing his legs. "I mean 'no,' in the sense that I am literally unable, because I have no idea what this is about. But beyond that, 'no' in the sense of I would not. The door hadn't even shut when y'all started pissing on me being here, acting like it's beneath your professional standard. Like lawyers and the warden at the crazy house are two pegs up from reporters. And then you ask me for help. So, no."

"We don't call it a 'crazy house,' " Lantigua said, "and no one in polite society has for a very long time. It's a mental health treatment facility."

"I guess you'd be up to speed on the terminology," Sully said. "How long you been here?"

"Since 1962 as a graduate student intern, since 1976 as executive director."

"Ah. Thank you. So the problem with your point of view, like I was saying, is that I'm the only one your patient wants to see. Why? Who knows? Maybe because I was there that day in the Capitol, or maybe because he's got a crush on me, maybe because he's just fucking crazy. I'm here to listen to what he has to say. Any of you who don't want to be here, hey, there's the door."

"Reckless," Wesley said.

"Wes, I been stared down before," Sully said, "by people with guns who knew how to use them. You, you just look constipated."

Lantigua ignored the exchange and sighed, as if he were dealing with very small children. He flipped open a folder on his desk. Then he slid a sheaf of papers over to Sully.

"Waivers and confidentiality agreements." When Sully arched his eyebrows, Lantigua hastily clarified, "The confidentiality just applies to our policies and procedures, the privacy of other patients. Some of whom have a certain degree of notoriety."

"You're worried I'm going to try to cop an interview with Hinckley on the way out?" Sully said.

Lantigua lowered his chin and gave Sully his best bureaucratic look, letting it sit over a two-second silence. "Just sign the form, Mr. Carter. Or, as you say, don't. Now. Is everyone done? Thank you, thank you. Fine. I'll leave these here. Now. If you would follow me."


When they came into the ward, Sully was the last in line, save for the linebacker-sized orderly trailing them all. His eyes flew over the floor, taking it in, the patients wandering about, the big windows showing the fading gloom outside, the cloud cover ending the day early, the television on but not loud. The walls were dingy and aged, the paint was dull, the floor was shined but there was a dull yellow sheen to it.

And there, in a lime-green chair in the television room, dressed in jeans and a white pullover shirt, untucked, sat Sly Hastings. His close-cropped hair was under a White Sox cap and his face was averted, looking out the window. Uncle Reggie sat next to him, muttering and looking at the television, then turning to take in the entourage.

Sully cut his eyes away from the pair as soon as he saw Reggie start to turn his way. It wasn't fast enough. There was a glint of recognition in the man's eyes. He started to raise up, point. And, before he got fully out of his chair, Sully saw, from the corner of his eye, Sly's right hand rise up the man's back, grab his shirt tail, and jerk him back down.

No one else noticed.

Lantigua led them down the hall to the far end, past room 237, to a secured door that looked just like all the rest. He swiped the magnetic card that hung on a lanyard around his neck, looked in, and them stepped back, holding the door open to let them all in, the air flat, stale, recycled, and yet charged, like someone had cut all the ions loose and they were rocketing around the ward, colliding, crashing into one another, changing, reforming, shaping into something yet unseen.

Inside the conference room, the patient sat at the end of a long wooden table, head down. He could be dozing. You could think that, that tousled hair, the slack shoulders, not looking up, no recognition at all that the people he had summoned were filing in. He was wearing the same loose, standard-issue white jumpsuit he had worn earlier. His forearms were on the table, little plastic cuffs binding them together, his black hair pulled back in the same ponytail, a few strands loose and unmanaged, hanging over his forehead. He was looking down at his hands when they all filed in. An orderly flanked him on either side. One of them was Jamal, who studiously avoided eye contact with Sully.

At the back of the room, opposite the door, a tripod held a small video camera. The guy operating it wore a St. E's uniform and a tired expression, leaning back against the wall, his camera already honed in and focused, cleaning his fingernails, ignoring the new entrants, too. Looking like he was getting overtime for this but now thinking he had better things to do.

Janice went to the near side of the table and sat. Sully, who had started in after her, now reversed his steps and went to the far side, the right. He wanted the man looking at him, not at his attorney. Wesley sat at the head of the table. Lantigua slid past Janice to get to the front of the room, the door closing and locking behind him. He moved between Jamal and George, the former stepping back to allow him the space. Lantigua looked up and motioned to the videographer, with a hand rolling forward, and said, "You can start it now." He looked at the camera, expectantly, until the man pointed back at him. Lantigua bent down and whispered in the patient's ear. George nodded but did not look up.

Lantigua buttoned his coat, looked at the camera, and stated the date, location, and the people in the room. "We are here at Mr. Waters's request, including one media representative, as he wants to make a brief statement. He has made this decision after full consultation with counsel, though he is proceeding against her advice. I myself have interviewed Mr. Waters at length about this procedure. I reluctantly conclude he is competent to do so, no matter how ill advised."

He looked around the room, nodded, and said, "As we have all agreed, there will be no questions. Mr. Carter, do you have your recording device?"

Sully took the slender recorder from the inside pocket of his backpack, turned it on, hit the 'record' button, and slid it toward the front of the table. "It's directional," he said. "It'll pick up from there just fine." He pulled out a small notebook and a pen as backup.

Lantigua nodded. "Okay then. Mr. Waters. Proceed." He walked to the back of the room, standing by the video camera.

George looked up. His shoulders were rounded, the eyes distant. He looked as he had when Sully first walked into his cell earlier in the day.

"I, uh," and he coughed, bringing his hands to his mouth, covering it while he coughed again. "Thank you all for, ah, coming. This will only take a moment."

He rolled his neck, audibly popping the vertebrae. When his eyes opened again, they were still muddled, and he looked either down at the table, or up at Sully. He started speaking slowly and picked up speed and volume as he went. Making eye contact, Sully, leaning forward into the edge of the table, looking at the irises, would swear what he saw in them was fear.

"My, um, statement is, like . . ." He coughed again. Nervous. "My, um, name isn't Terry Waters. Never has been. It is George Harper. This, uh, as of today, became known to Mr. Carter. I killed Barry Edmonds not for or against any Indian cause. I could give a shit about that stuff. I had petitioned him, about the care of my mother here at St. E's, before her death here seven years ago. He was, ah, her local representative at the time, the representative of the place where she had come from. And, ah, Edmonds, he, well, I'd say he ignored that. He ignored what I told him. Or tried to tell him. There were letters, lots of letters, with documentation, and I, ah, called—about what was happening here, to patients here. So time went by. I had to figure out a way to arrange my own meeting. My mother, Frances, as Mr. Carter no doubt knows by now, was mutilated by a lobotomy by Dr. Walter Freeman, the patron saint of this shithole, as was my grandmother. My mother spent the last twenty something years of her life here as a . . . a vegetable. She was sexually assaulted, over and over again, I learned, for sport. On the ward. Orderlies putting their cocks in her mouth. Turning her over and butt-fucking her over the side of the bed. Taking pictures. I visited her as a child, as a teen, as an adult. You, Dr. Lantigua, you ignored me over and over—"

"Wait, wait, wait," Lantigua cut in, pressing forward, trying to cut him off. "Turn the cam—"

"—and though neither you nor your malignant staff recognized me, doctor—I suppose it has been several years now, and I took the time to gain some weight, you know, a little beard, color my hair—let me say it is so nice to finally be back . . . home."

Janice was standing now, Wesley was sitting there, spreading both hands, palm up, in the air, like what the sweet fuck is this, and still, though the atmosphere in the room had changed, although the temperature felt like it had rocketed north, his implacable voice kept talking, still looking at Sully, as if drawing strength from him to continue.

"I was so concerned you would recognize me, Dr. Lantigua! But your incompetence is only matched by your lack of diligence, by the horrific torture chamber you call a hospital. I have been on these grounds three times in the past month, posing as an electrician. In this very building. It was so easy to walk in and out that it was tedious. Even Mr. Carter was able to walk into my room this morning. We had a nice chat."

Janice whipped her glare over to him now.

"You did *what*?"

Ezekiel, the lawyer, was looking from Harper to Sully and back again, Lantigua was still yelling at the man with the camera, "Off! Turn it OFF!" Sully alone was still looking at George, and so he was the only one who saw him make a small movement and reach, with his hands in their plastic cuffs, into the waistband of his pants.

Later, Sully would never be sure which came first, Lantigua's short, sharp bark of surprise, or the thick heavy boom that shook the building like a strike from a mortar shell. The recorder on the table slid sideways, the overhead light swayed, and a single fleck of paint, loosened by the blast, came fluttering down from the ceiling, until it came to rest, like a bone-white snowflake, at the right edge of the brown table.

"Sweet—" Janice said.

Harper pulled a small black circular remote from the waistband and held it in his palm. "Do you know you can get anything brought inside this place, for almost nothing? That the staff can be paid to do almost anything? That the gas lines in this building are so *very* old?"

He pointed the remote at them, like it was a weapon. He smiled, almost beatifically now, his gaze still resting on Sully. "But what I have always needed, these years of planning, I only learned recently, to truly make my work known, was my very own . . . *reporter*."

He pressed the button.

The explosion blew the chairs across the room and the people out of them. It rocked the concrete-block walls and collapsed the ceiling. Fire and smoke billowed in the abyss above, advanced in waves down toward them, then retreated before coming forward once again, with more force, hungrily sucking up the oxygen. The overhead light fixtures dropped, shattering, sparking, noise lost in the shock waves. Blackness fell, electric blue light shot through the air.

Sully was thrown back against the wall, then scrambled on all fours back in the direction of the table, but hit the crown of his head on the edge. He went down hard. He covered his head and scrunched his legs under him, trying to present a smaller target. He rolled over a body that was not moving. No idea where George was, his recorder gone; his notebook, history. But even then, over the smoke and reverberating air, over the sound of debris collapsing, over the screams from the front of the room, over the sound of chains moving and the metallic click of the door swinging open into the hall, he could hear Lantigua's strangled cry: "Get him, goddammit!"

## THIRTY-THREE

GLOOM AND MOANS came from outside the door. The sputtering of dying light fixtures. Flames. Figures staggering down the hallway.

Then the door swung back shut and everything went black. The totality of it swept over Sully, leaving him grasping to the left and right, trying to get his bearings. The collapsed overhead fixture flared again. His eyes began to adjust. The exposed hole in the ceiling was giving off a faint orange glow, flames licking in the distance.

Debris, from the air vents above the room, shards of jagged iron pipe. Behind him, the camera was overturned, on its side, the red "recording" light still on and the man beside it, on his back, his head gashed open above the forehead. He didn't move and Sully crawled toward him until he could make out the deep cut in his neck, the real bleeder, shrapnel, some piece of flying metal taking him out. Then he stopped crawling that way. Ezekiel lay against the far wall, facedown. Jamal, he could see now, was lying on the floor in the rear of the room, not moving.

Janice Miller, flat on her back, eyes open, dark blood coming out of her ears, a spike of pipe buried in her chest.

The door, the door.

Fire, smoke, George, the other patients in the ward—all of that was loose and deadly and on the other side, but staying put was a death sentence. Any fool could tell that from the flames advancing above, the smoke descending now into the room in a thick, deadly cloud, causing him to retch and spit.

What he needed was a straight line to the exit . . . which was where? How had they come upstairs? His mind was foggy; steps and elevator, both?

The door was illuminated by the ghastly orange from above. Crawling forward, tapping each hand and knee to the floor to test it for glass, he made it to the wall. Then, sliding along it, to the door. He groped upward, and yanked it open. He stayed on his knees, below the smoke.

Streetlights from outside, coming in from the big scenic window, gave the room illumination. Sirens, in the distance. A revolving red emergency light hanging from the ceiling. From somewhere below, boiling up the stairwells, came an indecipherable roar, loud but not enough to muffle the screams in the distance, the clanging of what sounded like a metal tray dropped on the floor. Scurrying figures ran past him. The control room looked like it had taken a direct hit from a shell, shatter-proof windows spider-webbed with cracks, its once-locked doors standing open.

"Sly," he hissed. "Sly *Hastings*."

There was a gunshot a moment later. Then two. There was a rumbling to his right and a herd of patients came stampeding down the hall. Their faces distorted, the leaders slamming doors shut in front of them as they ran, the doors bouncing back, the herd still coming, bearing down on him, smoke billowing behind them.

He braced himself against the wall and they swarmed past him in a rush until one man reached out, grabbed his sport coat, and pulled him forward and off balance, the man holding on to his jacket, pulling them both down and rolling onto the floor. Feet tripped over them, more bodies falling. Sully rolled and got himself back up but not before the patient rolled with him, Uncle Reggie rolling over him, screaming, "White devil! White devil!"

Sully got two hands on the man's chest and pushed him, hard, and Reggie was back up and scrambling, running down the hall after the rest. Sully sat up, cursing, breathing, lost as to where to go, the explosion still ringing in his head.

From the darkness, from a shadow in the corner of the ruined room, a tall, lanky figure advanced on him. No rush to his movements. The features of Sly Hastings emerged as he came closer, his baseball cap gone, a long, thin cut on his right arm. He kneeled into a squat beside Sully, looking up at where the ceiling had been, the flames above them. Loosely, in his right hand, handling it as casually as if it were a cup of going-cold coffee, was a semiautomatic.

"The fuck," Sully shouted, making himself heard over the dull roar, the pops, the yelling in the deep recesses in the building, and, aware of it only now, smoke detectors *beep-beep-beeping*. He ran a hand down his leg—it was stinging—making sure there was no gash.

"Gas line, boiler," Sly shouted back. "Brother down the street from one of my properties wanted to get the insurance. Cut a gas line. It went about like this here."

"Where's Harper?"

"Who?"

"The crazy fuck we're here for!"

"That Indian? Got none. That thing blew, me 'n Uncle Reggie got thrown halfway to the televisions. Great big hole in the floor opened up. Ceiling collapsed. Motherfuckers running."

"You see anybody else from that room? Lantigua? The lawyers?"

Sly shook his head. "You hear them gunshots, though?"

"Counted three," Sully said, waving his hand to the right. "If that's what they were. Could have been another floor. Could have been the stairwell. George set this fucking place to blow. He's got a remote, it's pegged to some sort of explosives. On the gas lines, like you say."

"Why he want to do that?"

"His mom. Died hard in here. I think he took it personal."

Sly surveyed the damage. "You don't say."

The flames were lighting up the outside of the building now, flickering below. The floor, he could see now, had sagged. The wiring above them was hissing. Smoke began to appear as thick ropes in the air.

"You know how to get out of here?"

Sly jerked his head toward the control booth, the observation station, whatever it was, and the mass of collapsed debris that filled the hallway behind it. "Used to."

Sully cursed, then tried to stand. "Help me up, brother. Damn."

Sly pushed off the balls of his feet and rose above him, offering a hand. Once on his feet, he leaned backward, tested his arms, coughed.

"The smoke," Sly said.

They started down the far hall, away from the control booth, moving deeper into the building, stepping over a blown-off door, chunks of ceiling. Water was now running in a slow stream over the floor.

Sly, slowing, bending down, then rising back to full height, wincing. "Sewer line."

Fifty feet farther on, Sully turned into a darkened stairwell as a piece of ceiling fell behind them, collapsing in flame. When he turned back to look? The control room had started to burn.

He hesitated, though. There was no way to tell if, or when, police or firemen were coming. It was probably less than an hour before he and everyone else in the place would die of smoke inhalation, and that was without another explosion atomizing them all.

The firefighters might break open the doors, blow out the reinforced glass at the entrance. They might do that, sure. But they were not going to come rushing into a burning building filled with the criminally insane, rapists, child killers and throat chokers, knife-wielding cocksuckers and necromancers, grown men who once-upon-a-time had carried their prepubescent nieces from the car to the beach so that they could fingerfuck them while pretending to just have their hands under their hip.

No, no, no. The cavalry wasn't coming. They'd let Canan Hall burn to smoking rubble and call it a public service. He and Sly would be two more crispy critters at the bottom of the pile when the smoke cleared.

They got down the stairs at as good a clip as they could muster, given the darkness and the smoke. But as they came down one flight and then the next, the noise grew louder and more frantic. Sully was in the lead by a step until, before he had fully realized what was happening, they had caught up and run into the herd.

The patients were stacked up against a double door, a large red EMER-GENCY EXIT sign above it. Forty or fifty of them. They were leaderless and scared and angry, all of them talking, some yelling. The crowd was milling at the edges, packed in tight at the core.

Sully pushed his way forward, twisting to slide through a narrow gap of flesh here, lowering a shoulder to push through a narrower opening there, thinking the door ahead was open and the crowd was bottle-necked. It was one of the times he was glad to be next to Sly Hastings, except that when he realized the door was still locked, and turned to move backward, Sly was no longer there.

Instead, not six inches from his face, loomed the gaunt and wizened features of a patient, pressed up against him in the crush. He was, unlike the rest, utterly calm.

"Locked emergency exits," he said, looking Sully in the eye, "and they call *us* crazy."

Another explosion rocked the building then, the sound of shattering glass and flying steel somewhere above and behind them, the blast waves drowning out everything else. The patients scattered, some pounding against the door with renewed ferocity, the rest turning and clambering over Sully, pushing him backward, stampeding now for the steps back up, toward the flames.

Trapped in the tidal surge, he ran with them, helpless. "Sly! Sly!" It didn't matter. No one heard. No one paid attention. Keeping his feet moving, picking them up at the knees—he did not want to fall down in this bunch—they all came back up one flight. Half the tribe banged open the entry door and took off down the hallway. The flames were licking up the side of the walls. The other half kept to the stairwell, heading up to the third floor, where he and Sly had just come from. Sully started after them and heard two, three gunshots, all in quick succession. The patients turned as one and came roaring back, nearly knocking him over. He hung onto the railing, survived the flood, and made it up to the third-floor landing.

"Sly!" Nothing.

He tried it one more time, louder. He could make a run for it on his own straight down the hall, looking for another way out, but running into the herd again filled him with dread. So he stayed bent over, running quick for the control room. Something in there had to show the exits. Ten, twelve steps down the hall, his right foot and then his left caught on a heavy weight in the middle of the floor. He cursed and went tumbling, falling hard, landing on his chest, barely able to get his arms out in front of him. He slid and rolled over.

He came to a stop on his back and looked up, the orange and yellow lighting, the flames and the darkness. Standing over him and pointing a gun at his head was Sly Hastings. After a second, he pulled the gun back.

"It being hard to see up in here," Sly said, "maybe you and me ought to stick closer."

Sully pushed himself up and made out two bodies on the floor, both wearing the white patient uniforms, both shot in the head. "You did this?"

"It got bottled up downstairs," Sly said, looking down at the bodies. "I yelled at you to come on and thought *you* was right behind me. I get up here, something blows, and these dudes," he nudged the body of the nearest with a toe, "come running out the door. The lead two, them right here, they come at me full tilt. So I took what you call executive action."

The fire was on the floor now, down the hall, licking at the ceiling.

Panels that hadn't been blown out were now smoldering, then puffing into flame.

Sly, taking it all in, calculating. "You don't think that motherfucker locked us all in."

"Actually," Sully said, "I'm giving eight to five he did."

## THIRTY-FOUR

THE BACK STAIRWELL had no emergency lights. When Sully opened the door, the blackness gawped at them, swirling with dust and smoke trails.

"We gonna choke, we go down there," Sly said, stepping back. "We get down there, the basement? And that door is locked? We fucked."

Sully looked into the blackness. "Prop this door open. Here. With that thing, whatever it is. That's going to let some air out, give us something to shoot for if we have to come back up on the hot foot. It's seven or eight steps to a landing, two landings to a floor. So two right turns equals one floor, am I right?"

"So?"

"We need four floors to get to the basement, so that's eight right turns. The doors are all straight out from the stairwell. Eight right turns, plow straight ahead, we'll hit the door."

"Then what?"

"We're in the basement."

"This goddamn building start collapsing though—"

"Like your options here, do you? Try to shoot out shatterproof glass and jump fifty feet? Put your shirttail over your nose. It ain't going to take us fifteen seconds to be at the basement door."

They ducked into the stairwell, a deep breath into blackness. Sully led, reaching out to find the railing and then, with that in hand, rushed down the steps, spinning at each landing, and then down, down again. The smoke was thickening. His eyes were burning. He took a slight breath and the air burned his mouth and throat. He retched. And then he was at the bottom level and he walked forward hurriedly like a blind man, one arm extended, until it hit the basement door. His hand found the bar to open it and he leaned a shoulder into it, shoving hard and, sweet baby Jesus, it opened onto a wide hallway of concrete-block walls and a low ceiling.

It was, by comparison to the upper floors, quiet, save for the sound of a steady, hissing rain. It came down on his head. The sprinklers. Here, way down here, the sprinklers had kicked in. Emergency lights, too, the floor in a dull, sickly glow. It was a long, wide hallway, opening onto several rooms. Down the hall, at the entrance to one room, lay two bodies, one of them bearing the white jumpsuit of a patient, the other a business suit, almost on top of each other. With Sly above him, gun raised, Sully turned the bodies over.

Head shots, the both of them, entrance wounds in the forehead. The second corpse was that of Wesley Johnston, the AUSA. "Holy shit," Sully whispered. "Wes."

"Walked right up on them," Sly said. "They didn't see him coming. Or didn't expect no shit from him. The Indian have a gun?"

Sully, eyes fixed on Johnston for a moment—the top half of the man's head was just gone, splattering along the walkway and walls behind him—tried to picture how it had gone down.

"He's not an Indian. He didn't have a gun upstairs, but he's been in the building before. All this, it's been a setup. So he hid a piece. Wes, here? He was either trying to get out, or to get George." He looked up. "Our boy is down here or he just left."

Sly nodded. Sully stood. They moved forward slowly, Sly in front, Sully two steps behind. Fifty feet down, they came to a swinging double door with a porthole window set in each. Stealing a glance through the left window, the room inside looked familiar, but not something Sully could immediately place. He hissed at Sly, who flanked the other door.

Sully eased his door open a few inches. By the pale dim emergency lights overhead he could make out not a storage room or exit ramp but what at first appeared to be an operating theater. It was empty. They both went in. The small row of elevated seats and the operating table, stainless steel with a hole in the middle. The table could be tilted, up or down. It dawned on him.

"The autopsy room," he said to Sly. "Where the good doctor Freeman used to string them up on meat hooks."

"What?" Sly said, but only half listening. He moved ahead, halfway across the room, stopping. "You see this shit?"

Sully came forward, moving off to Sly's right in the half darkness. "See what shit? I mean, it's just—"

He stopped, both in forward movement and advancing thought.

The body of Eduardo Lantigua was on the far side of a gurney, one arm caught in a strap. A steel ice pick had been driven through his right eye and protruded, sticking up a good six inches. As Sully stared, trans-fixed, horrified, Lantigua's mouth opened in a soundless gawp. The waist of his suit was dark, the table under him wet. The fingers slowed, scratched at the underside of the stainless steel table, finding no pur-chase. His remaining eye wandered, untethered from reality.

The mouth opened wider.

Sly raised his right hand and fired, one, two, three times, into the man's chest, blowing holes in flesh and vital organs, the sound echoing in the tile chamber like a series of detonations.

"The f—"

"No way," Sly said, looking at the corpse, "I'm listening to anything that comes out of that mouth."

Sully hissed at him. "George is down here," he said, "and you, you shooting, you're telling him right where we standing."

A cold, taut shiver worked its way up his spine, the first tingling of panic. There had to be an exit. Had to. But George Harper was somewhere between them and it—if he wasn't already gone, locking them in behind him.

This part of the building, it had to open onto a drive of some sort, an alley. St. E's was a century old. Canan Hall, it was built on the sloping, western grounds. This basement—its very architecture argued for there being a delivery entrance.

"The bodies," he said aloud, finally. "The autopsies. They wouldn't have brought the bodies up through the building. There has to be an exit off this room. Gotta be there." Gesturing forward to the far set of double swinging doors.

Sly nodded. He moved to the rear set of doors, paused to look through one of the porthole windows, and slipped through.

Sully stayed by the base of the gurney, waiting. In spite of himself, he looked down at what had become of Lantigua. Forty-five minutes earlier, the man had been in charge of this particular universe. Now, look.

He heard the door swing open. He looked up to see Sly slip back into the room from the same set of double doors he'd just left.

But something was wrong. Sly's features had gone wrong. Something was off. His nose appeared here and his eyes there and there was a sheen—

The mist, the sprinklers

—and Sly Hastings, the killer of so many men in so many places, kept walking and walking toward him and the gun wait what was coming up no Sly was looking at Sully with eyes lit from within but not making eye contact and—

"Sly? You find the ex—"

—the gun was leveling, the barrel the barrel deep and dark and unending—

Nononono not not not

—and the last thought to fly through Sully Carter's mind before Sly

Hastings fired three rounds from twenty feet away was that this is how his mother had died. Her killer looking into her eyes. The bullets slamming into her face, her forehead, scissors flying, knocked out of one of her shoes, crumpling dead onto the pathetic linoleum floor of her pathetic beauty salon in their pathetic town. None of it meant anything and never had.

## THIRTY-FIVE

BULLETS SPLIT THE air. He felt the *pfftttt pfftttt pffit*. It knocked him from his feet.

The world fell away. The back of his head hit the wet concrete.

After a moment, to his surprise, he felt little rain drops on his face. Mist.

He found he could open one eye. His head was turned to the side. Sly's Air Jordans, right in front of him were smeared with bright red blood.

"You gonna want to get up," he heard Sly say, sounding far away, like he was calling out down a tunnel.

It became clear, after a moment, that Sly was talking to him. He found that he couldn't roll to his right, so he rolled left, flat on his back, the mist from the sprinklers falling onto his face, into his eyes. Sly was standing over him but not looking at him.

Sully, blinking, looked over to his right.

There, no longer breathing, not fifteen feet from the corpse of Eduardo Lantigua, sprawled on his back, his white jumpsuit drenched in blood, was the bear-sized bulk of Reggie Hastings.

His hair was thick with blood and specked with gore. He had taken one round to the forehead, just off center.

Sly dropped to a squat beside the body, rubbing a hand across one jaw, looking at the mess that had once been his uncle. The last link to his own generations, what he'd said. Sly looked wrong. He looked hollowed out.

Sully coughed. He worked a hand to the back of his head, a lump rising. "Jesus, Sly."

Sly didn't say anything. He leaned over and flicked at Uncle Reggie's left hand. It still held a jagged sharp of iron pipe. "He come in the back door there. Must have been tracking us from upstairs. Holding a finger up to his mouth, telling me to be quiet. Coming up back of you."

Sly, still looking at his uncle, the blood flowing across the concrete floor. It was mixing with the water from the sprinkler now. The mist, it was beading up on Uncle Reggie's face, which was untouched below the eyebrows. Tiny dewdrops, clean, pure, little bubbles of absolution that held and then dissolved and ran.

"Thought you were a devil," Sly said. "Said it the other day. Upstairs, he saw you come in again? Said you had talons coming out your sleeves. Claws."

"But—"

"Didn't mean, like a, a like, bad white person. He mean, like you had red eyes and could fly and possess people and shit." He paused, still looking at the corpse. "Think. The world, you get up every day of your life? There's winged things and people who can't die. Fangs. They, all of 'em, can talk inside your head without nobody else hearing. That's, you know, not a sentence. It's everything you're ever going to be, to have."

Sully pushed himself up. He coughed again and looked at Uncle Reggie and Lantigua and felt like he was going to vomit.

"You, you didn't have to do that," he said, closing his eyes against the sudden vertigo.

"Didn't do it for you," Sly Hastings said, as tenderly as Sully had ever heard him say anything.

*    *    *

"I'm walking out of this place, the last time," Sly said, standing. "Them back doors, you were right. Down the hallway, big double door."

"It's not locked? George, he forgot it?" He felt himself coming around, standing.

"Ask him, it's his escape hatch."

"Why you say that?"

"Because I just shot him. He was following Uncle Reggie there, ten steps back, like he was using him for a guard. Maybe he told Unc he'd get him out. Come through the door, looked real surprised to see me."

Sully, jolted, whipped around. There was nothing, no one, just the shadows and the mist from the sprinkler. "Where—"

"Winged him," Sly said. "Hit the floor, scrambled back out. Missed the next shot, him falling like that, and then he was up and gone."

"Then, he's, he's—"

"Somewhere back thataway," Sly said, nodding toward the darkened halls leading back into the asylum. "Which is why we're going out thisaway. My experience with shooting people, they don't like to get shot twice."

Sully was still wheezing, trying to keep up. "Yeah, yeah, but . . ."

"But nothing. I ain't studying this shit no more. Half the police, the fire department, they're up there on King Avenue. You'n go up there, you want. But Lionel's down the hill there, edge of Simple City."

Simple City, it dully bounced across his mind. Sly, using the name for Benning Terrace, the housing projects just beyond the boundary wall of St. E's, where he'd come of age—and where no one would ever say that they had seen him, this night or any other.

"I can't," Sully said. "Gimme that gat, you going."

Sly turned. "Say what?"

Sully stood, woozy, the idea coming to him, making a fetching motion with his right hand. "The Glock. Gimme. George, he wants to flatten this whole place."

"So?"

"Can't. Can't let him. There's . . . there's people still upstairs. He's using me. Used me. To set this up."

Sly shook his head. "This ain't—"

"I don't got time, brother. Come on. Come on now."

Sly shrugged his shoulders and shook his head and underhanded the Glock to him.

"Hey shit," Sully said, "don't—"

"You not going to shoot him with that."

"Don't sell me short," Sully said. "I got business with this little bastard."

There was a blood trail.

Thick red drops, spreading on the wet floor, led back through the swinging double doors. This presented him with a problem before he was ready to consider it: Smash through on a dead run? Turn sideways and slide through? There was no way to tell where George was on the far side, whether he was deep in the bowels of the building or bleeding out just a few feet farther on. Sully came to the near left side of the doors, reached his right arm out and pushed the swinging door as hard as he could, then flattened against the wall.

Nothing.

Then the door came bouncing back to him and, as it did, he caught it with his right hand, putting the pistol in his left, and pushed it back, coming in quick and low behind it, bent at the waist until he was in the hallway.

The blood drops led straight across the hall into a room behind another set of double doors. He blew through those doors, finding himself in a huge, dark supply room. On his right was a long row of tall steel racks, packed with ancient tools and saws and knives and steel pans. He cut that way, throwing his right leg out front and tucking his left beneath him and sliding across the water-slicked floor behind the racks.

Still nothing.

He got to his feet and peered through the racks back into the open walkway of the room. The blood stains that had fallen there still led forward, drop by drop. The even intervals showed a steady pace, the man neither running nor averting his path. He knew where he was going and wasn't hurried, not even after taking a bullet.

"Damn," he whispered. George had been setting this up for God only knows how long. He knew where he was headed. He knew the exits. Sully, unconsciously, tapping the gun against his hip, his equalizer, his security blanket.

The emergency lighting overhead flickered, a bulb exploded to his left, and he raised the gun, nearly firing on reflex. *Fuck fuck fuck*, he thought, peering at the blood drops. Had to move. He walked as silently as possible around the racks, now stepping parallel to the blood drops, moving deeper in the storage room. He was tracking Harper as he would a wounded bobcat.

This lasted the length of about a dozen steel racks. Here, the blood stopped dripping and turned into a stagnant puddle. George had stopped here. Kneeling now, head up, Sully scooted to the top side of the puddle. Two feet farther on, there were more drops. He followed them for ten feet, twelve, getting close to far door—and then they stopped. He walked all the way to door, another fifteen feet. Nothing.

He went back, getting down on his knees. The floor was dark and wet. Three reddish maroon drops, a neat little trail of plasma popcorn. The drops were fat at the bottom and thin at the top. The droplets radiated outward—back toward the way he'd just come.

"Fuck me," he whispered.

The little shit heel had doubled back.

"**HEY, GEORGE?**" **HE** called out, pushing back through the door of the storage room. The sound of the fire above was distant but there were crashing thumps every now and again, the building collapsing, coming down above him. There was no longer any way out above, he knew that now. There was only straight ahead. He wondered if Sly had escaped before George had doubled back. He raised his voice, louder. "George? It's me, Sully. Remember our bond? Let's talk about it."

Three steps, four, five, eyeing the blood drops as he moved. The walkways in the supply room formed a Y around the junk and storage that had accumulated over the past century. Nothing looked like it had been used in a decade. Cabinets and cases and carts and gurneys stacked high with boxes and crates, all under a thick coat of now-wet dust, the walkways barely wide enough for a gurney to be pushed.

Harper had come to the crux of the Y, stopped and then moved off to the right, toward the far side of the autopsy room. This lead to the hallway outside the double doors Sly had gone through and found . . . the exit. Of course. The building blueprint popped into his head, a schematic as drawn from above. Supplies had long ago come in this rear door, while the bodies had gone out.

George hadn't retreated. He'd just looped around the autopsy room and gone around them.

Along the wall to his right were warped cabinets, lined with bottles and glasses. He reached over, grabbed one by the neck, turned and underhanded it high in the air, back down behind him, the bottle rotating end over end backward, until it crashed into the floor, shattering on impact. Then he did the same with another bottle, leaving it a little short of the other, then smashed two more right behind him, the floor now a carpet of glass shards.

With his back protected, Sully moved forward once more, gun up. Soft as the rain, he slipped through the swinging doors, sliding his head and chest through, then shuffling his feet. This gave him a clear view of the hallway. It stretched fifty, maybe sixty feet to the exit.

The steel double doors, leading outside, were slightly ajar.

The night and sounds of sirens, the *waaannhh waaannhh waaannhh*, poured through the gap, flashes of the rotating red and blue lights of the police and ambulances and fire trucks splashing onto the yard from the street above.

Just before the door, in the middle of the hallway, sat an orange plastic chair. It looked to be a refugee from the late 1960s. In the slightly curved seat stood two legs. These led to the jumpsuit-clad torso of George Hudson Harper. The white fabric was stained with dark blood at his chest and the left leg.

Sully blinked. George had removed the cheap fiberboard panel of the ceiling and was working at something above. His head and shoulders and arms were up there. The upper left leg was heavily bound, the blood from the bullet hole still oozing. George kept his weight off of it, just a toe touching the chair.

Sully crept forward, transfixed. It became apparent the blood on the chest was splotched from the outside but not pulsing from the inside. It wasn't his. Lantigua's, likely.

It was a surreal scene—a bleeding, headless apparition in the hallway of an insane asylum, standing daintily, like a beauty queen bringing up her heel to better display the calves.

From the ceiling, a cluster of wires dangled, suspended in air, ending in some small black blob. Sully blinked, took two silent steps closer. It was an egg timer.

"Hey, Boo," he said.

The headless body in front of him froze. Then the shoulders stooped and George's face appeared below the fiberboard. He had a large cut on his right cheek, which wasn't bleeding. It was just a red stripe. Their eyes held and George's were dilated and wild and then he stuck his head back into the ceiling.

"Your friend left a few minutes ago. I thought you already had. He left the door open. You need to go."

Sully walked around him to the double doors, pushing one of them all the way open, making sure Sly wasn't dead on the pavement out there, an ice pick sticking up from his face. Then he turned back. "George. It's over. This is over. You, you, you fucked this up. They, this place, they were terrible to your mother and you had them and then, sweet Jesus, you're as sick as the rest of them. Now get the fuck down."

"Sixty seconds, Sully." George brought his head and arms down out of the ceiling again, his wiring finished. He put one hand on top of the chair back for balance and stepped down, bringing the wounded leg down lightly. The connecting cord to his plastic cuffs had been sliced through. The cuffs were still on each wrist, like jailhouse jewelry.

"I need you to leave," he said. "You, you, you owe it to my mother, to tell her story."

George dragged the chair across the floor to the side of the wall, metal legs scraping. The man was weirdly calm, the energy of earlier dissipated and gone, now sounding more like a tired husk than a mass killer.

"Nobody knows it but you, Sully."

He had not expected this. The mother, Frances Harper, she did deserve some coda, some measure of justice. The dead didn't get that from courts or the law. They got it only from stories that outlived them. He was the person who could do that.

"Goddammit, George, don't make me kneecap you. You're not blowing any more shit up." He glanced up at the wiring, the egg timer. "Cut that cord. Turn it backward. Or off or whatever."

George was limping toward him, slowly. "You can't reach the timer or the wiring, Sully. Forty-five seconds. You're going to die in here, you don't leave. You can do something for our mothers. You're the last one." Sounding exhausted.

Sully dropped the barrel of the gun and pointed it at George's good knee and pulled the trigger. He flinched, expecting a detonation, but heard only a click. The Glock did not kick. He pulled the trigger again and got the same dry-firing snap.

The thing was empty. That was what Sly had been trying to tell him. "God—"

He saw the open O of surprise and fear curling up at the edges of Harper's mouth give way to open-faced confusion, the features twisting, the eyebrows coming down, and then George bull-rushed him, plowing into him with a lowered shoulder.

Sully's knee gave way, the force of the tackle knocking him backward, gun flying out of his hand, hitting the wall beside him. His shoulder crashed into the double doors, knocking them wide open. They both stutter-stepped outside, into the rain, an awkward dance pair, and then Sully fell, his ass hitting the pavement before his head snapped back, cracking against it. George grunted and rolled off him. Sully blinked, vomit bubbling in his throat. George was up, running back through the doors, pulling them closed behind him.

Sully fought to get to his knees. The revolving lights of the police and ambulances and fire trucks spun at the far end of the building, the vertigo returning. He stood and careened sideways, nearly falling, nausea sweeping over him. He righted himself and lurched back to the doors.

They were locked.

"George!" He bellowed, tugging at the handles. His hand, wet, slipped. He wobbled backward, struggling for balance, pinwheeling his arms, and then he turned, seeing the free-floating forms of the patients in their white jumpsuits wandering the grounds, in the grass, aimlessly heading this way or that, the lights of the city off to his right over the river, and then he got his feet under him and he was staggering downhill, down toward the cemetery and the dead and he tripped and fell face forward, the mud and soaked grass rushing up at him and then the world blew up behind him, the sad lost dead world of George and Frances Harper and Reggie and the nameless rest, the dark orange flames billowing high into the night.

## THIRTY-SEVEN

"JOSH, BUDDY, EASE up on the throttle."

The boy, his unbuckled life jacket loose around his shoulders, was bringing them up the Potomac late in the afternoon. Washington lay to their right, Virginia to their left. They were under the Key Bridge, easing up to the Three Sisters. There were a dozen other boats, half of them yachts, party music thumping from the decks, anchored in the river, this little canyon between the bluffs, the houses way up there, the cars on the George Washington Parkway. The light in August fell from the west in a descending haze, the sun dropping behind the hills, the day feeling worn out from the heat, the humidity, half the river falling in shadow, half still in the amber light. Late on Sunday afternoon, Josh's last day in town, the weekend after the horror show.

"I'm barely *going*."

"The wake, brother. Let's not rock it up on the other guys. Go to port here, get us in the shadows, drop anchor."

"Which one's port again?"

"We been over this. How many letters in 'port?'"

"Um, four."

"How many letters in 'left?'"

"Four."

"You at the helm and facing forward?"

"Yes."

"Well then."

Alexis, sitting beside him on the back bench of the boat, gave him a playful elbow in the ribs. "Be nice," she hissed.

"'So which direction is left?'" Sully whispered back, imitating Josh's high voice. Then, louder, to Josh, "Star student. Kill the throttle. Here."

Josh did, and the motor, which had been a low thrum, cut to silence. They drifted, a breeze coming, them passing from sunshine into shadow. Josh went to tend to the anchor. Alexis pulled her knees up to her chest, still holding her beer bottle in the left hand. She had his Saints jersey pulled over her two-piece, her concession to the season starting, her show of excitement about their trip to see them play in the Dome in October.

"Wow," she said, "chilly in the shade."

"So," he said, leaning back in the seat, putting his right arm around her shoulders, "you're taking the photo editor job."

"For a year, anyway," She yawned, getting sleepy now, the sun, the skiing, the heat, the beer. They'd been out all day. She leaned her head over on his shoulder. "I like it. I like sitting in place for a while."

"And you, this spring, telling me to get my ass back abroad."

"Meant it."

"Mmmm."

"A break every now and then, you know. Not the worst thing. Facials. Workouts at the gym. Yoga."

"Christ. Yoga."

"Started. Who knows."

He turned his mouth to her ear. "If you stay here," he whispered, looking up at the bluffs on the Virginia side, "I'll keep you next to me. Safe."

She looked up at him, her hazel eyes flecked with green, her body warm against him, legs crossed at the knee, this living *thing*, allowing herself, he saw, to be as vulnerable as a woman of her life and experience could be. She was going to complain. He felt her body tense. She was going to good-naturedly tell him to bugger off, their version of flirting. But then he felt, under his touch, her body relax, release. It passed between them.

She took her eyes off his and looked over the river. The yellow golden light there, on the D.C. side. He felt her breath rise in her lungs, her chest, and let go.

"I know," she whispered. She raised her head, then bopped it lightly against his chest, her hair wet against his skin, against his scars, as softly as a cat leaping from couch to floor.

His phone rang. It was up by the wheel. Josh looked at it, picked it up, and underhanded it back to him. "Unknown number," he said.

"Why did . . ." and Sully caught it, left-handed, against his hip. He ordinarily would ignore it, but with the story finally on 1-A today, the centerpiece, the whole sordid family epic of George and Frances and St. E's, the place that had killed them both, maybe it was Eddie calling him from his home line, something urgent.

"This is Carter," he said, putting some attitude behind it.

There was a series of clicks and hisses, some static down the line.

"Mr. Carter?" a voice finally said.

He recognized Lionel's voice before the second syllable of the first word. It jolted him off the vinyl seat, a quick step forward, moving to the front of the boat. The temperature, the air, it cooled over his shoulders. He put the phone tight against his jaw.

"Hey now."

"You know who this is?"

"Sure I do."

"Then let's don't fuck around," Lionel said. "I's calling to let you know I was taking over from the previous administration."

"Really now."

"He say to tell you he retired. He say, he's just a building owner now, runs his apartments. Not into the life no more."

"I have to say," Sully said, "I am not shocked to hear this."

"He say to tell you don't be calling him no more."

"Not surprised about that, either."

"Don't come around, neither. He say that, too."

"Okay."

There was a beat.

"So, like, whatever. I got no beef with you, mister."

Sully found himself nodding. "Ditto."

"You need to know something, you call me, we see what we can work out."

"I'll, I'll be seeing you, Lionel," he said, clicking off the call. He tossed the phone on the front seat of the boat. Should have thrown it into the river, that's what he thought. People finding him when he didn't want to be found.

Turning, he saw Alexis and Josh, sitting next to each other on the back bench, both looking at him, apprehensive, wondering what was going on, what was with the sudden bitterness to his features. He could see it in them, written under the skin, that sense of dread—of the unknown, of things in the shadows that had fangs and claws and walked on two feet. They were seeing it in him. He was looking at a reflection of himself.

In that instant, he felt something shift inside of him, a long-ballasted weight that came unmoored. It drifted through his chest. *Let go of it*, the night voices said. The voices he heard before sleep, usually an indistinct mumble, whispered inside his head, for once with perfect clarity. The weight rose through him like a balloon. *Let go of it*. The murder and violence and horror. A blood-red balloon, rising. He willed it to go. At least, he tried to, that afternoon on the river. He would remember that later, how he had willed the muscles in his face and in his heart to relax.

Then he forced a smile to his lips and peeled off his shirt, just that quick, put his gimpy foot on the mat, then put his good one on the rail and pushed off. Sully Carter, over the side, poised in the darkening air, his arms out, the balloon rising fast above him, finally loosed, weaving skyward. He did not look upward to watch it. The evening chill fell over his skin. "Who's with me?" he called.

He saw Josh rising, taking the bait, before he hit the water.

# ACKNOWLEDGMENTS

**AS IN ALL** the Sully Carter books, I have worked factual events into a fictional universe. I have slightly altered the geography of the city, the layout of St. Elizabeths, and the architecture of several buildings to suit Sully's purposes.

In 1998, Russell Weston stormed the U.S. Capitol building, gained entrance, and killed two guards before being subdued. Long diagnosed as a paranoid schizophrenic, he was held at St. Elizabeths for a time. He remains in a federal psychiatric hospital.

Walter Freeman researched the mentally ill at St. Elizabeths and helped perform the first lobotomy in the United States, at George Washington University Hospital. He later pioneered the transorbital procedure. His ice picks, barnstorming trips across the United States, and autopsies at St. E's are all historical details. The dates of his final lobotomies—carried out in D.C.—roughly match the historical narrative.

The history of St. E's is largely as described. The mentions of T. S. Eliot and Rosemary Kennedy are from historical records. St. E's has been vastly downsized. Most of the former campus now houses the U.S. Coast Guard and the U.S. Department of Homeland Security.

The fictional is everything else.

As always, I'm indebted to everyone who makes this particular railroad go. Most notably, my adorable spouse Carol, who runs everything from the locomotive to the caboose. She has her very own cowbell.

I am very lucky to be represented by the redoubtable Elyse Cheney Literary Associates—Elyse, Alex, and Sam—thank you for that voodoo that you do.

At Viking, Allison Lorentzen gave Sully Carter a home to call his own, and has made all three of the books about him better. Thanks also to Rebecca Lang, Bennet Petrone, and Diego Nunez.

My day job for the past sixteen years has been at the *Washington Post*, one of the free world's great newspapers. I'm indebted to my editors, Lynn Medford and Steven Ginsberg.

Elsewhere, Jack El-Hai, author of the definitive biography of Freeman, *The Lobotomist*, first wrote an excellent book, and then entertained further questions from me. For anyone interested in the history of the mentally ill in the United States, the PBS *American Experience* documentary in which Jack appears, also titled "The Lobotomist," is as well done, sad, and horrifying as the book.

Freeman's papers and tools are housed at the George Washington University Library in the Special Collections Research Center. I thank the staff, none of whom are reflected here, for their assistance. The autopsy pictures that Sully sees there are historical items but are no longer on public view. The ice picks are.

The Honorable Russell F. Canan's stellar defense-counsel work took him to St. E's to meet with clients on many an occasion before he became a judge at D.C. Superior Court. He patiently answered my queries about that process and about some of the basic legal language employed in C-10 hearings—although I changed almost everything about all of it. Former Assistant U.S. Attorney June M. Jeffries is always thoughtful when I ask about the mysteries of her profession.

The Committee is the Committee and what happens there stays there. Love all y'all.

Last, hugs to Chipo, Drew, and Paige. You guys are awesome. Erika, sweetheart, we love and miss you every day. You are with us everywhere we go.